Sharon Sala will touch your heart

"Sala [has a] rare ability to bring powerful stories to life."
—*RT Book Reviews*

"Charming…Sala creates realistic characters that make you laugh and care."
—*Thoughts in Progress*

Welcome to the Blessings, Georgia series

You and Only You

DISCARD

"A delight."
—*Fresh Fiction*

"Starts strong and leads to a riveting climax."
—*Booklist*

"Charming…Sharon Sala makes Blessings, Georgia, a vastly entertaining place to visit."
—*BookPage*

"Engaging, heartwarming, funny, sassy, and just plain good!"
—*Peeking Between the Pages*

"With colorful characters and an enticing story line, Sala's new series proves to be amusing and appealing."
—*Romantic Reads and Such*

I'll Stand By You

"An amazing story by a true storyteller…Sala once again shows why she is a master of the romance genre."

—*RT Book Reviews*, 4.5 Stars

"Small-town romance with humor and heart and a heaping pinch of reality…the characterization is rich and varied."

—*The Romance Dish*

"A joy to read…Ms. Sala nails small-town living. I want more."

—*First Page to the Last*

"A heartfelt and emotional love story…incredibly uplifting and gratifying."

—*Book Reviews and More by Kathy*

you
and
only
you

Originally published as
The Curl Up and Dye

SHARON SALA

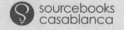
sourcebooks
casablanca

Published by Sourcebooks Casablanca, an imprint of Sourcebooks, Inc.
P. O. Box 4410, Naperville, Illinois 60567-4410
(630) 961-3900
Fax: (630) 961-2168
www.sourcebooks.com

Originally published in 2014 by Sourcebooks Landmark as *The Curl Up
and Dye*.

Printed and bound in Canada.
MBP 10 9 8 7 6 5 4 3 2 1

Some people's lives are all about who they used to be instead of what they became. They stay so wrapped up in youthful successes that they fail to recognize the opportunities for growth.

It almost always takes a life-altering experience to shake them out of their past into living in the now. Some of those rides are quite bumpy. Some of the ruts they are in are too deep and they give up and quit, too afraid to step out of their own shadows.

This book is for the ones who make it through and come out with a new appreciation for being an adult.

Welcome to the present. It's a great place to be.

Chapter 1

Blessings, Georgia
November

LILYANN BRONTE ALREADY KNEW HOW FAST LIFE could change. Her past was a road map to prove it. But on this particular Friday in the first week of November, she experienced one of those déjà vu moments as the Good Lord hit Rewind on the story that was her life.

She was sweeping the front sidewalk of Phillips' Pharmacy, where she worked, when she heard the low, sexy rumble of a hot-rod engine. The skin crawled on the back of her neck as a shiny black pickup truck went rumbling down Main Street.

Before she could see the driver, sunlight hit the windshield, reflecting directly into her eyes. At the same time she went blind, she heard him rack the pipes on the muffler, just like Randy Joe used to do when he picked her up for their Saturday night dates. But that was a long time ago, before he went away to war in Afghanistan and got himself killed.

She had no idea who was driving this truck, and when she looked again, it was turning the corner at the far end of the street and then it was out of sight.

For LilyAnn, seeing that truck and hearing the pipes rattle felt like a sign. Was it the universe telling her she was living in the past? Because if it was, she already knew that. Or was it Randy Joe sending her a message, and if it was, what was he trying to say?

As she resumed sweeping, a car drove up and parked in front of Dalton's Fitness Center next door. It was Rachel Goodhope, who ran the local bed-and-breakfast in Blessings. She got out wearing her workout clothes and waved at Lily as she ran inside.

Lily eyed the woman's big boobs and toned body and began sweeping in earnest. Rachel looked good for a woman in her late forties, and everyone knew she liked to stay fit. She was on her third husband, and there was talk he might be getting the boot before long. No one could actually put their finger on what the problem was with Rachel and her marriages. Some said it had to do with her choice of men, while others hinted that Rachel would be a hard woman to please. Still, she obviously saw the need to stay fit in case she was ever in the market for husband number four.

Lily was of the opinion that any woman with a backbone and the nerve to speak her mind should be difficult to please. Her great-great-grandma, Delia Bronte, had put a musket ball through a Yankee captain's hat during the War of Northern Aggression because he had not taken it off his head when he forced his way into her house. Lily liked to think she had a little bit of that in her, as well.

Just thinking about that Yankee intruder and her great-great-grandma's gumption made her push the broom a little harder across the sidewalk. But seeing that truck had set her to thinking about the past, and before she knew it, she was knee-deep in memories long since gone.

—◦◦◦—

LilyAnn had been a constant source of pride for her parents through all her growing-up years. When she reached high school, she lost her braces and grew boobs, hitting her stride with a bang. She became an honor student, a cheerleader, and was voted prettiest and friendliest every year by her class. When she was chosen head cheerleader her senior year, Randy Joe Bentonfield, the star quarterback, also chose her for his steady girl. She was over the moon, and her parents rejoiced in the moments in which she excelled.

As the year progressed, she marked another milestone by being named homecoming queen, then another when the announcement was made that she would be the valedictorian of her high school graduating class—two more notches in a high school career on a fast track to success.

But it wasn't until she won the title of the Peachy-Keen Queen that her parents broke out in full braggadocio. Lily felt as if her life could not get any better. But as the old saying goes, once you've reached the top, the only place to go is downhill.

On the morning of September 11, 2001, two planes flew into the World Trade Center in New York City and another one into the Pentagon. When the fourth one was taken down by the plane's passengers, crashing into a cornfield killing all on board, the world suddenly stopped turning on LilyAnn's axis. It was no longer about her.

National outrage followed the shock as young men and women from all over the country began enlisting in the army, including a lot of the young men in Blessings.

Randy Joe was one of the first to sign up. She cried

herself silly, after which they made love. Randy Joe was so full of himself about being a man going away to war that he gave her a promise ring before he went away to boot camp. He came back long enough to have his picture taken in his uniform and then he shipped out, returning a month later in a flag-draped casket.

People said it had been a good thing he'd had that picture taken beforehand because he'd come back to Blessings in pieces, no longer fit for viewing.

His death devastated Lily, but at the same time, it thrust her back into the spotlight. Now she had a new status—the almost fiancée of Blessings' first war casualty. She dropped out of college that year and wore black, which went really well with her long blond hair. She visited his grave site every day for a year, and people said what a faithful young woman she was, grieving for her lost love in such a fashion.

When a new semester of college rolled around, she didn't go back. She was still paying visits to the cemetery, although as time between visits lengthened to weekly, then monthly, people still commented that LilyAnn was such a sweet thing to remember her dearly departed in such faithful ways. And because she'd lost her way and didn't know how to move past her first love or the success of her prior milestones, she took the mantle of bereavement to a whole new level.

One year turned into two and then three, and going to college was something other people did as everything became a blur. Her daddy had a heart attack and died, which turned her mama into a widow, and Lily barely remembered her dreams for the future and had forgotten how to get there.

The worst were the times when she could no longer bring Randy Joe's face to mind. At that point, the guilt would set her to eating a whole pint of chocolate-chip ice cream, just because it was his favorite treat. It didn't revive her memory or renew her desire to move on, but it did pack on the pounds.

The years came and went without notice until Lily was eleven years lost. Now she only visited his grave when she thought about it and had unwittingly masked her emotions with a bulwark of extra weight.

She had no status in Blessings beyond being one of two clerks at Phillips' Pharmacy and the daughter of Grace Bronte, the widow who married a man twelve years her junior whom she met on an online dating site and proved all her critics wrong by living happily ever after in Miami, Florida.

Between the loss of Randy Joe and the abdication of her only living parent, LilyAnn had lost her way. She was stuck in a rut: too afraid to step out for fear of getting too close to someone and getting left behind all over again.

—⁓—

At least, that's how Lily *had* felt, until today when the sun got in her eyes and she'd heard the rattle of those pipes. She felt off-center, like she was trying to balance on one leg, and became convinced that truck was an omen of great change.

As soon as she finished sweeping, she went inside and began her day. Today was Friday, which meant she would get her hair done during her lunch hour. But she had to wait for Mitchell Avery, the other pharmacy clerk, and couldn't leave until he arrived.

When Mitchell finally clocked in less than five minutes under the wire, she grabbed her jacket, turned the key to the cash register over to Mitchell, and headed out the door.

The sun was directly overhead, and the morning breeze had quickened to a stiff wind. She shivered, wishing she had worn a heavier jacket. She caught a glimpse of herself in the plate glass windows of Dalton's Fitness Center and then quickly looked away. It was always a shock to see what she looked like now. She didn't feel like a big girl, but she was one. She quickened her step, suddenly anxious to get off the street, out of sight and judgment.

When she reached The Curl Up and Dye, she was relieved. This was a safe place, a place where people came to get pretty. If only there was a place where people could go to get their lives back, she'd be the first standing in line.

The bell over the door jingled as she walked inside. The owner, Ruby Dye, who everyone called Sister, was already smiling, which prompted Lily to smile back.

"Hey, LilyAnn. How's it going, honey? Boy, that wind is sharp today, isn't it?"

Lily nodded as she hung up her jacket. "Yes, it's getting cold. I sure hate to see winter coming."

"I kind of like it," Ruby said. "The short days and long nights give me time to den up with a good book and some popcorn, or watch old movies on the cable channel."

The last thing Lily needed was more time to eat through the loneliness.

"I guess," she said, as she sat down at the shampoo station.

As soon as Ruby put the cape around her neck, Lily leaned her head back in the sink and closed her eyes. Getting her long blond hair washed by someone else was pure luxury. When Ruby began scrubbing and massaging Lily's scalp, the tension in her shoulders began to ease. By the time they were through and she was back in the stylist chair, Lily was two shades shy of having been put into a trance.

Ruby eyed the young woman, watching the way Lily looked everywhere but in the mirror at herself. If only there was a way to get her out of the rut she was in.

Ruby's eyes narrowed thoughtfully as she combed some styling gel into Lily's wet hair and then reached for the blow-dryer.

"I don't suppose you're interested in a new hairstyle?" Ruby asked.

Lily frowned. "I wouldn't know what to do with it."

"No matter. One of these days we'll figure something out," Ruby said.

Her thumb was on the Power button when they all heard the sound of a hot rod passing by. Whatever the driver had done to that engine, it rumbled like a stereo with the bass set on high.

Lily's eyes widened. It had to be the driver with the truck like Randy Joe's. She swiveled her chair around so fast to get a look that Ruby got the round brush tangled up in her hair.

"I'm sorry. Did that pull?" Ruby asked, as she began trying to unwind it.

Lily was oblivious. "No, no, it didn't hurt," she muttered, still craning her neck to see the driver.

And then to everyone's surprise, the truck pulled up

to the curb in front of the salon and parked, the driver racking the pipes one last time before killing the engine.

Vesta and Vera Conklin, the twin fortysomething hairstylists, had been eating their lunch in the break room and came out to see what the noise was all about.

Mabel Jean Doolittle was the manicurist, a little blond with a scar on her forehead from having gone through the windshield of her boyfriend's car. She called it her reminder to never date anyone that stupid again.

She was finishing off a polish for Willa Dean Miller, who ran the local travel agency, and all the women in the shop turned to look as the driver walked in.

He was a thirtysomething hunk in a tight, long-sleeved T-shirt tucked into a pair of fitted Wrangler jeans. He had wide shoulders, long legs, slim hips, and a face bordering on cute rather than handsome, but he was working with what he had just fine.

He immediately swept the dove-gray Stetson from his head, revealing dark wavy hair, and smiled at the room like a star granting an audience to his fans.

Even though Vesta had yet to meet a man worth her time, she wasn't yet dead and buried. She handed Vera her bowl of salad and scooted toward the counter.

"Welcome to The Curl Up and Dye. Can I help you?" she asked.

"I sure hope so, darlin'. My name is T. J. Lachlan and I'm new in town. I inherited the old Bissler house from my great-uncle Gene and am staying there while I'm fixing it up to sell. I came in to get a haircut and learned the local barber is in the hospital. When I saw your Walk-Ins Welcome sign, I wondered if I might trouble one of you fine ladies for a trim."

"Sure, I have time," Vesta said.

Vera glared at her sister, then smirked. "No you don't, Vesta. Sue Beamon is due any minute." She set the bowls with their food back in the break room and sauntered to the front of the store and introduced herself.

"Welcome to Blessings, Mr. Lachlan. My name is Vera, and I'd be happy to cut your hair."

"Y'all can call me T. J., and isn't this something. Excuse me for saying this, but twins are truly a man's finest fancy," he said, and then flashed them both a wide grin.

They didn't know whether to be insulted or impressed by the sexual inference, and Ruby could see it was about to get out of hand.

"Vesta, there comes Sue, so Vera can pick up the walk-in. Welcome to Blessings, T. J. Take a seat and we'll get you fixed right up."

She arched an eyebrow at the twins as a reminder that this was a place of business, then turned Lily's chair around and the blow-dryer back on. Because LilyAnn's hair was so long, it always took a while to dry. She began working the round vent brush through the lengths while keeping an eye on the clock. Lily only had a limited amount of time, and Ruby didn't want to make her late.

It wasn't until she was about through that she realized Lily was staring at the stranger as if she'd seen a ghost.

Ruby paused. "Hey. Are you okay?" she whispered.

Lily blinked, and when she met Ruby's gaze in the mirror, her eyes were filled with tears.

"I'm fine, Sister. He just reminded me of someone." Then she shook her head and looked away.

Ruby's eyes narrowed. This was the first time she could remember the woman even showing an interest in another man. Even if it was a negative interest, it was better than nothing.

"How about we do something a little different with your hair? Maybe pull the sides away from your face and fasten them up here at the crown…or maybe at the nape of your neck? Hmm? What do you think?"

She pulled the sides back and held them up at the crown to show Lily what she was talking about.

Lily frowned. Pulling her hair away from her face like that only emphasized her double chin.

"I don't know. I guess," she muttered.

"Good," Ruby said. "A little change never hurt anyone."

With an eye still on the clock, she quickly finished Lily's new look.

"There you go. Look how pretty you look like this, and just in time to get back to work before Mr. Phillips can complain."

Lily frowned again. She felt naked—like she'd revealed too much of herself. She didn't much like it, but it was too late to change it. She slipped into her jacket and grabbed her purse before scuttling toward the front like a crab going sideways across a beach. Her head was down and her shoulders slumped, operating on the theory that if she couldn't see the hunk, then he couldn't see her.

"Same time next week," she said, as she handed Ruby her money and bolted out the door like the place had just caught on fire.

But what had caught fire was LilyAnn's lust. She hadn't felt stirrings in her belly like that since the last time she'd seen Randy Joe naked. Only then she'd been just as naked and proud of her body, not like now.

Not once in the last eleven years had she given her changing shape much thought. It had never been an issue to her existence until today. The stranger was hot like Randy Joe and drove a fine fancy truck, just like Randy Joe. And once upon a time he would have looked at LilyAnn and wanted her…just like Randy Joe. But that man sitting in Vera's styling chair would never give her a second look.

So the question was…what, if anything, was she going to do about this?

She sailed past the fitness center without looking at her reflection and hurried into the pharmacy, anxious to get something else on her mind besides wondering what T. J. Lachlan looked like naked. She'd heard some men looked good in their clothes but not so much without them, and knew it had to do with the size of their stuff. While she wasn't one to judge a person on looks, she was seriously giving some thought to "what if?"

Her boss, Mr. Phillips, saw her coming in and waved her over.

"Hey, Lily, we just got in a new shipment. As soon as you can, come back to the pharmacy. You can check them against the invoice for me."

"Sure thing," she said, and stowed her purse and jacket, then got to work.

By the time five o'clock rolled around, she was exhausted in mind and body. She hadn't given her life this much thought since the day after Randy Joe's funeral.

"I'm leaving now," she said.

"Have a good evening, LilyAnn," Mitchell said, and waved good-bye.

Lily waved. "You too, Mitchell."

The air was even colder now than it had been at noon. She pulled the collar of her jacket up around her neck, ducked her head into the wind, and started home. Even though it was only ten blocks from here, she was wishing she'd driven.

She was almost at the corner when someone honked, then shouted out her name.

"Hey, LilyAnn!"

She paused. It was Mike, her next-door neighbor, who'd braked out on the street.

"Want a ride, honey?"

She nodded and ran out into the street, circled the back end of his car, and got in.

"Thanks. It sure got cold today, didn't it?"

Mike Dalton nodded, but he was eyeing her new hairstyle.

"I like your hair pulled back like that."

She blinked. "Oh, thanks. I'd forgotten all about it. It was Sister Dye's idea."

"Well, it was a good one," Mike said. "Were you busy today?"

"Yes, were you?"

He nodded. "Yeah, when it gets closer to the holidays, people always come in more often. I guess they want to lose a little extra because of the holiday food and parties."

"Right," Lily muttered, and pulled her jacket a little closer around her stomach.

Mike sighed as he accelerated. He wanted to grab

LilyAnn and shake her. She talked to him, but she never looked at him. How could one woman be so oblivious? He'd loved her since the tenth grade and every day of his life since, but she'd never seen him like that.

When Randy Joe Bentonfield finally got to first base with her in high school, every boy knew it just from the smirk he wore the next day. And when Randy Joe finally hit a home run, Mike seriously considered beating the hell out of him just to wipe that smile off his face. As it turned out, he didn't have to. An IED in a foreign land wiped Randy Joe straight off the earth. Back then, Mike was sorry as he could be that Randy Joe was dead, but he wasn't going to lie and say he wasn't sorry she was free again.

Only it had done him no good. He'd spent the last eleven years living next door to the woman of his heart, hoping one day she would really look at him and knowing if she did, he wouldn't have to say a thing. It would be impossible for her to miss the love on his face.

He stopped for a red light.

"Are you doing anything special tonight?"

She glanced at Mike. "No, are you?"

"It's all-you-can-eat shrimp night at Granny's Country Kitchen. I don't have any leftovers. Wanna go eat with me?"

She shrugged. "I guess. But I need to shower and change clothes first."

"Me too," Mike said. He would have loved a little more enthusiasm, but he'd take what he could get. "Wear something warm, for sure."

"Yeah, for sure," she muttered, and then saw Willa Dean waving at them as she locked up the travel agency for the night. She smiled and waved back.

"Ever want to travel?" Mike asked.

"Hmm? What? Oh, I don't know. Once I thought I would like to see Jamaica, but I never thought much about it since."

"Your mom is in Florida. Why don't you ever go see her?"

LilyAnn shrugged. "I don't much like her husband, and he doesn't much like me."

Mike frowned. "How do you know he doesn't like you?"

"Last time they came to visit, he made the comment that I was nothing like my mother. It felt like a dig."

Mike's face flushed a dark, angry red. "You never said anything before."

"So? What could you do about it?"

"I could have punched his damn face," Mike muttered.

Lily gasped. "Well, of course you could not. That's Mama's husband."

"Yes, and you're her daughter, and he owes you some respect."

She sighed. "I know, but don't ever say anything to her, okay? She's happy. I don't want to spoil that."

The light turned green.

Mike drove through the intersection, still fuming. By the time they got home, it had started to rain.

"Yucky weather," Mike said. "Are you still okay with going out?"

"Sure. I won't melt."

He laughed. "You're the best. You've got an hour to make yourself gorgeous, and then I'll be knocking on your door, okay?"

She rolled her eyes as she opened the car door. "It would take longer than an hour to make that happen."

Mike grabbed her by the wrist, stopping her exit. "Don't talk like that, okay?"

She frowned. "Like what?"

"Like putting yourself down. You're beautiful, LilyAnn."

"Not anymore," she said. "I'll be ready when you are."

She got out and ran toward the house. As soon as she unlocked the door, she waved and went inside.

Mike just sat there. What the hell kind of a spell had Randy Joe put on her that she'd willingly died with him? What was it going to take to dig her out of that grave?

He backed up, pulled into his own driveway, and got out. The cold rain was a slap-in-the-face wake-up call to run, but he didn't. He was so pissed at her and at himself for being such a hopeless romantic. He needed to cool off, and this was as good a way as any.

He thought about putting up a sign in his front yard to get her attention but was afraid it would be ill-received. There wasn't anything wrong with a gentle nudge, but he was afraid that an "I love LilyAnn" sign would be more like a slap in the face, and he wouldn't risk rejection.

Whatever.

He stomped into his house, shedding clothes as he went. By the time he got to the bathroom, he was carrying an armload of wet clothes and was naked as the day he'd been born. He caught a glimpse of himself in the mirror and stopped for a judgmental scan, ticking off the pros and cons.

Good six-pack, check.

Lean muscle mass, firm body, check. Brown hair, but in need of a haircut, check.

Green eyes, still in pissed-off mode, check.

And then there was his face.

In need of a shave, but otherwise okay. His features were even. His nose wasn't too big or too small. Except for the bump on the bridge from being broken twice, it was fine. He had what his mama had called a stubborn chin, which probably explained why he hadn't quit on LilyAnn. He was just stubborn enough to believe that if he waited long enough, she would finally love him.

He dumped the wet clothes on the bathroom tile, grabbed the razor and shaving cream, and got down to business.

Chapter 2

AS SOON AS RUBY AND THE GIRLS CLOSED FOR THE day, they went straight across the street to Granny's Country Kitchen to eat supper.

Ruby had spilled permanent solution on the leg of her pants and smelled a little like a chemistry lab, but the scent was quickly lost in the aroma of shrimp and hush puppies as they walked in the door. Granny's served shrimp three ways on all-you-can-eat night: fried, grilled, and boiled in the shell, which was served cold. The sides that came with it—coleslaw and hush puppies—were generous servings, so it didn't take long to get full.

They were still sitting in a corner booth when Mike and LilyAnn came in. Ruby elbowed Mabel Jean.

"Those two should be a couple, don't you think?"

Mabel Jean eyed them and shrugged. "I think Mike is interested, but I don't think she is."

Ruby frowned. "I know, but it's weird. They do stuff together all the time, but it's like they're brother and sister or something."

Vesta leaned over her twin to add her two cents to the conversation.

"She's all wrapped up in what was, not what could be."

Ruby nodded. "That's for sure. I wonder what it would take to make her take a better look at Mike Dalton. I think he's adorable."

Vera pointed to a basket on the table. "Anyone gonna eat that last hush puppy?"

"You can have it," Ruby said.

Vera didn't have to be told twice and quickly popped it in her mouth.

"I'll get more," Vesta said and waved down the waitress.

Mike and Lily took a seat in a booth on the other side of the room, unaware they were the topic of anyone's conversation.

Ever the gentleman, Mike helped her off with her coat before she slid into the booth, but she didn't thank him. She was already focused on the waitress taking orders as Mike sat down on the other side.

"I'll have iced tea," she said.

"Me too, and we're both having the all-you-can-eat shrimp. I'll take mine fried, and LilyAnn wants to start with grilled and the cold peel-and-eat shrimp with extra cocktail sauce, please."

It never occurred to Lily that Mike had not only ordered exactly what she wanted without asking, but also knew what she liked best. He was such a fixture in her life; it seemed obvious he would know.

Mike tore off the end of the paper on his drinking straw and blew it at her, then grinned when it hit her square on the nose.

She rolled her eyes. "You always do that, I know you're going to do it, and yet you catch me off guard every time."

His eyes narrowed briefly. "That's because you don't pay attention, LilyAnn. If you did, you'd see the world in a whole new light."

That sounded like one of those double entendre

comments, but before she could ask him what he meant, a new group of diners came in. She felt the cold air that came with them and glanced up, just as her heart skipped a beat. It was the new guy again, with a trio of losers who frequented the local bar. So she knew where he was hanging out if these were the first friends he'd made, which wasn't encouraging news. She blinked and then looked away.

Mike caught a look on her face that he hadn't seen in years, but it was gone so fast he decided that he'd imagined it.

"Hey, Mike. Hey, LilyAnn. How's it going?"

Mike looked up. It was Rachel Goodhope and her husband, Bud.

"Hello, Rachel…Bud… Looks like everyone had the same idea tonight. Granny's cooking supper, right?"

"Well, we know it's not me. I do enough cooking at the bed-and-breakfast," Rachel said, then threw back her head and laughed.

The sound of her laughter was just enough to catch T. J. Lachlan's attention. Lily saw his head come up as he swept the room until he located the woman. The look of lust on his face was impossible to miss.

Lily glanced at Rachel just long enough to notice her form-fitting pants and sweater. Black was a good color on her. But when she realized Mike was talking to Bud about Rachel's workout habits, her shoulders slumped unconsciously.

"Rachel is pretty faithful about the workout regimen we set up. You should come sometime. I know you're still laid up from that fall off your four-wheeler, but I have a really good masseuse on the premises. She could help you with those muscle cramps."

"I'll give it some thought," Bud said.

Lily frowned. Not only did she not know that Bud Goodhope had suffered an accident, but she also did not know Mike had hired a masseuse.

"When did that happen?" she asked.

Mike shrugged. "She's been there almost six months."

Before Lily could comment further, the waitress returned with their food, and after giving Mike a long lingering look, Rachel and her husband moved on.

For a short time Mike and LilyAnn were involved in passing salt and pepper and trading sauces. When they began their meal, they ate with few words between them.

Lily rarely took her eyes from her plate. She didn't want to look up for fear someone would be looking at her, so she kept peeling shells and dipping shrimp.

From Mike's perspective, something was going on with her, but he couldn't figure out what was happening. She was always quiet, but tonight she was completely withdrawn. Finally, he slid a hand across the table and patted her hand.

"Hey, you."

She looked up. "What?"

"Are you mad at me? Did I do something wrong?"

Lily's stomach knotted. Mike was too observant.

"Of course I'm not mad at you. I have no reason to be."

He smiled. "Thank goodness. It's just that you were so quiet, I thought…"

She shrugged. "Sorry. I've been thinking a lot lately."

"About what, honey?"

Her eyes narrowed. "About the fact that my life is going nowhere."

Mike's heart skipped a beat. *Oh my God! Is this LilyAnn waking up?*

"So where do you want it to go?" he asked, and then dunked his shrimp in her red sauce because his was all gone.

She wouldn't look across the room. There was no need baring her soul to Mike. He wouldn't understand.

"I don't know for sure, but I'm in a rut. I need to make some changes, but I'm not sure where to start."

"Start with something easy to identify," Mike said.

She nodded. "Yes, I'll think about that."

He beamed. "If you need help or advice, you know where I live."

She laughed, and like Rachel, the sound carried over the noise in the busy room.

—*w*—

Once again, T. J. Lachlan's head came up as he scanned the room. He couldn't identify the woman who'd laughed, but he was a man who operated on gut instinct and that was a sexy laugh, which meant he was interested in the pursuit, although thanks to his deceased mama and his ex-wife, whatever trust he might have had in the opposite sex was gone. One had abandoned him and the other had taken all his money and run off with his best friend. He'd been down on his luck until learning that he'd inherited his uncle's place. This was going to be his ticket to better things and if he broke the hearts of a few bitches along the way, so much the better.

The men he was eating with were simply a means to an end. Being the new guy in town, he'd used them to insinuate himself into the social life. He didn't know what his future plans were, but he liked to walk on the wild side. However, it was already apparent the Wilder brothers would never get him into the right social circles he needed to be in to unload the big house. So, it's what he got for picking his connections in a bar. However, it was one night and one dinner, and he was seeing people he'd already met. It was time to say hello to the ladies from The Curl Up and Dye.

"Hey guys, next time the waitress comes back around, tell her to bring me some more fried shrimp and another Coke. I'll be right back."

He got up, leaving the Wilder brothers to their shrimp plates, and sauntered across the room, making sure to nod and smile at the people at every table he passed. By the time he reached the booth where the girls were sitting, they were coming to the conclusion he had to be a player.

"Just look at him," Ruby muttered. "He's working the room. All he needs is to pull out a deck of marked cards and find his first sucker."

Mabel Jean smiled.

"If he's playing strip poker, I'll volunteer," Vesta said, then looked at her sister and snickered.

Ruby grinned. The twins didn't trust men, but it appeared they weren't above using one now and then if the mood hit them just right. Personally, she wouldn't touch T. J. Lachlan with a ten-foot pole. He reminded her enough of her ex-husband that it made her want to deck him where he stood just to watch him bleed.

"Well, I'll be. I think he's coming over here," Ruby said, and wiped the grease off her fingers as he kept coming toward them.

"Evening, ladies," T. J. said. "Thanks for recommending this place. It's great."

"No problem," Ruby said, eyeing his dining companions. "I see you've already met the Wilder brothers."

He rolled his eyes in a self-deprecating manner. "Yes, I was introduced to them this afternoon."

"Which means you must have been playing pool at the Eight Ball, because that's where the Wilder brothers conduct their business," Vesta said, then smiled brightly.

T. J. frowned, uncertain if these women were making fun of him or honestly oblivious.

"Yes, well, when you're new in town, you meet all kinds of people," he said.

Ruby put her elbows on the table and leaned forward, as if she was dying to hear his answer.

"What's your occupation, T. J.?"

"Uh, well, I'm…uh, between jobs at the moment. But I work in construction. When I inherited my great-uncle's house, I backed off of taking any jobs until I get it fixed up to sell."

"Ah…construction is a hard job," Vera added, frowning sympathetically.

T. J. nodded. "Yes, ma'am, that it is. So, I'll leave you to your meal. I just wanted to be neighborly and say hello. Y'all have a nice evening, and I'm sure I'll be seeing you around."

"Yes, I'm sure," Vesta echoed.

The women were smiling as he turned around, but as soon as he got out of hearing distance, they put their heads together and started picking his story apart.

"He may know how to remodel a house, but he does not work in construction," Vera muttered.

"How do you know?" Ruby asked.

"Because he shook my hand when he paid me earlier, and it was smooth as a baby's bottom. Even if he wore gloves, there would be calluses or a scar or two."

"Hmm, wonder what he's up to?" Ruby asked.

"Chances are we'll all find out sooner or later," Mabel Jean said, and grabbed her ticket. "I gotta get myself home. See you guys tomorrow, okay?"

"Absolutely," Ruby said.

A few moments later, they were out the door.

—⁂—

T. J. stopped by his table long enough to pick up the check. He eyed the total, peeled off a couple of twenty-dollar bills from the wad in his pocket, and left them on the table as he and his dinner companions left the restaurant.

Even though Lily had not looked at him again, she knew T. J. Lachlan was gone when she heard that hot-rod truck starting up in the parking lot. She reached for a drink, stifling a shudder like she used to when Randy Joe began taking off his pants.

—⁂—

It was still raining when Mike drove LilyAnn home. He had the heater on inside the car, making the windshield fog up inside. He was hot for the woman in the seat beside him, and she was as cold as that rain falling outside. Desperate for something to talk about, he picked the first thing that came to mind.

"That Rachel Goodhope is something, isn't she," Mike said.

Lily frowned. She had *not* been thinking about Rachel and was just the tiniest bit irked that Mike had.

"How so? I hadn't given her another thought," she muttered.

Mike laughed. "I just meant that she's something of a man-eater and so outrageously blatant about it. Old Bud is either oblivious or super confident about their relationship. You can tell just by the way she acts that she's always looking for the next Mr. Right."

Lily frowned. "How do you know that?"

He shrugged. "I don't know. I guess it's just a guy thing. So, did you have a good time tonight? I know I sure did. You're easy to be with, lady."

Lily smiled. "Thanks. You're a really good friend to me, Mike. I appreciate that."

Mike's smile slipped.

"Yeah, that's me…everybody's best friend," he muttered.

Lily was a little taken aback by the tone of his voice, but then they were pulling up in her driveway and it was too late to ask what was wrong.

"Thank you for supper."

Mike stared at her face in the glow of the dashboard light, wishing to God he had the right to pull her into his arms for a good-night kiss.

"Yeah, any time," he said, and settled for running his finger down the side of her face. "If you figure out that change-your-life stuff and need my help, you know where to find me."

She nodded. "Thanks again," she said, then ducked her head and ran through the rain.

As soon as she turned on the porch lights, Mike

backed out of the driveway, then pulled up into his drive and got out. He was so weary of hiding his feelings that it was depressing. He went inside and turned on the television, then went to make some coffee. He needed to work on the books for the fitness center, and it would give him something to think about besides the fact that his next-door neighbor was probably taking off her clothes.

Lily was too antsy to sleep. She changed into her pajamas, put her hair up in a ponytail, and decided to paint her toenails. It wasn't like anyone would see them, but it was a calming task and she needed to think. She chose a pale pink shade, sat down on the floor in front of the TV, and pulled her knee up beneath her chin and began to brush on the color.

She had one coat on and was about to begin the second coat when her phone rang. She frowned as she glanced up at the clock. It was almost 9:00 p.m. She jammed the brush back in the bottle and then set it aside as she reached for the phone.

"Hello?"

"Hi, LilyAnn. It's me."

Lily leaned back against the sofa as a big smile spread across her face.

"Mama! What's going on?"

Grace laughed, which made Lily shiver with longing. She missed her mother a lot.

"Nothing is going on," Grace said. "Eddie and I were just talking about Thanksgiving and wondered if you had made plans."

"No, no plans."

"How would you feel if we came back to Blessings for Thanksgiving? Think you could put up with us for a couple of nights?"

"Yes! Oh my gosh, that would be wonderful!" Lily said.

Grace laughed again. "Good! I have to say, I know you're not a baby anymore, but you'll always be *my* baby, and I've been missing you something fierce."

Lily's eyes filled with tears. "I've been missing you, too, Mama. This is the best news ever. So do you know what day you're planning to arrive?"

"The day before Thanksgiving, which means we'll be there Wednesday and Thursday night, and then Friday morning, we'll head on to Savannah to see his daughter and family. She recently had a baby, so Eddie and I are officially grandparents. I can't wait to see it. It's a girl."

Lily's smile slipped a little, but not much. She was perfectly willing to share her mama and tried not to think about how far away she really was from living a life that complete.

"That's great! I'll bet Eddie is excited, too."

"Over the moon," Grace said. "So…we'll be there in time to help with cooking. Be sure and invite Mike to dinner, too. I haven't seen him in ages."

"Yes, I will."

"I guess I should have asked if he's still single. If he has a girlfriend, she might be expecting him at her place."

Lily frowned, remembering how Mike had talked about Rachel Goodhope. "No girlfriend that I know of."

"Okay then. Well, we'll be there before you know it… Oh, and Eddie says to tell you hello."

Lily rolled her eyes. That was a lie and she knew it.

"Yes, well, you tell him I said hello back."

"I will, and honey...I can't wait to see you. I need a hug from my Lilybug. See you soon. Bye-bye."

"Bye, Mama," Lily said.

Lilybug was a nickname from her past, back when life was perfect and definitely worth living. She pulled her knees up again to finish painting her toenails, but tears were welling and she couldn't see her feet. Defeated in every way that mattered, she lowered her head and began to sob. She cried until her head hurt and her eyes were red and swollen before she managed to pull herself together. Feeling sorry for herself went nowhere.

She put the polish aside and got up to go wash her face. The floor was cold beneath her bare feet as she headed to the bathroom. She splashed water to cool her burning eyes and, as she was reaching for a towel, caught a glimpse of herself in the mirror. The woman she saw felt like a stranger. She leaned forward, glaring at her reflection.

"What have you done to yourself, LilyAnn? Where the hell did you go?"

Disgusted, she pushed away from the mirror, dried her face angrily, and stomped back to the living room to turn off the television. She'd had enough of this day. Maybe tomorrow would be better.

She went through the house, checking locks and turning out the lights, before she crawled into bed. She set the alarm, then turned out the bedside lamp, rolled over onto her side, and closed her eyes.

—∿∿—

Mike was standing at his bedroom window in the dark, just like he did every night, waiting for that last light to go out. He knew it was in her bedroom, and he knew she was finally in bed. He reached for the window, flattening the palm of his hand against the chill of the glass. As always, there was a distance between them that time and location could not span.

"Good night, my love. May tomorrow be the day that when you open your eyes, you see me."

Chapter 3

LILY WOKE ABRUPTLY AS THE ALARM BEGAN TO SOUND.

"Lord have mercy," she muttered, as she turned it off and got out of bed.

She staggered to the bathroom, then down the hall to the kitchen to make coffee. She turned up the thermostat on the way, wishing she'd thought to get her house shoes. The floor was cold.

As soon as she had the coffee going, she started toward the pantry, then stopped, reassessing her options. Mama and Eddie would be here in three weeks. She knew what they'd be expecting, and a part of her wanted to shock them, especially Eddie. And she wanted T. J. Lachlan to look at her like he'd looked at Rachel Goodhope. If she got the attention of the hot new guy in town, it would almost be like before—almost like having Randy Joe back.

But taking Eddie down a notch and getting T. J. to see her was a big feat. How could she make that happen?

Without thinking, she grabbed a bowl out of the cabinet and the cereal from the pantry and began pouring, then stopped. She looked down at the bowl brimming with sugar-coated cereal, then looked over at the carton of half-and-half.

Sugar and cream.

She paused, put part of the cereal back in the box, traded the half-and-half for skim milk, and ate with an eye on the clock. Recently she'd been walking to work because she liked being outdoors, but it was also good exercise. If T. J. Lachlan stayed around long enough and she lost some weight, she was convinced she could catch his eye. The thought was exciting. For the first time in years, she was looking to the future.

Fifteen minutes later, she was dressed and out the door, carrying a bag with her work shoes and iPod. Her steps were long, her shoulders back. She didn't know she had an audience and, if she had, would have thought nothing of it. Mike was just a childhood friend, not the man she wanted to take to bed.

Mike was surprised to see LilyAnn walking to work again. He started to call out and offer her a ride and then noticed the bounce in her step. He couldn't remember the last time he'd seen that and decided not to mess with a good thing. He waited until she'd passed before going out to get in his car, then went in the opposite direction. He didn't want her to think he was spying on her.

It was noon when Lily shifted into the next phase. Instead of going to lunch, she put her tennis shoes back on, grabbed her purse and iPod, and headed next door to Dalton's Fitness Center. Her stomach was in knots. Once upon a time she'd been good at trying new things. It was time to get back in the habit.

She pushed the door inward and then headed for the counter and the man behind the desk.

He looked up, smiling.

"Hello there, LilyAnn. It's good to see you."

"Hello, Stewart. Can I pay for a visit at a time without becoming a member?"

"You can pay for a month at a time. Would that work for you?"

She nodded. It would take way more than a month for what she intended to do.

"Yes, that would be fine."

She wrote out the check, then followed him to the women's locker room. He gave her a locker key and told her he'd wait for her outside while she stowed her gear. Then she grabbed her iPod and locker key and followed him back into the gym area.

Stewart paused. "So what did you have in mind? Do you just want to tone up, or is this part of a new diet regimen?"

"I want to lose weight and decided to begin with some exercise during my lunch break," she said softly.

Stewart nodded. "Okay, then I would recommend starting on the treadmill. I noticed you didn't bring a change of clothes, so I'm assuming you plan to go back to work afterward?"

She nodded. "But I can bring a change of clothes next time."

"Whatever works for you. If you'll step up on this treadmill, I'll show you how it works. You can increase or decrease speed and incline to suit yourself, but I recommend we start with a slower speed. You can amp up after you've been at this a while, okay?"

"Okay."

She watched as he explained how to work it. After he walked away, she dropped the iPod in her pocket, put the earbuds in her ears, and hit Play. The music began as she started the treadmill, but it felt like much more had just happened. She'd just taken a huge step back into public life.

At first she felt awkward and anxious on the treadmill, like she was going to either walk off the front of it or roll off the back. It took her a few minutes to get the hang of the pace and then she found a rhythm. The music was moving her spirit, and her feet were moving the blood in her body faster than it had pumped in years. Before she knew it, thirty minutes had come and gone and she wasn't nearly as tired as she'd expected to be.

There were people coming and going the entire time she'd been on the treadmill, and to her relief, not a one of them paid her any attention. She was intent on maintaining her pace as the iPod shifted to another download. But when she heard the first notes, her heart dropped. It had been ages since she'd listened to her playlist, and she had completely forgotten the song was there. Before she knew it, tears were running down her face, but she kept on walking, trying to outrun the pain.

Mike had been busy with errands all morning. By the time he was finished, it was almost 12:30. He came in the back door, dumping supplies as he went, then washed up before going into the gym area.

The last thing he would have expected was to see LilyAnn on one of his treadmills, but the moment he saw her, a surge of excitement swept through him.

This is great! She was serious when she said she wanted to change.

He didn't know whether to ignore her and leave her in the zone or walk by and at least acknowledge her presence. Her chin was tilted slightly toward her chest and he could see the earbuds, which meant she was listening to her iPod. His instinct was to not bother her—until he saw the tears. He was halfway across the room before he realized he'd taken a step. Without saying a word, he walked up right beside the treadmill and pulled the earbuds out of her ears.

LilyAnn flinched. Mike! Where had he come from? When he put the earbuds in his ears, she groaned.

Mike wasn't surprised that it was country, because that was her favorite music genre, but the moment he heard Alan Jackson's voice and the words to the song, his heart dropped.

Damn it to hell.

He looked up at her, then purposefully ignored the tears and opted for upbeat.

"Hi, honey. Great to see you. However, unless you were planning to go straight to a funeral from here, 'Where Were You When the World Stopped Turning' is not exercise music. Be right back."

She watched him walk away with her iPod. A few moments later he came back, dropped her iPod, without the earbuds, into one of her pockets and put a different iPod in the other pocket and popped her earbuds back in her ears.

He stood there, waiting for her reaction. It was an old country song, but it was one that wouldn't send her back into mourning the loss of her boyfriend. George Jones singing "White Lightning" always made him laugh, and he and LilyAnn had the same sense of humor. He hoped it would hit her the same way.

One moment she'd been wallowing in a song that had

been an anthem to Randy Joe's war, and now this. She looked up at him and grinned.

He pulled an earbud out of her ear. "My job is done here," he said, then poked it back in, tweaked her nose, and went to wait on a customer.

Lily upped the treadmill speed to keep up with the rhythm, moving in a much happier frame of mind, and before she knew it, it was time to get back to the pharmacy. She stopped the treadmill and hurried to the counter.

"Thanks for the music," she said, and slid Mike's iPod back across the counter. "Gotta hurry or I'll be late."

"Good to see you here, honey," he said softly.

She paused. "It's a start," she said, and ran to get her things out of the locker, leaving the key on the counter as she headed for the door.

Rachel Goodhope was coming in as Lily was going out. She saw the beads of sweat on Lily's upper lip and the pink tinge to her cheeks. When Rachel realized the woman had been working out, the look on her face was nothing short of shocked.

"Well, uh…hello, LilyAnn."

"Hi, Rachel. 'Scuse me. I'm going to be late." Lily pushed past her and kept going.

Rachel's eyes narrowed as she watched the tall blond duck into the pharmacy next door, then shrugged it off and headed toward the counter.

"What'll it be today?" Mike asked. "Spinning or treadmill?"

Rachel tossed her red hair and gave Mike a brilliant smile.

"Spinning, I think." She stroked her hand up and

down her leg in a suggestive manner. "I need to work on my thighs."

"Then spinning it is," Mike said, and handed her a locker key. "There's a bike open now. I'll put a towel on the seat so they'll know it's taken."

Rachel wiggled a finger at Mike and smiled. "You're the best. Be right back," she said, and headed into the women's locker room to lock up her purse.

Mike knew she was flirting, and she wasn't the first woman in town to do it. He ignored her, just like he ignored the others. His heart was taken. Even though they didn't know it, they were beating a dead horse.

He grabbed a clean towel and laid it on the bike seat, then moved over to the weights to spot a local who was lifting. He knew the guy was a loner and tried hard to fit in, but he seemed at ease in the gym. Here, the guy didn't have to compete against anyone but himself.

He noticed Rachel come out of the locker room and climb on the bike, then forgot she was there.

Had Rachel known that, she would have been irked. She came here on a regular basis because she'd marked Mike Dalton as a possible candidate for husband number four. The fact that Mike didn't know it was of no consequence. Rachel operated on the principle of "what Rachel wants, Rachel gets," and somehow it always fell into place.

─ww─

Lily was busy putting up new stock, mostly oblivious to the customers coming and going. She opened the top on another box of painkillers, checked to make sure the unit price was the same as the shelf price, and then began sliding the bottles into place. She heard footsteps coming down the aisle and absently stepped to the side to let them pass as she continued to work. Instead, the footsteps stopped and then someone tapped her on the shoulder.

"Excuse me, lady. Where can I find Band-Aids and alcohol?"

She turned around and for a split second lost the ability to speak. It was T. J. Lachlan in all his manly glory. Black hair, brown eyes, and a shade of a dimple in his right cheek. Then she caught herself and quickly answered.

"Next aisle over, about midway down," she said.

He nodded without even meeting her gaze and walked away.

Lily felt his disregard and accepted it, but it didn't make her sad. In fact, it reinforced her intent. She hurried to finish shelving because it was almost her quitting time. As soon as she was through, she carried the empty boxes outside to the Dumpster, grabbed her things, and waved good-bye to Mitchell as she went out the door.

The air was chilly, but she'd had the foresight to wear a warmer jacket today. When she passed the fitness center, she wouldn't look at her reflection. This was just day one; no time to start judging progress. As soon as she got to the corner she crossed the street and, instead of heading home, went to the Piggly Wiggly.

Gladys Farmer had been a checkout clerk at the supermarket since LilyAnn was a kid. She couldn't imagine the place without her. When Lily walked in, Gladys saw her and spoke, just as she did to everyone who came in, even while she was scanning groceries for another customer.

"Evening, LilyAnn."

"Hi, Gladys," she said, and headed toward the produce department pushing an empty cart.

She began loading it up with vegetables she liked to eat raw, then vegetables to cook, and finished up with a couple of different kinds of fruit before moving to the meat department. She chose a big bag of frozen chicken pieces and a small ham, which was leaner in fat than red meat, and it was already cooked, which served her purpose, too.

After adding skim milk, high-fiber cereal, and a dozen eggs, she was good to go. She had a moment of regret for buying so much stuff when she remembered she was on foot, but she kept moving toward the front. She wheeled into line at the checkout to wait her turn and hadn't been there long when someone wheeled up behind her.

"Well, hello, LilyAnn. Long time, no see."

Lily turned around and stifled a groan. Polly Winston, her high school nemesis.

"Hi, Polly."

Polly eyed her old schoolmate with a satisfied smirk. LilyAnn might have beaten her out from being crowned Peachy-Keen Queen years ago, but she'd gone to hell in a handbasket afterward. The blond bombshell of Blessings High was overweight and dowdy. God was good.

"How's your little mama doin'?" Polly asked.

"Just fine. She and Eddie are coming home for Thanksgiving. It'll be great to see them again."

Polly smirked. "I guess it was hard to see your mama move away, leaving you behind."

Lily wanted to slap that look off her face, but resisted the urge.

"Actually, it wasn't hard at all. Mama was real sad after Daddy passed. I'm glad she's happy again."

The smirk slid a little sideways, but Polly persisted.

"I guess. It's a shame you never managed to get over Randy Joe and all."

Lily arched an eyebrow. "Why, whatever gave you the idea I was still grieving for Randy Joe?"

The smirk was gone. Polly frowned. "Well, you didn't marry or even date anyone else. I just assumed—"

Lily interrupted. "Now Polly, you know what they say about the word 'assume.' It makes an ass of you know who." She giggled for effect. "Actually, I just never found anyone else in town interesting enough to bother with. By the way…how's Darrell? I heard he had another wreck. Is he okay? My stars, I'll bet your insurance premiums are through the roof."

Polly's mouth opened, but she was so shocked she didn't know what to say. Not only had LilyAnn just stood up for herself, but she'd also done a fair job of bitch-slapping Polly right back for that dig without touching a hair on her head.

"Uh… Well, I…"

"Oh. Gotta go. I'm next," Lily said, and wheeled her cart right up to the counter and began unloading her groceries.

LilyAnn was so mad she was shaking, but she wouldn't let on. She carried on a conversation with Gladys as she paid for her things, but didn't remember a single word of what they'd said by the time she got outside.

The air was sharp, and the sun was about to set. If she hurried, she would get home before dark. And if she didn't, it wouldn't matter. This was Saturday night, the night when a good number of the citizens had places to

go and people to see. It wasn't like she'd be walking a
dark street alone.

Her stride was long as she headed for home with the
bags bumping against the sides of her legs. The first five
blocks weren't so bad, but the wind was picking up, and
with the sun about to disappear, the temperature was
dropping with it.

As she was approaching another intersection, she
heard the sounds of a vehicle braking and someone
calling out her name. She turned to look and then
smiled as Mike came running. He took the sacks out
of her hands.

"Get in the car before you freeze to death, woman."

She didn't have to be told twice. She jumped in the
front seat as he put her bags in the back, and then off
they went.

"Did you have car trouble, honey?" he asked.

"No. I just felt like walking and forgot I was going
to get groceries. Totally my bad. Thanks for stopping. It
was getting cold."

"Any time," he said, then slammed on the brakes just
as a shiny, black pickup truck ran a stop sign and sped
through the intersection in front of them.

LilyAnn recognized the truck *and* the driver and
shivered just a little as the sound of that hot-rod engine
rattled her senses.

"Stupid jerk," Mike muttered.

Lily blinked. She didn't like to think that T. J.
Lachlan might be a stupid jerk with flaws, but he *had*
been speeding.

"Yeah, dumb," she said, and looked away as they
drove on through.

A couple of minutes later, Mike pulled up in her driveway.

"You go unlock the door. I'll get your groceries," he said.

She did as he asked, then held the door aside as he carried her things inside.

"In the kitchen?" he asked.

"Please," Lily said, and followed him in.

He set the bags on the counter and couldn't help but notice the amount of healthy stuff she'd bought. He didn't say anything, but he was pleased. Yet another sign that she was serious about change. If only he could figure out how to insinuate himself into her sights.

She was already putting up groceries and missed the look of longing on his face.

"Is there anything else you need me to do?" he asked.

"Uh…no, oh, wait! I almost forgot. Do you already have plans for Thanksgiving?"

Mike's heart leaped. "No. Are you inviting me to dinner?"

She nodded. "Yes. Mama and Eddie are coming, and Mama wanted me to invite you."

Disappointment shredded the little bit of hope he'd just felt.

"Your mama said to invite me?"

"Yes. Hand me those bananas, will you?"

He dropped them in her hand.

"What about you, LilyAnn? Do you want me to come to dinner, too?"

Lily looked up and frowned. "Well, of course. What a silly question."

"Yeah, silly questions are my specialty," he

muttered. "So if you don't need anything I'll get out of your hair."

He walked out without saying good-bye.

"Thanks for the ride," she yelled, but all she heard was the door slam. She shrugged and promptly forgot about it.

—∞—

The Sunday morning ritual for most of Blessings was about the same—breakfast, then church, or early church, then brunch.

It all depended on the denomination. LilyAnn was a member of the Wesley United Methodist Church, and there was never a question of if she was going to church. It was simply a question of which service.

When she was little, her parents had taken her to the last one. Sunday school always began at 10:30 a.m. and preaching afterward at 11:15 a.m., and she'd been dressed for display, like the little doll she was.

Now she dressed to hide, and cooler weather was her friend. Jackets and coats, long-sleeved shirts and slacks hid a multitude of sins, which was good when you went to a church where people preached against them.

—∞—

LilyAnn eyed the sky as she carried the trash out to the bin behind the house. It was nearly half a mile to church, too far to walk in heels. The day was cold but clear, and she could take a walk this afternoon. Right now, she needed to hurry and get out of her sweatshirt and jeans or she was going to be late for church.

She ran back inside, shutting out the cold as the door

slammed behind her, and was on her way down the hall when the phone began to ring. She lengthened her stride to get to the bedroom to answer.

"Hello."

"Hey, it's me, Mike. Can you come over right now? I need some help."

It was the slight tremor in his voice that made her heart kick out of rhythm.

"I'm on my way," she said, and hung up the phone. By the time she got to the door, she was running.

She flew across her front yard and up his driveway, then around to the back door because she knew it would be unlocked.

"I'm here!" she yelled, as she ran in through the kitchen. "Where are you?"

"In the bedroom."

She'd spent half her life in this house playing with Mike when they were little and knew exactly where to go. But the moment she started down the hall and saw the blood, panic hastened her steps. The trail went all the way across the hardwood floor of his bedroom and into the bathroom. The door was ajar.

"I'm coming in!" she yelled.

Mike was leaning over the bathroom sink, wearing a pair of blue jeans and nothing else. Blood was pouring from a cut on his forehead, and there were smaller cuts and scratches on his torso. The Plexiglas shower door was in shards.

"Oh my God, oh my God, Mike! You fell!"

"I got dizzy. Slipped. Tried to get dressed, and this is as far as I got. I'm too dizzy to drive myself to the ER. Can you—"

"Sit down," she said, and slammed the lid shut on the commode, then grabbed a hand towel, folded it into a large pad, and pressed it against the cut. "Hold this," she said, and flew back into his bedroom, snatching a button-up shirt from the closet and a pair of house shoes from beside his bed.

Within a couple of minutes, she had him dressed and on his way down the hall, but he was leaning on her with every step.

"Where are your car keys?" she asked.

He pointed to the dish by the front door.

She grabbed them on the way out, pulling the door shut as they went. Her purse and driver's license were at her house, and that was just too damned bad. If they got stopped on the way to the ER for speeding, the police officer could kiss her fat ass.

By the time she got Mike in the car, all the color had washed from his face and she was getting scared.

"How long have you been bleeding?" she asked, as she backed the car down the driveway and took off, leaving rubber on the street as she accelerated.

"I don't know," he mumbled, and then passed out.

"Oh my God! Mike! Mike!"

But he wasn't talking. She grabbed the compress that had fallen into his lap and shoved it against his forehead, steering with one hand as she ran stop signs and red lights, thankful it was Sunday morning when the traffic was sparse.

She picked up a cop car two blocks from the hospital, but she didn't slow down. If he wanted to give her a ticket, he was going to have to do it there.

When she didn't slow down or stop, the cop hit the

siren and accelerated, trying to catch her. She pulled into the ER bay with him on her bumper. When she got out running and covered in blood, the cop's attitude changed as he jumped out of the cruiser and followed her to the passenger door.

LilyAnn recognized the officer as a former classmate and started issuing orders.

"Lonnie, get me some help! Mike is unconscious!"

Every angry comment Officer Lonnie Pittman had been planning to deliver shifted into nervous energy as he dashed into the ER, coming back moments later with a doctor, a nurse, and two orderlies pushing a gurney.

"What happened?" the doctor said, as they dragged Mike's bloody body out of the car.

"He fell in the shower. I don't know how long ago, because he'd lost a lot of blood by the time he called me. It was a bad fall so he may have internal injuries, too. He has cuts and scratches all over his upper torso. Don't know about the rest of him because he was wearing blue jeans when I showed up. All I know is that the shower door was Plexiglas and it was in pieces."

"Are you his wife?" the nurse asked.

The question startled Lily. She'd never thought of Mike in that way. "No, but…I guess I'm the closest thing to family here in Blessings. We grew up next door to each other and still live in the same houses."

"Follow me inside. Maybe you can help with some of his medical history."

Her voice was beginning to shake. "I need to move the car."

"I'll do it," Lonnie offered. "Meet you inside."

Lily followed behind as they wheeled Mike in. Her

heart was hammering so hard that it was difficult to catch her breath, and she couldn't look at the blood on her clothes without wanting to cry.

Mike was the invincible one. Seeing him so pale and still brought back memories of her daddy's heart attack. He had gone from the emergency room to the funeral home in less than two hours, and this was a horrible reminder of that day.

After giving them all the pertinent information regarding age, birth date, address, and so on, she referred them to Mike's family doctor for medical info. It was all she could do. Before she knew it, they were wheeling him into surgery.

Lonnie Pittman found her in the surgery waiting room. When he handed her the car keys, her hands were shaking so hard that she dropped them twice before she got them in her pocket.

"I'm sorry I was speeding," she whispered.

"Yeah, well, unusual circumstances and all that, but damn it to hell, LilyAnn, don't ever do that again. Call an ambulance next time."

She nodded.

He sighed. "Is there someone you want me to notify? Does he have a girlfriend? Maybe his pastor?"

"No girlfriend," she said, and then frowned. "At least none that I know of. I'll call his parents as soon as I know what to tell them."

"Where do they live?"

"Denver, Colorado. They moved there after his dad retired. That's where his sister's family lives."

"Okay. Well, remember what I said."

Unaware there were tears on her cheeks, she looked up.

"I will, and thank you."

He patted the top of her head. "You're welcome, LilyAnn. Hope he's okay."

She didn't know when Lonnie left. Her gaze was fixed on the doors at the far end of the hall. Mike had to be okay. She couldn't imagine life without him somewhere in it.

Chapter 4

IN A TOWN THE SIZE OF BLESSINGS, WORD SPREAD FAST about Mike Dalton's accident. Within an hour, customers and friends alike began showing up in the waiting room to check on his condition. Seeing LilyAnn sitting there with her clothes covered in blood just made the situation worse. The fear on her face set the tone for the room as silence grew.

And then Ruby Dye showed up. Someone had asked for prayers for Mike Dalton at her church, and the moment service was over, she had headed for the hospital. When she saw LilyAnn and the shape she was in, Ruby gasped in horror.

"Honey! What on earth happened? Are you okay? Is any of this yours?"

It was the sympathy that did Lily in. She started to cry.

"No, Sister, it's all Mike's. He slipped in the shower. He had a bad cut on his head, and they were talking about internal injuries."

"Well, bless his heart," Ruby said. "Soapy surfaces, I guess."

Lily shrugged, about to agree, when she remembered something Mike told her.

"No. He said he was dizzy. Oh my gosh! I forgot about that. He said he got dizzy."

"From the head injury, I'm sure."

"No, no, it was before he fell. Mike used to get inner ear infections a lot, and they always affected his balance. I need to tell the doctors. I should have remembered. They need to know."

"You can tell them later. Right now he's where he needs to be."

Lily nodded as she wiped her eyes and blew her nose.

"Is there anything I can do?" Ruby asked. "Do you want some clean clothes? I can go to your house and get whatever you need. Is there anything we can do for Mike?"

Lily thought of what his house looked like when they left it.

"There's blood all over his house, and the shower door is in pieces."

Ruby patted her hand. "I'll get the girls from the shop, and we'll take care of that. Can I bring you anything from your house? Make me a list. Tell me where to find the stuff, and I'll do it gladly."

Lily felt weight coming off her shoulders. "Are you sure?"

"Absolutely," Ruby said.

Lily leaned over, lowering her voice so no one else could hear.

"Mike is a private person."

Ruby whispered back. "Honey, we'll just clean up, not mess into his business, okay?"

"Okay. The back door at his house is open. The front door is unlocked at my house, too. I'll give you a list of stuff to bring from my house, including my purse and keys. If you'd lock both houses when you're through, I would appreciate it."

"Consider it done," Ruby said, and gave LilyAnn a quick hug. "I'll be back later with your things. Have faith, honey. He's going to be fine."

Lily sighed. "From your lips to God's ears."

Mike Dalton was in recovery when Lily finally made the call to his parents. It was the most difficult phone call she'd ever had to make. Just when she thought the call was going to go to voice mail, someone picked up.

"Hello?"

She recognized his mother's voice.

"Carol, hi. It's me, LilyAnn."

"LilyAnn. Oh my goodness. I haven't heard your sweet voice in ages. How have you been?"

"I'm okay. I'm sorry, but I'm calling about Mike. He's had an accident." She heard a gasp, and then Carol's voice began to tremble.

"Please tell me he's alive."

Lily groaned. "Yes, yes, I'm sorry. I should have said that first. I didn't mean to scare you, but he's in the hospital here in Blessings. He fell in the shower this morning. At first I thought it was just a bad cut on his head, but he passed out in the car when I was taking him to ER. The doctor said he had ruptured his spleen in the fall and came close to bleeding out. He's out of surgery and in recovery now. I waited to call until I knew what to tell you."

"Oh lordy. Hang on a minute. I need to get Don."

Lily could hear Carol calling her husband, and then moments later she heard him pick up an extension.

"LilyAnn, this is Don. Is he okay?"

"I haven't seen him yet, but the doctor assured me he came through surgery just fine. They don't expect a problem, but—"

"We understand…there's always a 'but' with surgery. And this couldn't have happened at a worse time for us. We're snowed in. Literally. Until they run the snowplows on our roads, we will not be able to get out of the house. I can make a call to see if they'll make an exception, but for now, we're stuck."

"Oh no, I'm so sorry," Lily said. "Look, don't worry, okay? I won't leave him on his own, you know that. I'll take care of him until you guys can get here, and I'll make sure he understands your situation."

Carol was crying, but Lily could hear the relief in her voice.

"You are a godsend, sugar. Thank God you are just next door. Did he say how he happened to fall?"

"He said he got dizzy. I forgot to tell the doctor, but you know what I'm thinking."

Carol groaned. "Yes. Inner ear troubles again. We went through that all through his childhood. I guess I thought he'd outgrown it."

"I'll be sure to mention it to the doctor," Lily said.

"Tell Mike we love him and that we'll be there as soon as we can get out, okay?"

"Yes, ma'am, see you soon."

A short while later, Ruby came by with clean clothes and LilyAnn's purse.

"Here you go, honey. Clean clothes are in the bag. Lord have mercy, I never saw so much blood."

Lily nodded. "I know. Scared me to death when I first saw it, too. Thanks again for what you did. It really helps."

Ruby hugged her. "That's what friends are for. You call me if you need anything else. Tomorrow's Monday and you know I'm off work."

"Yes, thank you, but I think I can handle everything else."

"Did you get in touch with his family?"

Lily nodded. "They're snowed in. They'll get here as soon as they can."

Ruby rolled her eyes. "I swear, Colorado is a beautiful state, but I could never live where it snows like that. I'd never get warm. Anyway, I'm off. Call if you need me."

"Thank you again."

Ruby smiled. "You're welcome."

As soon as she left, LilyAnn changed out of her bloody clothes and then made a call to Willy Green, the local fix-it man, to repair Mike's shower door. She had just finished negotiating a day and time for him to come by when she saw them bringing Mike down the hall from recovery. She breathed a huge sigh of relief.

A short while later, Stewart Friend, the desk clerk at the fitness center, appeared, red in the face and out of breath. He poked his head in the room, saw Mike asleep on the bed, and motioned for Lily to come out in the hall.

"Oh my God! It's true. I heard he was in the hospital, but I didn't believe it. Is he going to be all right?"

"They said yes, but he's going to be out of commission for a while."

"That's what I came to talk about. You tell Mike that I'll handle everything until he gets back. I know how he does everything, right down to daily deposits, and he trusts me. I've done it before. If I need help, I'll get my wife to come in and help me clean and work the desk."

"That's great. I'm sure he'll appreciate it," Lily said.

"Yes, well, I'd better go. I'll run by to make sure everything is set up to open tomorrow and then go from there."

"Thank you, Stewart. You are amazing."

Stewart shrugged. "I like Mike a lot. He's not just a good boss, he's a friend. So, see you later. Call if you need me."

Lily went back into the room with a lighter step. Yet another problem solved.

LilyAnn had been sitting by Mike's bed for almost an hour, studying the contours of his face. It was weird, but she felt like she was looking at a stranger—a good-looking stranger. She'd never seen him so still.

Well-wishers straggled in and out of his room, but as soon as they realized he was asleep, left their regards and quickly exited—all except for Rachel Goodhope.

The door was closed and visiting hours were over, and yet Rachel came in without knocking. She seemed surprised and then unhappy when she saw LilyAnn, but Lily didn't care. The moment she saw what Rachel was wearing, her intent for being here was obvious.

Despite the cold weather, her skirt was so short it barely covered her ass, and her black blouse was unbut-toned all the way past her décolletage. The red push-up bra beneath was doing a bang-up job of rearranging the "girls." They would have given Dolly Parton's boobs a run for their money, and the message Rachel was sending was loud and clear.

Lily knew Mike would *never* mess with a married woman, and since Mike could not defend himself, it was up to her to do it for him.

When Rachel started to walk in, LilyAnn shot up from her chair and quickly backed her out into the hall, closing the door behind them.

Rachel frowned. "What do you think you're doing? I came to see Mike."

Lily stood her ground. "But as you saw, he's asleep."

"I thought I would sit—"

"No."

Rachel's frown deepened. "Excuse me?"

"He's not up to visitors."

"You're here," Rachel sneered, then saw a look on LilyAnn's face that made her nervous. She pulled her purse against her chest as a subconscious shield.

Lily put her hands on her hips in a defiant gesture. "Yes, I am here, and I'm not going anywhere, either, so don't think you can sneak back in here later. I promised his parents I would take care of him until they can get here, which means you can't go in until the doctor says he's strong enough for visitors."

Rachel's eyes narrowed angrily. "You're overstepping your bounds."

Lily jabbed a finger between Rachel's abundant boobs.

"No, *you're* the one overstepping your bounds. Does Bud know he's on the way out? Does he know Mike Dalton is in your sights as hubby number four? Better yet, does Mike know that? I'd bet the deed to my house that the answer to all three of those questions is a big loud NO."

Rachel stifled a gasp, shocked that the fat bitch had picked up on that.

"How dare you?" she hissed.

Lily poked her finger a second time, jabbing harder as she lowered her voice.

"No! How dare *you*?" she whispered. "Your life is your business, and I don't give a damn what you do with it until you involve a helpless man in your cheating-ass scheme. Now you take your pitiful self out of my sight, or I might have to let it slip around town that poor Bud Goodhope is about to become ex number three."

Rachel's face was flushed and Lily knew she'd hit a nerve, but Rachel was still defiant.

"You don't know what you're talking about," she said. "Bud and I are fine."

"Then get your ass home and make sure it stays that way. People run all over me, Rachel, but that's because I *let* it happen. However, you don't mess with my friends when they can't defend themselves. Do you hear me?"

Rachel shrugged. "Fine. I didn't expect you to make such a big deal out of a simple visit to a friend."

"I'll give you a piece of advice. Next time you get dressed for a friendly visit to a single man, wear a skirt that covers your ass, button up your damned blouse, and leave the push-up bra at home."

Rachel's eyes widened in disbelief. "I can't believe you just said that," she gasped.

LilyAnn glared. "And I can't believe you wore that hooker outfit in public."

"Oh my God," Rachel said.

"Yes, now that I think of it, God is probably inter-ested in your intent, too, so I'd say that a prayer for

forgiveness is a good idea. While you're at it, say one
for Mike that he gets well, and tell Bud I said hello."

Rachel cheeks were red, her eyes flashing angrily,
but LilyAnn Brontë was a good five inches taller and
at least forty pounds heavier. Rachel wasn't getting
into a slap-fest with this woman, regardless of what
she'd said.

"Of course I'll say a prayer," Rachel said shortly, and
took herself back to the elevator as fast as she could.

Lily couldn't help but stare. That woman looked
cheaper going than she had coming. Her skirt was so
tight and her heels so high that while one butt cheek
went up, the other went down, like the pistons that used
to fire beneath the hood of Randy Joe's hot rod. As soon
as the woman disappeared, Lily went back into the room
and sat down.

Another hour passed before Mike began showing
signs of regaining consciousness. She was so relieved
to see movement that she quickly rang for a nurse.

"He's waking up, isn't he?" Lily whispered.

The nurse nodded. "He was one lucky guy. That cut
on his head was minor compared to the ruptured spleen.
If you hadn't gotten him here when you did, he might
not have made it. Just sit tight and talk to him if you
want. He'll come to in his own time."

The nurse was gone, but Lily's stomach was still
in knots, knowing how close he'd come to dying. She
pulled her chair a little closer to the bed.

"Hey Mike, it's me, LilyAnn. I would greatly appreciate it if you would open your eyes."

—◊◊◊—

The first thing Mike felt was pain, and the first thing he thought was why. Then he heard a voice.

LilyAnn.

Wherever he was, knowing she was there calmed him. He tried to move and then groaned.

The pain is in my belly—no, my head—no, my belly. He took a breath and then gasped. *For whatever reason, I hurt all over.*

Lily stood up so he could see her if he opened his eyes.

"Hey, Mike, it's me, LilyAnn. You're in the hospital, but you're okay. Can you open your eyes?"

He licked his lips, then felt something wet and cool against them.

"I can't give you water, but this might help," she said, carefully wiping his lips with a wet cloth.

It did, but he couldn't get that said. He tried to open his eyes, but they were so heavy.

She patted his arm. "Come on, sleeping beauty, open your eyes."

He pushed past the lethargy until he saw her leaning over him. So close, as close as she'd ever been, and he was too damn weak to do a thing about it.

LilyAnn smiled. "There you are."

"How…?"

"I brought you here. You fell through your shower door, cut your head, and ruptured your spleen. You've been in surgery, but you're going to be okay."

Now he remembered the fall.

"Damn."

"Well put," she said. "I called your parents. They're snowed in, but they said to tell you they'll be here as soon as they can get out and that they love you."

His eyelids were getting heavy again. "Love…" he whispered.

She patted his arm again. "They know you love them, too. It's okay, Mike. Just rest."

He was too sedated to clarify. It had been her, not his parents, that he'd been thinking about, but all things considered, it was just as well that he never finished the thought.

It was nearly suppertime before the doctor made his rounds and found LilyAnn waiting for him.

Doctor Rollins knew nearly everyone in Blessings, and LilyAnn was no exception. He smiled when he saw her sitting near his patient's bed.

"Hello, LilyAnn. I understand you're the hero in this episode. How have you been?"

Lily frowned. "I'm no hero, Doctor Rollins. I just helped a friend. While you're here, I would like for you to look in his ears. He mentioned that he'd been dizzy, and with everything that was happening, I forgot to mention it when I brought him to the ER."

"What about his ears?" Rollins asked.

"He has a history of inner ear infections, and I think that might be why he had such a bad fall."

"I see," Rollins said, as he stepped over to the bed to examine his patient. After checking Mike's vitals and the wounds under the bandages, the doctor pulled out his light and peered into each ear.

"Good call," he said, as he straightened. "They're both infected. I'll order some antibiotics for them, as well."

LilyAnn leaned back with a sigh, satisfied her job had been done.

It was dark before she left the hospital. Mike had awakened off and on, but never for more than a minute or so. Satisfied that he was in good hands, she grabbed the bag with her dirty clothes and left, pausing at the nurse's desk on her way out.

"Would you please put a No Visitors sign on Mike Dalton's door? His family lives in Colorado, and they're snowed in. I'm not sure when they'll be able to get here, and he's still so out of it he doesn't need the hassle of constant company. I have to work until noon tomorrow, and then I'll be here to run interference for him."

"Sure thing," the nurse said, and promptly made up a sign and went to put it on the door as LilyAnn headed for the elevator.

When she got in Mike's car to drive home, the blood on the front seat was a vivid reminder of what had happened, but he had leather upholstery, so she'd clean that up tomorrow. All she wanted to do was take a bath and get in bed.

Sunday night in Blessings was low key, and she was grateful for the lack of traffic. By the time she pulled up in Mike's driveway, she was shaking. It took her a few moments to remember she hadn't eaten a bite of food since breakfast. She grabbed her bag and locked his car, then walked across the yard to her house and went inside.

Her house was cold. She amped up the thermostat and dropped her purse and coat on the sofa as she headed for the kitchen. The thought of food actually turned her stomach, but she knew she needed to eat.

She dumped her dirty clothes in the washing machine and put them on soak in cold water, then peeled a banana and ate it slowly while she scrambled some eggs. She was used to living alone and thought nothing of the quiet, but tonight it was unsettling. She couldn't quit thinking about how scared she'd been, and how helpless she'd felt when Mike had passed out in the car.

The phone rang as she sat down to eat, but when she saw the caller ID, she let it go to voice mail. She didn't want to talk to Sue Beamon right now. Sue was a nice woman, but she was also a busybody, and the last thing Lily wanted was to be pumped for information.

As soon as she finished eating, she went into the living room to turn on the television, needing the noise to remind herself she wasn't alone in the world. After that, she headed for the bathroom to take a long, soaking bath.

The day dawned cold and gray; the air felt thick and damp. Lily dressed for comfort rather than work, knowing she was only going to be in the pharmacy half a day and then at the hospital until they ran her out.

She ran across the yard to clean Mike's car, and then headed back to her house to get ready for work. She dug out a pair of navy blue sweats, found a sweatshirt that matched, and put her long hair up in a no-nonsense ponytail. The final touch was an all-weather coat instead of a jacket, in case it finally rained.

Because she had dressed down to such a degree, she put on a little more makeup than usual to spruce up her appearance. She went out of the house with mascara and a light dusting of eye shadow to go with the rose-colored lipstick. From the neck up, it was the closest she'd come to looking like her old self in years.

When she got to the pharmacy, she went straight to the back to talk to the boss before they opened the doors for business. She found him behind the counter in the pharmacy taking inventory.

"Hey, Mr. Phillips, I need to take off at noon."

He frowned. "I don't know if…"

"I promised Mike Dalton's parents that I'd take care of him until they could get here."

His frown deepened. "Mike? What happened to Mike? The wife and I were out of town yesterday."

By the time she'd filled him in, he was in shock. "Good Lord, LilyAnn. You saved his life."

She shook her head. "The doctors saved his life. I just got him to the hospital."

"Still the same thing," Phillips said. "Of course you can take off. If I need more help, I'll call my wife. Margie doesn't mind helping out. Give Mike my best wishes."

"Thank you so much. I won't have to do this after his parents arrive."

"No problem," he said. "In the meantime, count these out for me."

And just like that, the morning began. When the doors opened later, nearly every customer who came in had heard about Mike's accident and headed straight for Lily. They all wanted details and updates, and for the time being, she was a hot commodity on the Blessings gossip chain.

T. J. Lachlan drove into town for some paint and caulking. The sooner he got the old house fixed up, the sooner he could sell it. He hadn't made up his mind what he would do afterward, but it didn't matter. He liked living without encumbrances that tied him to one place for too long.

It hadn't taken long to realize that hanging out with the Wilder brothers was not going to endear him to people in the upper levels of society, so he'd since steered clear of the pool hall. He wasn't above conning a widow or two if the opportunity arose, but that couldn't happen if he got a bad reputation here like he had back home.

He drove into town for breakfast and headed for Granny's Country Kitchen for sausage gravy and biscuits. When he pulled up to the curb in front of the café, he wasn't thinking about women, but his attention shifted the moment the café door opened and a pretty redhead walked out. He wasn't intimidated by the man on her arm, because what she was wearing had the "come fuck me" look.

Her long hair was obviously dyed. Her boobs were Dolly Parton–sized, another aspect he definitely admired. Her skinny-leg jeans outlined every lush curve from her waist to her ankles, and while her chunky white sweater hung loose around her hips, the V-neck plunged most indecently. He'd never seen a more blatant invitation, but that was all right with him. He liked fine women who favored a trashy look.

He got out quickly, intending to make eye contact before she got away, but he need not have worried. The moment she saw him, she fixed on his face like a mongoose to a cobra.

He felt the force of her gaze and for a split second got a dose of his own medicine. The tables had turned, he was the one under inspection, and it caught him off guard. Then she looked away, seemingly oblivious to his presence, but he knew it was an act for the man beside her.

"Morning," he said, tipping his hat as he stepped aside to let them pass.

Bud Goodhope smiled. "Morning," he said.

Rachel's sideways glance and the little smile on her face intrigued T. J. If he wasn't mistaken, he'd just been invited to check her out further. It was an auspicious beginning to a Monday morning and put a smile on his face as he walked into Granny's.

―――

Although The Curl Up and Dye was not open on Mondays, Ruby always used the day for a thorough cleaning of the shop. Dusting, cleaning windows, mopping floors; it all had to be done and this was the only day to do it uninterrupted.

She was at the front washing the inside surfaces on the plate glass windows when she saw T. J. Lachlan park and get out at the café across the street. At the same time, she saw Bud and Rachel Goodhope come out of the café and guessed that the bed-and-breakfast didn't have any guests or they wouldn't be eating out.

When Ruby realized Rachel was actually giving the stranger the come-on, she shook her head. The only thing that kept Rachel from hooker status was that she didn't charge men money. She married them first, then took them for all they had, after which she kicked them to the curb. Rumor around town was that Bud was on the downhill slide and didn't know it. It appeared that rumor was right.

Chapter 5

LILYANN HADN'T GIVEN A THOUGHT TO HER NEW lifestyle program when she stopped by her house on the way to the hospital. She was so busy with all that was happening that she grabbed an apple and a stick of string cheese and ate them on the way.

Once she arrived, her appetite appeased, she headed for an elevator. Now that she was here, she was anxious to get to Mike's room. He'd been out of her sight since ten o'clock last night, and she just needed to make sure he was okay.

When she got off on the fourth floor, she saw a number of people standing near the nurses' station but thought nothing of it. It wasn't until she got closer that she realized they were women from the Ladies Aide at the First Methodist Church, one of whom just happened to be Rachel Goodhope. LilyAnn was so pissed that she wanted to scream. The gall of that bitch! She was so determined to get in to see Mike that she was actually using the cover of the church to get into his room.

When LilyAnn passed the nurses' station, she paused long enough to wave and let them know she was there, then strode down the hall to Mike's room and went in, closing the door behind her.

"She just went inside!" Rachel cried. "I don't understand why we can't, too."

The nurse had already guessed this was part of the

reason Miss Bronte had asked for the No Visitors sign: too many well-meaning people too soon.

"She is considered family. Are any of you related to Mr. Dalton?" the nurse asked.

They shook their heads.

"She's no kin to him," Rachel argued.

"Oh, we know that, but she has been asked by Mr. Dalton's family to stand in for them until they can arrive from Colorado. I'm sorry, but rules are rules, and until Doctor announces Mr. Dalton is strong enough for guests, you'll have to leave."

The women left the plant they'd brought, along with a little card that said "We are praying for you," and headed toward the elevators.

Rachel was fuming. She knew she'd been bested and had to face the fact that she wouldn't see Mike until he got back to work. But that was fine with her. When she was there, LilyAnn Bronte was not. Then she would have him all to herself.

—∿∿—

Mike was sitting up in bed, glaring at the cup of chicken broth and the bowl of red Jell-O on his lunch tray. When he saw LilyAnn, his mood and pulse went up, as was evidenced by the sudden beep of the heart monitor. Thankfully, she didn't notice.

"I hope you brought me something to eat," he muttered.

Lily was so happy to see him awake and making sense that she wanted to hug him. Instead, she laughed.

"Sorry. Looks like you're on a liquid diet for a while."

Mike frowned. "Lots of help you are. Save my life and then let them starve me to death."

When she laughed, the sound did crazy things to Mike's heart, making it very difficult to maintain that frown.

"At least drink the broth," she suggested.

"You taste it and then say that to me again."

She shrugged as she took a quick sip. Her eyes widened as the tepid liquid oozed down her throat.

"Ick. Okay. It's definitely missing something," she said, then saw a packet of salt beneath his napkin and stirred it into the mug. "Try it again," she said.

He took a small sip. "Yeah, that helped. Thanks."

Lily beamed. "You're welcome. Have you heard from your parents yet?"

"Dad called early this morning. He said Faith's husband rented a helicopter to come get them. It took them to the airport and he's having them flown here in the company jet, so they should be here within five or six hours."

Lily's eyes widened. "Wow! What does Faith's husband do, anyway?"

"I have a dummied-down explanation about his company making something that is part of the guidance system on army jets."

"Way to go, Faith," Lily said, as she plopped down in the chair beside his bed.

He frowned. "Yeah, I guess every woman wants to marry a rich man."

Lily frowned back. "No, Mike. Most of us just want to love the man we marry."

His heart dropped. "Yeah, so at the rate you're going in the love department, I assume you've taken yourself off the market?"

The tone of his voice was only slightly less shocking than what he'd said.

"What on earth made you say a thing like that?"

"I don't see you dating. I don't see you even interested in dating."

Before she thought, she spouted off, "Maybe that's because you aren't paying attention."

All of a sudden he felt light-headed as the blood drained from his face. Now the diet and wanting to change her life were beginning to make sense. Son of a bitch! It was happening again, and just like before, he was not part of the equation.

"I guess I wasn't," he said softly, then shoved the tray away, leaned back, and closed his eyes.

"You didn't eat your Jell-O," she said.

"I don't want my Jell-O."

She frowned. "Okay, I just thought—"

"I'm going to rest now. Stay if you want, but I don't feel like talking."

LilyAnn knew he was mad, but she didn't know why.

"Okay. I'm here if you need me," she said softly.

I will always need you, LilyAnn. You just don't need me. But the thought went unsaid.

―⁓―

Lily knew something was wrong—very wrong. Mike had turned off communicating. Every time she tried to get him in a better mood, he either looked right through her or wouldn't look at her at all.

The entire afternoon passed with hardly a word spoken between them. His supper tray had come and gone, and he'd rejected it as blatantly as he was rejecting her. Her stomach was in knots. She couldn't go home tonight without knowing what was wrong. After the shift changed and the new nurses came on the floor to do rounds, the room was finally quiet again. Lily took it as her chance to try and straighten things out.

"Hey, Mike?"

He glanced over at her. "What?"

"Are you mad at me for some reason...or am I reading too much into this, and it's just because you're in pain?"

His nostrils flared slightly. She could tell she'd struck a nerve.

When he didn't answer, she persisted. "Have I done something wrong?"

He closed his eyes and leaned back against the pillow for so long that she thought he wasn't going to answer, and then she realized he was staring at her.

"No, LilyAnn, you haven't done anything wrong. I'm the one with some issues to face."

She frowned. "Like what? Is there anything I can do?" She thought there were tears in his eyes but decided she was mistaken.

"No. This is all on me. You've been telling me something for eleven long years, but I didn't want to hear it. Now I get it, and I've got to figure out what comes next."

She stood up, her hands suddenly shaking. "I don't understand. This sounds so final. If I've done something to ruin our friendship, I'm sorry. I'm so sorry. You're my best friend."

"You don't need a friend, LilyAnn. You need to get a life. Obviously you're moving on. I wish you all the happiness."

"Moving on? I'm not moving—"

All of a sudden the door swung inward and Mike's parents rushed in.

Carol was in tears, and Don looked anxious.

"Mike! Oh my goodness, honey! I'm so sorry. Are you okay? How do you feel?" Carol cried. Then she slid her arms around his neck and hugged him gently, but with fervor.

Mike winced as he managed a grin.

"Hey, Mom. Hey, Dad. Great to see you. I'd have taken a header sooner if I knew that's what it would take to get you to visit."

Their laughter was one of relief as they turned to Lily. Carol came toward her with her arms outstretched.

"LilyAnn, sweetheart! I shudder to think what might have happened to Mike if you hadn't been there for him. Thank you! Thank you so much!"

Lily suffered their hugs and kisses, somehow managing to react normally, but her heart was breaking. Something awful had happened between her and Mike, and she didn't understand.

"I'm so glad you're here," Lily said. "Mike needed you guys. Faith really came through for you, didn't she?"

Carol rolled her eyes. "Faith's husband is a jewel. We feel blessed to have him in the family."

Lily smiled and looked at Mike, but he was, again, ignoring her and talking to his dad.

"So, Mrs. Dalton, how long can you stay?" she asked.

"We're definitely staying through Thanksgiving."

Lily smiled. "Great. You're having it at my house. My mom and Eddie are coming here for Thanksgiving before going on to his daughter's house. She just made him a grandfather for the first time."

Carol clapped her hands. "I am so excited to see Grace again and to meet her husband. It will almost be like old times."

Lily looked at Mike again, but this time he was staring out the window, seemingly oblivious to the conversation.

"Yes, like old times," she said. "So, I'm going to leave you guys to have private time with Mike. I'll see you soon. Come for supper tomorrow night…around seven if you can make it."

"That sounds wonderful."

Lily wrote down her cell number. "Here's my number. Call me if you need anything…anything at all. I still work at Phillips' Pharmacy."

Carol laughed. "Blessings is an amazing place. It's very comforting to know things never change here."

Lily felt like crying. She had to get out before she came undone.

"I'm leaving now. Mike, you know where I am. Call if you need something."

"Now that Mom and Dad are here, I won't bother you again," he said.

She managed to smile as she made a smooth exit and held it together on the way home. But by the time she pulled up in her driveway, tears were running down her face. She got into the house, turning on lights as she went, and made it all the way to her bedroom before she collapsed on the bed, sobbing uncontrollably. Her heart hurt to the point that it was hard to breathe. Mike was on the mend. His parents were here. They were all having Thanksgiving together. She should be happy. So why did she feel like someone had just died?

One week later

"Lily! LilyAnn! How much are these cough drops? I don't see a price on them anywhere."

Lily glanced up from the cash register, at the woman waving to her from an aisle away.

"It's on the shelf," she said, and kept ringing up Willa Dean Miller's purchases.

Willa Dean leaned over the counter in a conspiratorial manner.

"The reason Sue Beamon can't see the price is because she's too vain to wear her glasses," Willa Dean muttered.

Lily managed a smile, but it was hard to find the joy in even the simplest of things.

"We all have our vanities," Lily said.

Willa Dean frowned. "I guess."

"That will be forty-two dollars and fifty cents," Lily said, as she dropped the last item in the bag.

Willa Dean ran her credit card through the scanner, signed her name on the screen, and then glanced over her shoulder. Sue Beamon was her next-door neighbor, and she was heading this way. She'd been trying to corner Willa Dean for a solid week, and she wasn't in the mood to be grilled about anything.

"Thanks a bunch, LilyAnn," Willa Dean said. She grabbed the receipt Lily handed her and sailed out of the store before Sue could get to the checkout counter.

"Well, shoot," Sue said, as she laid the bag of cough drops on the counter. "I wanted to talk to Willa Dean."

"You guys live on the same street," Lily said.

Sue shrugged. "I know. But these days she's always

working or gone. And when she leaves on her little
shopping trips, she leaves Harold behind. Kinda weird,
if you ask me. I think something is up."

Lily frowned. "You shouldn't say that. Someone
could get the wrong idea and start a rumor about Willa
Dean that wasn't true."

Sue blinked, taken aback by the not-so-subtle scolding.

"Well, yes, of course you're right. I was just…uh,
how much do I owe you?"

"It comes to three dollars and seventeen cents."

Sue counted out even change, took the receipt and her
cough drops, and hustled out of the store.

Lily sighed. It was Friday, almost noon, and where
the heck was Mitchell? Her head hurt. Her neck hurt.
She couldn't wait to get to The Curl Up and Dye for that
shampoo and head massage that Ruby gave her.

And just like that, Mitchell came hurrying in the
front door, waving as he went to put up his things. He
came back just as quickly. She dropped the register key
in his hand.

"Go, girl. You look like you need a break," Mitchell said.

"I need something," Lily muttered.

She left the pharmacy with a less than hurried step.
When she passed the fitness center, she couldn't help but
look in. Stewart was behind the counter, and she could
see his wife in the back. She knew Mike wouldn't be
back to work this soon, but she couldn't help but look.

Just thinking about Mike made the ache in her heart
worse. Day before yesterday, he'd come home from the
hospital, and when she'd gone over that evening after
work to say hi, Carol had said he was asleep. Lily had
tried again last night with the same result, and this time

she knew Carol was as uncomfortable lying as she was getting the rejection. She wouldn't go back. She knew when she wasn't wanted. She just didn't know why.

As she waited at the corner for traffic to pass, she heard the rumble of T. J. Lachlan's hot-rod engine and turned to look. The lure of new territory was still there, but not as appealing as it had been. She needed to be okay with Mike more than she wanted to see if she could attract a man. But she couldn't fix anything when she didn't know what was broken, and Mike wouldn't talk to her. All she could do was focus on changing her attitude, and hopefully her social life would change with it.

When the shiny black truck passed by the corner, she looked away. She didn't want anyone's attention. She just wanted her headache to go away, and the beauty shop was the best place to make that happen.

The bell jingled as she walked in the door.

Ruby waved at her from the shampoo station.

"Come on back, girl! I'm ready for you."

Lily hung up her coat, dropped her purse by Ruby's styling chair, and sat down in front of the shampoo bowl.

Ruby fastened a cape over her clothes and patted her shoulder.

"Lean back, honey, and we'll get this pretty hair washed in nothing flat."

Lily sank backward like she was sliding into an old footed tub full of bubbles, took a deep breath, and then closed her eyes. The water was warm on her scalp. Ruby's chatter was going in one ear and out the other, which was fine. Most of what she said was information and didn't require a comment.

When she squirted shampoo on Lily's head and began

to work it into her hair, using long, steady strokes to scrub it clean, Lily felt like crying. Logically, she knew it was because the tension was releasing in her neck and shoulders. But when Ruby actually began massaging her scalp, tears welled. She sniffed as she fumbled for a tissue to wipe her nose, unaware that the tears were already rolling down her face.

Ruby was shocked. Not once in all the years she'd been doing LilyAnn's hair had she seen her exhibit real emotion of any kind. Then she remembered how rattled Lily had been at the hospital after Mike's accident and immediately thought something must have happened to him. She leaned down.

"Honey, what's wrong? Is Mike okay?"

Lily began swiping at her cheeks. "I'm sorry, Sister," she mumbled. "I don't know what's come over me. I guess I'm just tired."

Ruby didn't push the issue, but she didn't think that was it at all. She finished the shampoo and rinse, then moved Lily back to the styling chair and worked some setting gel into the long, silky strands. Without saying another word, she grabbed the blow-dryer and brush and got down to business.

LilyAnn felt numb. She was only vaguely aware that the last customer was gone and that Mabel Jean had followed Vera and Vesta to the back room to grab a little lunch before their next appointments showed up. She wouldn't look at herself—couldn't look at herself without wailing, so she stared down at the toes of her shoes instead.

Ruby noticed the tears hanging on LilyAnn's lashes. She could almost feel her sadness. She liked her a lot, and when something was wrong in Ruby's world, she had an overwhelming urge to fix it.

"Listen up, girl. We're alone, so talk to me. Is something wrong with Mike?"

It was the word "Mike" that did it. Lily covered her face with her hands and sobbed.

Ruby's heart skipped a beat. "Honey. Is it Mike? Did he get worse? What's happened?"

"No, he's not worse. He's mad at me, and I don't know why."

Ruby stifled a huge sigh of relief. "Well, bless your heart. What happened?"

Lily was sobbing loud enough that it brought the other three women out of the back room.

"I don't know what happened. That's what's so awful. One minute we were fine, and the next thing he just shut down. I asked him if it was something I said, but he got all weird and said something about me getting on with my life and…and… I don't know. I just can't get him to talk to me anymore."

The women looked at each other, then at Lily, then back at each other again. They'd already discussed the fact that they thought Mike was sweet on her.

The twins came closer. One handed Lily a handful of tissues, while the other one went to get a wet hand towel to wipe the mascara running down her cheeks.

Lily wiped her eyes, unaware she was smearing the mascara even more, and then blew her nose.

Ruby laid down the blow-dryer and spun the chair around so that Lily was facing her.

"You and Mike have been friends too long to let something like this get out of hand. Let's see if

we can figure out what might have set him off.
Sometimes it takes a disinterested party to get the gist
of misunderstandings."

Lily waited as Vera moved into work mode and
began cleaning the mascara off Lily's cheeks.

"There now, sugar. You'll be just fine and no one will
know the difference."

Ruby pulled up a chair and sat down in front of Lily.

"You said you two were talking. What about?"

Lily shrugged. "I don't know. Just stuff."

"Think. Think hard. It might be the answer you need."

Lily closed her eyes, picturing the moment she
opened the door to his room and went in.

"He was complaining about the broth and Jell-O on
his tray. I put some salt in the broth and stirred it up, and
then he said it was better and drank it."

"That's good. What happened next?"

"I asked him if he'd talked to his parents. He said he
had and that Faith's husband sent a chopper for them
because the roads were impassable, then flew them here
in his company jet. I made a comment about Faith hitting the jackpot or something like that."

Ruby frowned. "What did Mike say?"

"Something stupid, that he guessed all women wanted
to marry rich men. I told him that wasn't so. That most
of us just wanted to marry a man we loved."

Ruby leaned back. "And what did he say then?"

"Oh…I think something to the effect that he
thought I'd taken myself off the market and wasn't
interested in that. I asked him why he would say something so stupid."

Vesta and Vera looked at each other, arching their

eyebrows knowingly as Mabel Jean scooted closer to Ruby.

"Then what?"

"I don't exactly remember. I've tried and tried to think what it might have been that I said, but nothing made sense."

"Try. What did you say next?"

Lily sighed and closed her eyes again, picturing Mike's face.

"I think it was when he said I never showed interest in men, and he didn't think I was interested in dating anymore."

"And what did you say to that?" Ruby asked.

"Oh, I just popped off. I said he obviously wasn't paying attention or didn't know everything about me, or something like that."

Ruby sighed.

The twins elbowed each other.

Mabel Jean patted Lily's knee.

They all got it. Trouble was, just because they knew didn't mean they should blurt it out to Lily. She needed to figure this out on her own.

Ruby glanced at the others and shook her head, then picked up the blow-dryer to finish the job.

"So, basically you told Mike you were already dating. Wow! I didn't know this. Who's the lucky guy?"

Lily frowned. "No, I didn't."

Ruby pretended surprise. "Oh, I'm sorry. I thought that's what you meant."

Lily's frown deepened. Surely Mike hadn't thought that, too. But even if he had, why would he act so weird? It wasn't like they had those kinds of feelings for each other.

"Well, I didn't mean that," Lily said, and glanced at the time. "We need to hurry so I don't get back late."

"Sure thing, honey. Just a few more minutes here and we'll have you looking like a glamour girl."

Lily snorted beneath her breath. Sister was sweet as anything, but she had just lied through her teeth and they both knew it.

By the time she was through, Lily only had a few minutes to get back to the pharmacy. She threw on her coat, put her purse over her shoulder, and started out in a long, hurried stride.

Chapter 6

WHEN MIKE WALKED IN THE BACK DOOR OF THE FITNESS center with his dad, it felt like he'd been gone a month instead of just over a week. It was his first trip here since the accident, and even though he couldn't stay, it felt good to be out of the house and back in his own environment.

He was on his way to the front desk when he saw a woman walk by the front windows. Her head was down, her shoulders slumped. She looked like she'd just lost her best friend. It took him a moment to realize it was LilyAnn, and when he did, he felt like he'd been sideswiped.

Was he responsible for that? He knew he'd hurt her feelings by shutting her out, but she'd hurt him, too. Still, he *knew* why he'd reacted so harshly, while she didn't have a clue. He knew he was a coward for not confronting her years ago, and turning on her like this now, right after she saved his life, must have felt to her like he'd cut her legs out from under her. He was heartsick and mad at himself. Damn it! Why did life have to be so hard?

His dad walked up behind him. "Is that LilyAnn? She looks upset."

"Yeah, she does," Mike muttered, and then Stewart saw him and shouted out a big hello, which alerted the clients. After that he was caught up in the commotion.

It wasn't very long before he began to tire, and his dad called a halt.

"Hey, Mike, I think you've been on your feet long enough, don't you?"

Mike was already shaky.

"As much as I hate to admit it, you're right. So, Stewart, you're doing a great job. I really appreciate you and your wife stepping up like this. I'll see you again soon, okay?"

"Absolutely! Really good to see you up and about," Stewart said, and then went back to the front desk as Mike and his dad exited out the back.

Mike eased into the front seat of the car. This trip was over with, but there was one more stop he wanted to make.

"Hey, Dad, I need you to drive me up the street to The Curl Up and Dye. The barber is still out of pocket, and I want to get my hair trimmed."

"Sure thing," Don said as he drove out of the alley and back onto Main Street.

A couple of blocks up, he pulled to the curb in front of the shop.

"It'll be good to see everyone again, but you know your mama is going to whip the both of us when she finds out we've been to the beauty shop and left her behind."

Mike grinned. "You're right about that, but I'll take the blame. Right now she's so glad I'm still alive she won't be mad."

Don was still chuckling as they got out. The bell over the door jingled as they walked in.

Ruby glanced up.

"Hey, girls! Look who's here! My goodness, Mike,

it's so good to see you up and around." Ruby gave him a quick hug. "And Don, you look all tan and fit! I can't remember the last time we saw you in here. Where's Carol?"

"Back at Mike's," he said. "She doesn't know we're here, which means we're both gonna be in trouble."

Ruby laughed. "So what can I do for you?"

"Does anyone have time to give me a trim?" Mike asked.

"I do," Ruby said. "Sit yourself over there in the shampoo chair, and I'll make you pretty."

"That'll never happen today," Mike said with a sigh, and gladly took a seat.

Ruby shook her head as she fastened the cape around his neck. "You've got it going on and you know it."

As soon as she got his hair washed, she moved him to her styling chair, then combed her fingers through his hair, testing the texture and thickness.

"You just want it trimmed, right? No new style or anything?"

"Right, just a trim."

"Then here we go," she said, as she picked up a comb and her scissors and began to snip.

Mike's dad sat down in an empty chair to watch, and without either man realizing it, Ruby wound the conversation around to LilyAnn.

"So you're feeling okay now?" Ruby asked.

"Getting better every day," Mike said. "I just stopped in at the fitness center for the first time since I got out of the hospital, but it will be a while before I can spend much time there."

"Good thing Stewart is so dependable," Ruby said.

"Yes, it is," Mike said.

"And speaking of dependable, I'll bet you're thanking your lucky stars LilyAnn lives next door. As my daddy used to say, she sure pulled your bacon out of the fire."

Mike's gut knotted. "Yes, ma'am, she did," he said softly, and looked away.

Ruby's eyes narrowed. He was as bothered as LilyAnn had appeared to be. Dumb kids. Why didn't people just come out and say what's on their minds?

Don heard Lily's name and interjected. "We just saw her walk by the gym a short while ago."

"She was on her way back to work. She gets her hair done here every Friday on her lunch hour."

"Ah…that explains it," Don said.

Ruby nodded. "Yes, although I wouldn't be surprised if she went home early today. Not sure whether she was getting sick or if something else was going on, but I've never seen her so down."

Despite the fact that Mike couldn't face himself, Ruby spun him back to the mirror. He glared at his reflection, wishing to hell his dad would stop talking about Lily. He was like a little dog with a big bone. Once he got started on a subject, he chewed in the same place until he got himself an answer.

"Bless her heart," Don said. "I'll tell Carol to go check on her this evening. Did she say she was feeling bad? If she is, I'll happily run her up to the doctor's office."

Ruby shrugged. "You know…I'm not sure she's physically sick. I think she's upset about something else."

"Someone made her cry," Vesta said, as she sailed past the chair with an armful of clean towels.

Mike closed his eyes. *Damn it all to hell.*

"Cry? Girl, she was sobbing," Vera added.

Mike felt like crying, too. He'd fucked up, big time, but how to fix it? Or was it too late? What if there wasn't anything left between them to fix?

Don frowned. "I don't like to hear that. I wonder if she'd talk to me about—"

"No!" Mike said.

The conversation ended abruptly, but it was all Ruby could do not to click her heels in delight. She'd planted a big seed. Now it was up to Mike to cultivate it.

A few minutes later, Mike and his dad were on their way back home.

"You feeling okay?" Don asked.

"I'm fine," Mike said. "As for LilyAnn, I'll talk to her, but I pick the time, okay? You and Mom just stay out of it."

At first Don was a bit taken aback, and then he saw the red flush on Mike's face and hid a smile. He and Carol had pretty much given up that anything would ever come of Mike and LilyAnn becoming a couple, but maybe things were looking up.

"Yeah, sure, Son. No big deal."

"Thanks," Mike said.

When they got home, Mike went straight to his bedroom under the pretense of needing to rest, but the truth was, he couldn't pretend everything was okay. If his mother saw he was troubled, she wouldn't let it go. Then he'd have to explain, and there was no easy way to say that he might have just broken the heart of the only girl he'd ever loved.

—~~~—

T. J. Lachlan was standing on a ladder staring at a water
stain on the ceiling of the formal dining room, wondering if the paint he'd chosen would cover it up or if he
should use a primer first. The best way to find out was
for him to put a coat of paint over the stain, let it dry,
and see what happened. He ran the paint roller through
the paint tray and did his thing, then climbed down. His
belly growled as he glanced at his watch. It was already
after 2:00 p.m., which explained the hunger pangs. He
set the paint tray aside and headed for the kitchen.

It wasn't until he opened the refrigerator door that
he remembered he'd eaten his leftovers for breakfast,
which left him with less than a quart of milk and nothing but uncooked oatmeal to go with it. He couldn't
cook worth a darn and hadn't eaten a real home-
cooked meal since his ex, Laverne, disappeared with
Buddy. Then he frowned. Every time he thought about
Buddy and Laverne doing the dirty behind his back, he
wanted to hurt someone. Then his belly growled again,
reminding him that old news was poor fodder for an
empty stomach.

T. J. was in the mood for a burger and fries. He went
to get his coat and car keys, then drove into Blessings
with food on his mind.

Everything was going according to plan until he was
forced to stop at the edge of town. There was a three-car
pileup, and the wrecker and the police car were already
on the scene.

When he recognized the woman standing on the side
of the road as the hot redhead he'd seen coming out of
Granny's the other day, his pulse kicked. She'd been
with a man then, but she wasn't today, and in his mind,

that was opportunity knocking. He got out of the truck and headed toward her wearing what he hoped was a concerned expression.

---ᴧᴧ---

Rachel was pissed. She'd stopped at the stop sign like she was supposed to, only to have some drunk ram her from behind at high speed, shoving her out into the intersection where the oncoming car hit her broadside. It was a blessing the last car was not going too fast, and she considered herself fortunate that she had been wearing a seat belt and was still able to walk. The drunk who'd rear-ended her car had hit his head on the windshield, and the only ambulance in town at the moment had already taken him to the hospital.

The man who'd broadsided her was, unfortunately, driving without a license and still talking to the police. The upside was that she was alive and the only one who wouldn't be ticketed.

Bud was going to have a field day filing with the insurance companies. She'd probably get a new car out of the deal, which was great, but she was wondering what it would take to get a new husband with it. In her mind, she and Bud were a thing of the past. He just didn't know it yet.

She knew he was in Savannah, but when she had tried to call him, she figured out her phone had been broken in the accident. Now she was just waiting for the ambulance to come back and take her to the ER to get checked out.

A sharp gust of air went down the back of her jacket. She shivered as she pulled it close while looking for a place to get out of the wind. Her neck hurt, probably from whiplash, and she was beginning to ache in all kinds of places.

She heard another car pull up and stop and, when she looked up, saw the hotshot from the other day heading toward her with an intent expression on his face. She lifted a shaky hand to brush the hair from her eyes and hoped she looked better than she felt.

T. J. knew she recognized him. Good. That meant he'd made as deep an impression on her as she had on him. He took off his hat as he approached.

"Ma'am, my name is T. J. Lachlan. I'm Gene Bissell's nephew. Are you all right?"

The fact that he was related to a local suddenly made this less suspicious. She could work this to her advantage.

"Well, I've had better days. I'm Rachel Goodhope. Thank you for stopping."

"Can I offer you a ride somewhere or have you already called someone for help? Your husband, maybe?"

"My husband is in Savannah, and my phone broke in the accident. I'll call him later, but I would definitely appreciate a ride."

"Do you need to go to the hospital to get checked out?"

"I think so," Rachel said.

"Have you already given your statement to the police?"

"Yes. I was waiting on the ambulance to come back."

"Sit tight," T. J. said, and headed for the cop. "Officer, my name's T. J. Lachlan. I'm the late Gene Bissell's nephew." He flashed his driver's license. "I've offered to drive Mrs. Goodhope to the ER. Just wanted to make sure it was all right to remove her from the scene."

The cop glanced over at Rachel, who was looking pretty shaky.

"Yeah, sure. That's probably a good idea. If I have any other questions, I know where to find her."

T. J. flashed him a smile. "Yes, sir, thank you," he said, and then headed back to Rachel. "You're good to go, ma'am. Here, let me help you to my truck."

Rachel liked the feel of his arm around her shoulders and leaned against him as they walked. As soon as they reached his truck, he opened the door, picked her up, and set her inside.

"Excuse the familiarity. The truck is real high off the ground. I didn't want you to strain yourself."

"Yes, thank you," Rachel said, and lay back against the seat as he got in on the other side.

It felt good to be in out of the cold and off her feet. When T. J. got in behind the wheel, he flashed a big smile that did nothing for the butterflies already in her belly.

"Can you buckle up, or do you need help?" he asked.

"I can do it," Rachel said.

She was buckling up as he drove away from the scene.

Neither spoke, and in a few minutes, they were in downtown Blessings and headed for the hospital.

T. J. glanced at her. Her eyes were closed and her body was trembling.

"You doin' okay?" he asked.

Rachel opened her eyes. "Yes, I think it's just shock," she said. "I can't quit shaking."

"Bless your heart," he said, and put a hand on her arm. When she didn't complain, he left it there. A couple of turns later, he was pulling up at the ER entrance. "We're here. Hang on a second, and I'll go get a wheelchair."

"I can walk," she said.

"No, ma'am. Whether you admit it or not, you're not far from passing out. Just let me help you, okay?"

Rachel nodded as T. J. jumped out and ran inside. He came back within moments with a nurse pushing a wheelchair.

"Well, my goodness, Rachel. Were you part of that wreck?" the nurse asked, as T. J. helped Rachel out.

Rachel nodded. "Yes, and it's a wonder I'm still in one piece. I got hit by two different cars."

T. J. knelt beside her and casually laid a hand on her knee. "I'll be on my way now. They'll get you all checked out."

Rachel grasped his hand with a shaky grip. "Thank you for being so kind," she said.

T. J. flashed a big smile. "Totally my pleasure, ma'am. I hope you feel better soon," he said, and stepped aside as the nurse wheeled her away.

He told himself that if she looked back, he had it made, so he waited, watching, making bets with himself. And when she suddenly turned around and peered around the nurse to see if he was still there, he gave himself a silent thumbs-up for calling it right and waved back.

He swaggered all the way back to the truck. He made another bet with himself that the next time he saw her, they would go straight to his house for some sexual healing, as well. Married women were the best fucks. They were always grateful for the attention and already attached, which meant he walked away free when it was over. It never occurred to him that his ex-wife, Laverne, had fallen into that category, or wonder if his errant behavior with other women while still married to her

had caused her unexpected exit with ol' Buddy. The
sorry bastard.

—————~~~—————

By quitting time, everyone in Blessings knew about
the wreck. LilyAnn heard about it from at least a dozen
people, none of whom had actually witnessed the accident, but all of whom still seemed to have all the pertinent details.

She was sorry Rachel Goodhope had been involved,
but not sorry enough to give her a call to see how she
was. She listened absently as she rang up the shoppers' purchases while watching the back of the store.
Mitchell was putting up stock, and he never put it in
the right place. Eventually she wound up having to
move it to coincide with the shelf stickers the next
morning. She wasn't sure whether he was that dumb
or that lazy. Either way, it always made extra work
for her.

The pharmacist had a line in front of the checkout
window, and she had a line up front. Whatever was
going on with the citizens of Blessings, it appeared
they were all getting sick at once. She kept using hand
sanitizer and hoping for the best because she didn't want
what they had.

What she wanted was to go home.

She'd held herself together about as long as she could
today. The fact that she'd bawled like a baby at The Curl
Up and Dye was humiliating, but it had happened and
there was nothing she could do to change it. She had one
more day to get through, and then she had Sunday off. It
wouldn't come soon enough.

The door opened again, letting in a brief blast of cold air. Lily sighed. Would this day never end?

When the last customer in her line finally went out the door, she breathed a quiet sigh of relief, but it was short-lived as T. J. Lachlan came swaggering up the aisle toward the register. When he shoved a packet of condoms and a tube of K-Y Jelly across the counter, her heart skipped a beat. Without looking up, she swept them across the scanner and dropped them in a sack.

"That will be fifteen dollars and forty-four cents, please."

T. J. had expected the tall blond to react to the condoms with either a giggle or a blush. The fact that she did neither intrigued him. He paused, waiting for her to look up, and when she did, he was slightly surprised at how pretty she was—overweight but pretty. He'd had a fat girlfriend or two in his day and didn't mind it.

"Cash or credit?" Lily asked, waiting for him to react.

"Oh. Sorry there, honey. I guess I was daydreaming."

She didn't respond to his flirting, and it ticked him off just a little that he'd gotten zero reaction. Even if he didn't want her, he wanted her to want him.

"Cash it is," he said, and slid a twenty toward her.

Lily made change, counted it back to him, and handed him the sack with his purchases.

"Have a nice day," she said.

"You too."

Lily knew he was staring, but she couldn't bring herself to meet his gaze and looked at his shirt collar instead.

Giving her up as a lost cause, he grabbed his sack and hurried back to his truck. A trip to the supermarket was next on the list. If he was ever going to get that painting finished, he needed groceries in the house.

T. J.'s exit had momentarily emptied the pharmacy of customers, and Lily took it as a sign that it was safe to leave. She'd already stayed fifteen minutes past her quitting time and didn't want to get caught by having to help close. She waved at Mr. Phillips as she headed toward the front door with her things.

"I'm leaving now."

"Have a good evening, LilyAnn. See you tomorrow."

She buttoned up her coat and jammed her hands in her pockets as she started the walk home. When she passed by the fitness center, she kept her eyes in front of her and her stride long and even. Considering how weird Mike was acting, her one visit there was likely to be her last, because working out after work wasn't happening. She was too tired to mess with it at this time of day.

The streets were already filling up with traffic, mostly from the locals all heading to the football stadium. It was Friday night in Blessings, which meant high school football. She ducked her head against the cold wind that had come up and kept moving.

On a normal Friday night, she and Mike would be doing something together. Either going to a football game or having all-you-can-eat shrimp at Granny's Kitchen. Sometimes they just rented movies and made sandwiches and popcorn and stayed inside. Her heart hurt. The cold shoulder he was giving her felt as bad as when Mama had married Eddie and moved away.

Her eyes welled up all over again, but it didn't matter anymore. It was almost dark, and no one was paying any attention to her or what she was doing. Her reluctance to go home to an empty house was what prompted her to turn right instead of left at the next corner, and before she knew it, she was on the way to All Saints Cemetery. With all that was going on in her life, she had a notion that it was time to let Randy Joe know she was ready to move on.

It was about an hour before sundown, which gave her plenty of time to speak her piece before they locked the cemetery gates. The wind caught the hem of her coat and blew it into a bramble bush as she walked through the gate. For a moment it felt as if someone had grabbed it in an effort to hold her back, which gave her the creeps.

She reached down to pull it free and, as she did, saw Mr. Gerty sitting on a bench just inside the gate.

Everyone in Blessings knew Mr. Gerty. He'd been coming to the cemetery to visit his wife's grave on a regular basis for the past twenty years, and in the beginning, LilyAnn had seen him daily. While her visits had thinned out, his had remained steadfast. Lily thought that made sense, considering how many years he and his wife had been together before she died.

He was sitting on the bench with his chin down, the coat collar pulled up around his neck.

"Bless his heart, he drifted off to sleep and is going to wake up in the dark," Lily muttered. "I better wake him up and send him on his way." When she got closer, she called out. "Hello, Mr. Gerty!"

Lily knew he was hard of hearing, and sat down on the bench beside him and patted his arm.

"Hey, Mr. Gerty! It's getting dark. Time for you to go home."

This time the silence was shocking.

"Oh no," Lily mumbled, and reached for his hand. It

was colder than the air—and stiff. Her vision blurred as she felt for a pulse. There was none. "Sweet Lord."

Her eyes were already filling with tears as she dialed 911.

"911. What is your emergency?"

"This is LilyAnn Bronte. I'm out at All Saints Cemetery. Mr. Gerty is here sitting on a bench, and I think he's dead."

"Oh my word!" the dispatcher said. "Stay on the line with me while I dispatch an ambulance."

Lily dug in her purse for a tissue. A few moments later, the dispatcher was back talking to her.

"Have you tried to do CPR?" she asked.

"No, ma'am. I don't know how long he's been sitting here like this, but he's way past that. He's very stiff and his skin is cold."

"I'm sorry. Are you okay?" the dispatcher asked.

Tears were running freely. "Not really. Can I hang up now?"

"I want you to stay on the phone with me until the ambulance arrives, okay?"

"Yes, ma'am," Lily said and, a few seconds later, heard a siren approaching. "I hear a siren now."

"Just stay with me until they arrive," the dispatcher said.

LilyAnn nodded, then realized the dispatcher couldn't see her, but it didn't matter because a police car had just pulled up at the gate, and the ambulance was turning the corner.

"The police and ambulance are here. I'm hanging up now."

She disconnected without waiting for permission because she needed to blow her nose.

Lonnie Pittman happened to be the one on duty, and he recognized LilyAnn as he ran through the gate.

She looked up. "Hey, Lonnie. We keep meeting in the strangest places, don't we?"

Lonnie felt sad. LilyAnn was crying, but she'd stayed beside Mr. Gerty. It was a very touching sight for a hardened cop. He squatted down in front of them to check for a pulse in the old man's wrist.

"Yes, he's definitely dead, and it appears that he's been so for some time. How long have you been here?"

"I just got here, saw him sitting on the bench, and thought he was asleep. I sat down to wake him up and then…" She shrugged and blew her nose again.

"You can get up now," he said.

LilyAnn looked at the old man and then shook her head.

"If it's okay, I'll just stay here until the ambulance arrives. He passed alone. I think I'll wait until they take his body away."

Lonnie sighed, then saw the ambulance, patted Lily's knee, and got up.

"They're pulling up now. Be right back."

Lily glanced at the old man's face. He looked so peaceful—like he'd just fallen asleep. She looked down the pathway toward the plot where his wife was buried.

At least he wasn't alone anymore.

Chapter 7

MIKE AND HIS DAD WERE IN THE FRONT YARD VISITING with Thomas Thane, their neighbor from across the street, when they began hearing sirens. Blessings was a small enough place that the sound of an emergency somewhere usually touched them all.

"I wonder what happened," Don said.

"I have a scanner in the house. I could go check," Thomas said.

"Never mind," Don said. "If it's bad, we'll all find out soon enough."

"I'm going to the porch to sit down," Mike said, and walked away, leaving them in the yard.

He was tired of the chitchat and hated that he was already feeling shaky, although, thanks to LilyAnn, his ear infection was cured. When he'd begun getting dizzy, he'd completely forgotten about his childhood propensity for getting inner ear infections and had only himself to blame for the accident.

As he sat, he could still hear the sirens and wondered again what was going on. He glanced toward LilyAnn's house. It was still dark. He frowned. Her car was in the driveway, but she'd walked to work again this morning. She should have been home by now.

A neighbor from down the block came outside, saw the men standing out in the yard, and came running.

"Did you hear? They found someone dead at All Saints Cemetery! Didn't give a name but—"

Mike stood up. The image of LilyAnn walking with her head down and her shoulders slumped, as if she bore the weight of the world, flashed through his mind. He began replaying their last conversation and the confusion he'd seen on her face. He'd been so lost in his own disappointment that he hadn't given any thought to what his reaction would do to her. All those years of grieving for Randy Joe and never moving on—he'd never thought about her being despondent enough to take her own life.

His gut knotted. If she *had* gone to that place in her head, the cemetery would be a logical place for her to do it. Right beside Randy Joe's grave.

Jesus, Jesus, Jesus. She wouldn't! Please, God, not LilyAnn!

The sirens stopped.

He walked off the porch, past his dad and neighbor, and stopped on the sidewalk. The streetlights came on as the sun finally set. He could hear the traffic from Main Street, which was only four blocks due north. Several cars went speeding past the street where he was standing, most likely thrill-seekers going to gawk at the cemetery so they could claim firsthand experience tomorrow at the coffee shops.

And still no sign of LilyAnn.

His heart was pounding and he wanted to cry. He'd never been this scared—ever.

Please, God, please.

And then he looked up the street, and the relief was so great that his eyes filled with tears.

His dad walked up behind him. "Hey, isn't that LilyAnn?"

Mike nodded.

"Her steps are dragging. I'm gonna walk up to meet her."

"Dad, no," Mike said.

Don stopped, then frowned. "Look. Whatever's going on between you two has nothing to do with the fact that I helped raise her. If you don't like it, go in the house."

Mike blinked. He hadn't heard that tone of voice from his dad since he turned twenty-one. His shoulders slumped, but he stayed put, watching. He saw his dad stop—saw LilyAnn say something and then cover her face with her hands. When his dad put his arms around LilyAnn, Mike swallowed a sob, turned on his heel, and went into the house.

"Hi, honey, where's your dad?" his mother asked, as he strode through the living room.

"Still outside. I'm going to lie down."

Carol frowned. Something was going on. She walked out onto the porch just as her husband followed LilyAnn inside her house. She waited. A few moments later, the lights began coming on in the house, and as they did, her husband exited, then started across the yard. When he saw her, he lengthened his stride, and when he got to the porch, he took her in his arms.

"Don! What's wrong?" Carol asked.

"I'll tell you in a minute. Right now I want to hold you."

Carol was a woman wise in the ways of men. Don Dalton wasn't a man for drama, so she wrapped her arms around his waist, hugged him back, and led him inside.

"Talk to me," she said.

Don sat down on the sofa, then grasped her hands.

"Remember Mr. Gerty?"

"Oh, yes…the retired postmaster. What about him?"

"LilyAnn found him on a bench at the cemetery. She thought he'd gone to sleep, but he was dead. She's pretty broken up about it."

"Oh dear Lord!" Carol gasped. "That poor girl, and poor Mr. Gerty, too."

"Where's Mike?"

"Lying down in his room."

"Well, he can get his ass up and go talk to LilyAnn," Don muttered. "I've had just about enough of this cold war between them."

Carol frowned. "I don't think we should meddle in—"

"I'm not meddling. I'm telling him a fact of life," Don said. "And set another place at the table. She'll be having supper with us tonight, and I don't give a damn how uncomfortable they both are. We're family and I want this crap over with."

He stomped out of the room.

Carol rolled her eyes, then got up and headed to the kitchen.

Don opened Mike's door without knocking. Mike was lying on the bed, staring up at the ceiling.

"Get up," Don said sharply.

"Why?"

"I said, get up. Get your ass across the yard to LilyAnn's and tell her to come eat supper with us."

"I don't want—"

"This isn't about what you want," Don said. "She doesn't need to be alone tonight. She found Mr. Gerty on a bench at the cemetery. He was dead. She's pretty broken up about it."

Mike swung his legs off the bed. "Oh shit," he muttered, and began looking for his shoes.

Don kicked them toward him with the toe of his boot. "I don't know what's going on between you two, but you're pouting and she's sad, and whatever the hell it is, fix it. We're having Thanksgiving dinner together next week, and I don't intend to eat across the table from you two with those hangdog looks on your faces. Understand?"

Mike stood up and fired back at his dad in the same angry tone.

"What's wrong between us is that I've been in love with her since the tenth grade and she has never known it. After all these years, she still doesn't see it, no matter how much time we spend together. Now she's on a big kick to restart her life because there's a new man in it, and once again, it's not me."

Don sighed. "I'm sorry. That's got to be the worst feeling in the world. But I have one question for you. I know you spend time with her, but have you ever once told her how you feel?"

Mike's face flushed. "No. I don't want to see the disgust and rejection."

"Then you have nothing to be pissed about. She's in the dark, son, and you're the only one with answers. Either put up or shut up, and quit making everyone else miserable with you. Now hurry up and get over there. Your mom's making a place for her at the table as we speak."

He walked out as abruptly as he'd entered.

Mike shoved a hand through his hair in frustration and headed for LilyAnn's.

—∿∿—

LilyAnn had made it all the way to the kitchen before she broke down in sobs. She kept remembering all the years she'd seen Mr. Gerty kneeling at his wife's grave, talking to her as if she was still alive. She'd done the same thing at Randy Joe's until she'd run out of things to say, mainly because their relationship was barely a year old before he passed, while Mr. and Mrs. Gerty had been married forty years before she passed.

They'd had a lifetime of history together.

She and Randy Joe barely had a year's worth of memories before he died.

While Mr. Gerty had been given twenty more years to live, he'd chosen to spend it with the dead. If fate hadn't turned her life around, she might have come to a similar end. Life was hard, but nobody promised it would be easy, and it damn sure wasn't meant to be wasted. The only good thing about the whole awful event was that Mr. Gerty's loneliness had come to an end.

She was getting up to get some tissues when she heard footsteps on the porch and then a series of rapid knocks, but she ignored them. Whoever it was, she didn't want company.

The knocks ended, but seconds later she heard a key rattling in the lock. She ran into the living room just as the door flew inward.

"Mike! What the fuck? I thought someone was breaking into the house."

"By using a key? And while we're talking, I can't believe you just said 'fuck.'"

She glared. "If I wanted company, I would have answered the door, and I felt like saying fuck because this has been a fucked-up day."

He sighed.

"Dad told me what happened."

She snatched the key out of his hand. "So now you know. What do you want?"

"I am to bring you over for supper. Your place has already been set. Dad has chewed my ass for making you sad, and I'm sorry on all accounts."

Lily's eyes narrowed angrily. "That is the most pitiful excuse for an apology I've ever heard."

"It's all I got," he said, and folded his arms across his chest.

She glared.

He glared back.

"Either you come with me, or Dad will come back and get you. Don't you get it? When our parents are around, we are no longer in charge of our lives."

She rolled her eyes. "Whatever. I have to wash my face."

"I'll wait."

"I'm changing the hiding place for the extra key," she muttered.

Mike wanted to put her over his knee. "Fine. Hurry up, okay? I need to sit down."

"Then for the love of God, sit down!"

She took the extra house key and dropped it in her pocket as she went to the bathroom.

Mike sat because it was that or pass out. He hadn't exerted this much mental energy on frustration since high school.

His phone rang. He looked at the caller ID and sighed.

"Hi, Mom."

"Is she coming?"

"She's washing her face."

"Good."

The line went dead. He disconnected and dropped the phone back in his pocket just as Lily came back.

He got up and opened the door.

She sailed out, locking it behind her, then dropped the key back in her pocket.

They walked across the yard in silence.

"We're here!" Mike yelled, as they entered his house.

"We're in the kitchen," Carol called.

Lily dropped her coat on the sofa and followed Mike to the kitchen.

Carol smiled and waved when she saw them.

"Sit, sit. Soup's hot and there's plenty for seconds."

"Smells wonderful," Lily said, as she scooted into a chair and unfolded the napkin in her lap.

The first bite was warm and comforting, and the conversation soon turned to innocent gossip about locals Carol and Don knew.

Mike snuck glances at LilyAnn every chance he got, but he was careful. His parents were too damn nosy about his business, and the last thing he wanted was them feeling sorry for him that he'd wasted his life loving a woman who didn't love him back.

Still, after nearly dying last week, there were far worse things than settling for second best. He was alive, and while there was life, there was hope.

~~~

Rachel and Bud Goodhope were playing cards with Willa Dean and Harold Miller when they heard the sirens taking off all over town.

"Oooh, I always hate that sound," Willa Dean

said, and stuck another chip in the guacamole dip and popped it in her mouth. "Yum, Rachel. You make the best guacamole."

Rachel smiled. "Thank you so much. Cooking is one of my passions."

Willa Dean wiggled her eyebrows at Rachel, and then they both broke into giggles.

"What's so funny?" Bud asked.

Harold rolled his eyes as he discarded a card and drew another.

"Don't ask them stuff like that. You know it has to do with sex. Once a woman passes forty, everything revolves around sex."

Willa Dean glared. "Harold, the best thing for you right now is to keep your mouth shut."

Harold's eyes widened and then he nodded. Ever since Willa Dean had caught him strutting around their bedroom in her underwear, she'd been hell to live with. He'd thought for sure she would divorce him and tell the world what he liked to do, but to his surprise, she did not. She'd taken matters into her own hands and bought herself a vibrator. Now when she disappeared into the extra bedroom, he took himself out of the house.

The sirens faded in the distance, then stopped.

"I wonder what's happening? Sure hope it's not another wreck."

"You were really lucky, girl," Willa Dean said.

Bud patted his wife's arm. "For that we are both very grateful."

"Yes, we're very grateful," Rachel said.

A few minutes later, their phone rang.

"Excuse me a minute," Rachel said, and got up to answer.

They could hear her talking in the other room, and when they heard her gasp and then cry out, they knew something bad had happened. A couple of minutes later she came hurrying back.

"You will not believe what happened. LilyAnn Bronte found Mr. Gerty sitting on a bench in the cemetery. He was dead and stiff as a board. Can you imagine sitting down beside that?"

"Oh dear Lord," Willa Dean said. "Poor Mr. Gerty. At least he's finally with his sweet Ina again. As for LilyAnn, I cannot imagine what she must be thinking."

Rachel was still smarting from the slap-down LilyAnn had given her and popped off before she thought.

"If I was a man friend of hers, I think I'd be huntin' me a new friend."

"What do you mean?" Harold asked.

Rachel discarded. "I'll take two," she said, and when Harold dealt her two more cards from the deck, she swept them up into her hands. "That's better," she said.

Harold liked LilyAnn. She'd sold him makeup at Phillips' Pharmacy for years without blinking an eye, even when she knew it wasn't Willa Dean's brand, and he knew she'd never said a word about it, so he wasn't letting the comment go.

"What did you mean about LilyAnn's men friends?"

Rachel shrugged. "Well, think about it. Randy Joe liked her and he died. Her daddy adored her and he died. She and old man Gerty have been hanging out at that cemetery visiting their loved ones for years, and now he's dead, too."

Harold laid down his cards and gave Willa Dean a look.

"I think it's time we get on home."

Rachel blinked. "What? We haven't had any of my bourbon cheesecake yet."

"It's like this, Rachel. I think the world of LilyAnn Bronte. She's one of the sweetest people in Blessings. She's had some hard luck, but not a damn bit of it is her fault. Randy Joe died in a war, not because he loved her. Her daddy died because he smoked and had a heart attack. And Mr. Gerty was in his nineties, for God's sake. I venture to say she didn't have a thing to do with his heart givin' out. I reckon he died from old age and grief."

Rachel blinked again. "Well, my goodness. I didn't mean anything by what I said."

Harold stood up. "Willa Dean, are you coming?"

She looked at Rachel and shrugged. "It is getting late and all. Thanks so much for everything. Next time it's at our house, okay?"

Rachel was stunned. She'd never had a man call her down like that. Ever.

"Yeah, sure… No hard feelings, okay, Harold?"

Harold gave her a long look and then shrugged. "No hard feelings, and I hope I don't hear any more of that crap about LilyAnn bantered about town."

"If you do, it didn't come from me," Rachel said sharply.

Bud was embarrassed, but that was nothing new. Rachel could be a bitch. He'd been on the receiving end of her sharp tongue a few times himself and was secretly tickled that old Harold had called her on it. He helped her clean up and then they went to bed without commenting about the situation, and the moment was soon forgotten.

Later on, they had two couples arrive at the bed-and-breakfast to spend the night. Bud registered them and got them settled into their rooms, while Rachel began planning the meal.

The next morning she was up before daylight making breakfast. She'd been at it for almost two hours and was frying up the last of the bacon when Bud finally walked into the kitchen.

"Hey, Rachel, how much longer before we set up the sideboard?"

Despite the cold day outside, her kitchen was hot and steamy. She glanced over at the tea cart she'd been loading and then back at the stove.

"About three minutes and you can take it out. Are they waiting? Please tell me they're not waiting."

"No, but I can hear them moving around upstairs and they did say they were checking out early."

Rachel reached for the tongs to take the remaining bacon strips out of the pan, and as she did, some grease popped out onto a hot burner, which caused a quick flare-up. Those flames flared back into the hot grease in her pan, and before she knew it, grease was popping and the flames were over her head.

She screamed and slammed a lid onto the pan. It smothered the fire, but not before she'd gotten a dose of the flames,

Bud was at her side in a flash, but it was after the fact. The fire was out. The bacon was burned, and Rachel's eyebrows and bangs looked like they'd melted.

"Oh honey, are you all right?" Bud asked.

Rachel was already wrapping a handful of ice cubes in a towel to put on the burn splatters on her arms.

"I guess. Thank goodness my clothes didn't catch fire." She glanced at the bacon she'd already cooked. "There's no time to cook more. What's there will have to work."

"That's plenty," Bud said. "You sit down and ice the burns. I'll put out the food and hold court. You don't need to come out unless you want to."

"Thanks," she muttered.

She could hear the couples gathering out in the dining room and sighed with weary satisfaction as they began tasting and exclaiming over the food she'd sent out.

The ice helped allay the pain of the small rising blisters on her arms, and when they felt better, she got up to go wash her face. That's when she saw her hair.

"Oh, for the freaking love of God! My eyebrows! My hair! Is Bud blind? I'm ruined!"

In a panic, she returned to the kitchen and began cleaning up the mess. As soon as the guests checked out, she was going to The Curl Up and Dye. Bud could clean up the rooms. She had a hair emergency.

———∿∿∿———

Vesta and Vera were working side by side doing haircuts, while Mabel Jean was cleaning up her station from her last customer.

Ruby was on the phone at the front counter when Rachel walked in. She glanced up and smiled, motioning that she would be off in a few seconds, and then noticed the condition of Rachel's face and hair.

"Hey, Moira, I have to go. I'll see you at 2:00 p.m. tomorrow."

She headed for Rachel with her hands outstretched.

"What on earth happened?"

"Oh, Sister, I had a little fire in the kitchen this morning," Rachel said.

"Are you in pain?"

Rachel was struggling not to cry. "Some. It feels like I've been stung by a swarm of bees. What can you do with my face and brows?"

"Come sit," Ruby said, leading her to a shampoo chair. She ran her fingers through Rachel's hair, then felt her eyebrows. "I think we can fix this so it doesn't look so shocking. Although the surface is singed, you still have brows. Do you trust me to do what I can?"

Blinking back tears, Rachel nodded, and with that, Ruby got down to work.

Rachel heard the chatter going on in the shop but was beyond caring about the gossip. She was too worried about becoming presentable again.

The bell over the door continued to jingle as people came in and went out. It was no big deal until Rachel realized one voice she was hearing belonged to LilyAnn. She was still smarting from the put-down the woman had given her at the hospital but didn't have a leg of indignation to stand on. The truth was she did have an eye on Mike Dalton. But to be fair, she had an eye out for any eligible male, and some who were not.

—∾∾—

Vera was manning the counter when LilyAnn walked in. They all knew about her finding Mr. Gerty's body but figured the less they mentioned it, the happier she would be.

"Hi there, sugar. What can I do for you?"

"I would like to change my hair appointment time next week."

"Okay, let's see what we can do. What day?" Vera asked.

"Mama and Eddie are coming in Wednesday for Thanksgiving, so if Ruby has an opening at noon on Tuesday or Wednesday of next week, it would be helpful. They'll be leaving sometime Friday, and I don't want to miss my visit because I'm getting my hair done."

"Hang on, let me check," Vera said. She scanned Ruby's appointment book, then looked up. "She can do you at 12:30 on Tuesday. How would that work?"

"It will be fine," LilyAnn said. "I'll just take my lunch hour thirty minutes later. Thank you so much."

"You're welcome, sugar. We'll still see you this Friday, right?"

Lily nodded.

"Okay then. So, you take care, okay?"

Lily nodded and left, grateful they hadn't mentioned Mr. Gerty. Work was a madhouse today. Everyone who came in wanted to talk about it.

But she wasn't the only one relieved to have escaped confrontation. Rachel breathed a sigh of relief when she heard Lily leave.

"Let's move over to my styling chair and see what we can do," Ruby said, as she wrapped a clean towel around Rachel's head.

Rachel did so with alacrity, hoping Ruby could perform, at the least, a small miracle. Between her recent accident and now this, she was wondering if God was trying to tell her to change her ways. She certainly hoped not. She liked her ways just fine the way they were.

She clenched her jaw as Ruby picked up her scissors and spun the chair around so Rachel could no longer see what was happening. At that point, like the wreck and the fire, it was out of her hands.

—∿—

T. J. Lachlan had finally finished painting the interior of the house and was moving on to exterior repairs. He'd been up in the attic often enough to know there was a leak in the roof, and he had a general idea of where it was. He'd climbed up on the roof an hour earlier, found the leak, and was in the process of patching it when he heard a noise down below. He looked over his shoulder just as the top rungs of the ladder began sliding sideways and then disappeared from sight. He heard a loud thud as the ladder hit the ground.

"What the fuck!" he yelled, and eased back to the edge of the roof just in time to see a large bull making an exit up the drive.

He didn't know where the bull had come from, but the puzzle was moot. The bigger question was: How was he going to get down? The house was two-story. The roof was steep. There was a chimney, but he was no Santa-fucking-Claus. He sat down and then took out his cell phone.

This was embarrassing as hell, but he was never going to get down without help. He could call 911, but if he did, everyone in town would know. It was hard to maintain a macho attitude when you were the joke of the week. The only local phone number he had on speed dial was The Curl Up and Dye. Even if he called them, he was wondering how they could help.

A cold gust of wind blew up the back of his jacket, which reminded him that spending the night on the roof was out of the question.

"The Curl Up and Dye it is," T. J. muttered, and started dialing on his phone.

———※———

Ruby turned off the blow-dryer, then picked up a teasing comb and a can of hair spray, eyeing what she'd just done for Rachel's hair.

"Just a few more minutes and we'll be done," Ruby said.

"Is it bad?" Rachel asked.

"No!" Ruby said. "Not at all! You'll see."

She worked quickly, giving Rachel's hair a liberal dose of hair spray before she turned the chair around.

"So what do you think?" Ruby asked.

Rachel couldn't believe it. She looked normal. A little different, but normal.

"How did you do that?" she asked, feathering the bangs across her forehead.

"You have more bangs than you did before. See, I pulled some more of your hair forward from the crown to cover what burned off. As for your eyebrows, I clipped the singed part off and reshaped them a little. It will all grow back, so don't think you have to live with this look forever."

Rachel was beaming. "You are a freaking genius," she cried.

"I like to think so," Ruby said as they went to the counter to pay.

The phone began to ring as Rachel was writing out a check.

"Hang on a second, Rachel, okay?"

Rachel nodded.

Ruby smiled her thanks as she answered the phone. "The Curl Up and Dye. This is Ruby."

"Uh… Hey, Ruby, this is T. J. Lachlan. Do you remember me?"

"Sure, I remember you, T. J. What's up? Do you want to make an appointment?"

"Not exactly. I have a problem, and your phone number is the only local number I had on speed dial."

"So, what's the problem?" Ruby asked.

T. J. sighed. "I'm embarrassed to say that I need help. I am stranded on the roof of my house."

Ruby's eyes lit up. "Stranded on the roof of your house? How did that happen?"

"I was patching a leak when someone's stupid bull got into my yard and knocked the ladder over. The bull's gone and I'm stuck. Do you know anyone in the area who could come out here?"

"I sure do. We'll find someone to get you right down. Hang on while I get the phone book to look up some names, okay?"

Rachel put a hand on Ruby's arm as she slid her check across the counter.

"What happened to T. J.?" she whispered.

Ruby was surprised Rachel knew him. "He's stranded on the roof of his house. Someone's bull got in his yard and knocked down the ladder. He needs someone to put it back up. He lives out at the old Bissell place."

"I can go," Rachel said.

Ruby arched an eyebrow. Everyone knew Rachel's propensity for chasing men.

"Well…"

"No, you don't understand," Rachel said. "The day I had the wreck he stopped and drove me to the ER. This is just my chance to return a favor."

"Oh! Well, my goodness, I didn't know that, but it definitely makes sense. If you're sure, I'll tell him you're on the way."

"I'm sure," Rachel said. "And thanks again for making me presentable."

Ruby smiled. "My pleasure," she said. "You take care now."

Rachel waved as she left, but she was already thinking about Lachlan and the possibilities that could ensue.

Chapter 8

RACHEL'S PULSE WAS RACING AS SHE DROVE OUT OF town toward the Bissell house. She glanced in the rear-view mirror a couple of times to reassure herself she was presentable enough for this little foray, and then shivered. It had been a while, four long years to be exact, since she'd had something besides Bud's fumbling excuse for romance. If he hadn't been so well-to-do, she would never have settled for the sixty seconds of wham-bam-thank-you-ma'am sex.

She was less than a quarter of a mile from her destination when her cell phone rang. When she saw it was from Bud, she rolled her eyes. Since she'd wrecked her car, she was driving his, which meant he was stuck at home. So should she answer and tell him the truth about what she was doing, or let it go to voice mail? Even if she let it go, her destination was no secret because the ladies at The Curl Up and Dye knew where she was going, and if they knew, then so would everyone else, which made the decision for her. She reached for her phone.

"Hello, Bud. What's going on?"

"I was just checking on you, honey. Are you still in much pain? Was Ruby able to fix your hair?"

"It isn't really pain. It feels more like a whole lot of beestings on my skin. And yes, my hair looks fine. She even managed to trim my eyebrows and keep me from looking like a madwoman."

"So, are you on your way home?"

"Not yet. I was just leaving the shop when Ruby got a phone call from Gene Bissell's nephew. Remember, he's the man who stopped at the wreck and took me to the ER."

"Oh yeah, so what about him?"

Rachel giggled, making it seem like a big joke on T. J.

"It's the funniest thing. He was calling her for help because their number was the only local number he had on speed dial. Said he was fixing a leak on the roof when someone's bull got in his yard and knocked down the ladder. He's stranded on top of the house, and it's that old two-story. Can you imagine? I'd be hanging on to the chimney with both hands."

Bud chuckled as Rachel continued her tale.

"So…seeing as how he stopped to help me when you were out of town, I offered to drive out and rescue him."

There was a moment of silence.

"Bud…honey…are you still there?"

"Yes, I'm here. So you're on your way to his house?"

"Bud Goodhope! Are you watching TV? I swear to my time, I would appreciate it if you would pay attention when I'm talking to you. I already said I'm on my way out there. So listen up, 'cause I'm not gonna repeat myself again. As soon as I put the ladder back up so he can get down, I'm coming home."

Bud was already backpedaling. He'd made her mad, and the worst thing that ever happened at their house was when Rachel got mad at him.

"Don't get yourself in a huff. I was just worrying about you, you know. You're still a little sore from the wreck, and then you went and burned yourself today. I just didn't want you straining anything."

She snorted derisively.

"You weren't all that worried about my well-being this morning when I got my ass out of bed at 4:00 a.m. to go make breakfast for our guests. And you were suspiciously absent for the next two hours, which tells me you went back to bed. You did, didn't you? So, you're worried about my welfare only when it suits you. Thank you so much for your concern. I will be home soon, and if I am in any way delayed, rest assured I will be calling your ass, despite the fact that you will not be able to help me now, any more than you were able to help me the day I had the wreck, because I am driving our only car."

She hung up before he could respond.

"That'll give him something to think about," she muttered, then realized she was at the turnoff, tapped the brakes, and took the turn.

T. J. was finished with the repairs. His stuff was packed up, and he was sitting near the edge of the roof waiting to be rescued when he saw a car coming down the driveway. The girls had come through for him in a big way. He breathed a huge sigh of relief and waved.

When the driver pulled the car up to the edge of the yard and got out, the last person he expected to see was Rachel Goodhope. He didn't know whether to look at this as a windfall or a huge embarrassment.

"Hi!" Rachel said as she hurried across the yard. "Who knew I would get to return the favor so soon?" she yelled.

"I sure appreciate this," T. J. shouted back.

"Give me a sec," Rachel said, and began manhandling the huge ladder.

She dragged it over to the house, then finally got it in the air and leaning up against the roof.

"Hang on to the end, and I'll pull it out to a better angle," she yelled.

T. J. waved to let her know that he'd heard and grabbed hold of both sides. As she'd promised, she pulled it back until it was at a good, sturdy angle, then got beneath it and grabbed hold with both hands.

"Climb down now. I won't let go!" she yelled.

T. J. swung a leg over and then went down backward, his tool belt bumping against the rungs as he went. The moment his feet touched hard ground, he breathed a huge sigh of relief.

"Lord have mercy! I sure appreciate that," he said, and turned around to shake her hand.

Rachel eyed his hand, then looked up at him and smiled.

T. J.'s heart skipped a beat. "Uh…"

"How grateful are you?" Rachel drawled.

T. J. grinned. "As grateful as you want me to be."

Rachel eyed the house. "I'd love to see what you've done with the place."

Hot damn. "I'd be delighted to show it to you."

"Can I see it all?" Rachel asked.

It was all T. J. could do to keep his pants zipped until he got inside.

"You can look at it for as long as you want."

"I don't have much time," Rachel said. "This time it'll have to be a hit and run. Maybe another time I can inspect it much closer."

T. J. led the way inside and locked the door behind them.

Rachel heard the click and turned around, her eyes narrowing seductively. Before he could move, she started to strip.

"Oh Lord," he whispered, and dropped his tool belt.

He kicked off his work boots and shucked out of his jeans, then realized how stupid he probably looked with a massive erection poking out from beneath the hem of his shirt and stripped it off, as well. He noticed the little red spots on her arms and neck, and then decided whatever she had, he'd risk catching it.

"My, my, I do so admire that," Rachel said, as she flattened her hands across his chest, then grabbed his hand and took him toward the sofa.

It occurred to T. J. that he was probably out of his element. He was so not in charge of what was about to happen, which heightened his excitement even more.

"I don't have all day," Rachel said.

"I'm gonna make you wish you did," T. J. drawled, and proceeded to push her down on the sofa and slide between her legs.

Rachel wrapped her legs around his waist and closed her eyes, determined to enjoy the ride.

Twenty minutes later, Rachel was on her way home and as smug as a barn cat with a rat in its belly. Sex with T. J. Lachlan was better than a good allover massage any day. She didn't have a tense muscle left in her body.

She glanced at the clock and smirked. They'd done the dirty, and she'd been dressed and gone in less than fifteen minutes, with a promise to make a return trip at a later date.

What she needed was a shower to hide the sex smell

on her body, but she had another idea that would solve the need for a shower and what to fix for lunch, both at the same time.

Once she got back to Blessings, she pulled into the drive-through at Charlie's Barbecue and ordered take-out. She'd walk in smelling like barbecue and fries, and that would be that.

Only a few minutes later, she was on her way home with a sack full of barbecue and a satisfied smile on her face. She pulled into the drive and parked, then shifted into defense mode, just in case it was necessary. She walked in the house with her chin up, carrying the sack.

"Something smells good!" Bud said, as he met her in the hall.

"I stopped at Charlie's on the way home and brought barbecue. After the fiasco at breakfast, I wasn't in the mood to cook another meal."

"Good idea," Bud said, and watched as she began taking things out of the sack. "Looks like we'll need plates and forks. Did you get extra sauce, or do I need to get ours out of the fridge?"

"I got extra," she said, and together they got their meal on the plates.

She was carrying them to the table, and Bud was right behind her with their drinks. When she sat down to eat, she flipped her hair back behind her ears.

Bud looked up and then frowned.

"Hey! You're missing an earring."

Rachel gasped. "Oh no! Those are my diamond studs!" She felt her ears and then moaned.

Bud's suspicious nature kicked into gear.

"So what were you doing out at that house to make you lose a goddamned earring?"

Rachel's eyes widened in disbelief and then narrowed angrily.

"I cannot believe you just said that!"

"I said it, and I'd be interested in your answer."

Before she could open her mouth, their phone rang. Bud got up to answer, stomping his feet with every stride that he took.

"Hello. Goodhope Bed-and-Breakfast."

"Mr. Goodhope?"

"Yes?"

"Hey, nice to meet you, sir. My name is T. J. Lachlan. Mrs. Goodhope was just out at my place to rescue me off my roof."

Bud was surprised the man was actually calling their house.

"Yes, I heard," he said shortly.

"Well, the reason I'm calling is that I just found a diamond earring outside when I went to put up the rest of my extra shingles. It was near where the ladder had fallen, and I guessed it might be hers. Would you ask her if she's missing one?"

Bud's stomach knotted. He knew before he opened his mouth that he was about to eat a butt-load of crow.

"Yes, she's already missed it," Bud said.

"Well then. I'm so glad I found it. I'm on my way into Blessings in a few minutes to go by the lumberyard and pick up some lumber to repair my tool shed. I'd be happy to drop it by your bed-and-breakfast."

"That would be great. I'm sure she'll be grateful. Thank you for calling."

"My pleasure, sir. Nice talking to you."

Bud hung up. When he turned around, Rachel was glaring.

"Uh…that was the Lachlan guy. Said he found your earring outside where the ladder was. He's bringing it by shortly."

Rachel stabbed a french fry and poked it in her mouth without answering.

Bud sat back down and reached for her arm, but she snatched it away.

"I'm sorry, Rachel. I guess I just got jealous."

"You guess? You guess?" She rolled her eyes. "What I'd like to know is why? I have *never* done a single thing to give you reason to distrust me, and you know it."

Bud was crestfallen and it showed. "I do know. I'm sorry. I said I'm sorry, and I don't know what else to say."

"Do me a big favor and don't say anything," Rachel said, then proceeded to add a little salt to her ribs and dug into them like a field hand.

The phone rang again.

"I'll get it," Bud muttered and once again strode over to the phone to answer. "Goodhope Bed-and-Breakfast."

"Hey, Bud, this is Ruby, down at The Curl Up and Dye."

"Hi, Ruby."

Rachel glanced up, suddenly curious why Ruby Dye would be calling her home.

"The reason I called is that I found the back of an earring on the floor beneath my chair and I'm thinking it might be Rachel's. It looks as if it might be real gold, and I know she has some nice jewelry. I actually swept it up with the hair I trimmed. Ask her if she's missing one."

Bud sighed. "She is."

"Great! Tell her I've already put it in an envelope for safekeeping and the next time she's downtown to stop by and pick it up."

"Yes, I'll do that," Bud said. "Thanks for calling."

He hung up, then looked at his wife and sighed.

"What?" Rachel asked.

"Ruby found the back of your earring at her shop. Next time you're downtown, she said stop by and pick it up."

Rachel rolled her eyes. "Well, that explains how I lost the earring to begin with, now, doesn't it?"

Bud nodded. "What can I say?"

"Nothing. You've already said enough," Rachel said, then got up with her nose in the air. "I'm exhausted. What with the fire, then the trip to the beauty shop, then out to wrestle that damn ladder up a two-story house, I'm going to take a nap. When Mr. Lachlan stops by with my earring, try not to make a bigger ass of yourself than you already are."

Bud's cheeks flushed angrily. "You don't have to be hateful."

"And you didn't have to act like a green-eyed fool."

She strode past him with her nose in the air.

A few moments later, Bud heard her slam the door to their bedroom. He sighed, then sat back down and ate his food in silence while Rachel got in the shower and washed the smell of sex off her skin.

When T. J. Lachlan showed up about thirty minutes later, the sight of him didn't make Bud any happier. The man was fifteen years younger than him, at least six inches taller, thirty pounds lighter, and good-looking. Bud wanted to punch him on general principle, but the man was polite and all business. He introduced himself, invited Bud out to the house for a beer any time he was in the neighborhood, dropped off the earring, and drove away.

Rachel was watching from her upstairs window. T. J. handled that like a pro, which made her realize he probably was. He was too good at sex and too smooth of an operator not to have been in this position before. What was it he'd said to her when she was taking her leave? Oh yes…he'd told her not to worry about a thing, and that he'd been shot at in rosebushes before. She sighed, hoping she hadn't bitten off more than she was willing to chew. T. J. Lachlan was just for fun. Someone like Mike Dalton was for keeps.

Four days later

Saturdays were always busy, but this one was crazy. It was the last weekend before Thanksgiving, and everyone was out and about, running errands and stocking up. Unless there was an emergency need for medicine, the pharmacy would be closed Thanksgiving Day.

Mitchell was already at work. She overheard him talking to an elderly lady about cats, and after the lady left, Lily picked up the conversation.

"Hey, Mitchell. Did I hear you tell Mrs. Bolliver that you had a cat?"

Mitchell nodded. "Yeah, her name is Cleopatra. I am her servant and that is all. If she's in a good mood, she lets me pet her."

Lily smiled. "That's funny. I didn't know you had a cat. You never talked about her before."

Mitchell shrugged. "You never asked me about that stuff before. So, you can go to lunch now," he said, and went back to facing an aisle.

Lily sighed. It was true. She'd worked with Mitchell for more than seven years and never once asked him a personal question. Proof again that she'd been living in a vacuum.

She exited out the back door. Mike's car was parked behind the fitness center. He still wasn't allowed to lift anything, but he was getting stronger every day, or so she heard through the grapevine. She wouldn't know because they were still at odds.

She pulled the collar of her coat up around her neck and put her head down as she walked into the wind. She had a destination in mind and a task that needed to be done. The sooner she got it over with, the better.

About four blocks down, she heard what was becoming a familiar sound—the rumble of T. J. Lachlan's hot-rod truck. When she got to the end of the block, she had to wait for traffic to pass, part of which was him and his truck.

She wouldn't look and was no longer sure she cared what he thought. As luck would have it, the old lady in the car in front of him stopped to wave LilyAnn across the street.

She lowered her head and moved quickly across the intersection in long, hurried strides.

A few minutes later, she was at All Saints Cemetery. She walked through the gates with purpose, heading straight for Randy Joe's final resting place.

The newly turned earth beside Ina Gerty's tombstone was a reminder of Mr. Gerty's recent demise, but there was no need to worry about him any longer. His troubles were over.

She glanced at it once, somewhat surprised his given name had been Joaquin, which set her to wondering what on earth would possess a woman to name a child Joaquin with a last name like Gerty. Definitely an oddity, but the world was full of them.

When she finally arrived at Randy Joe's tombstone, it dawned on her that this was the first time in eleven years she'd come without flowers. Maybe it was just as well, because her gift to him today was freedom. She was turning loose of the memory and all that came with it. Now he could be just another soul at rest.

Lily knelt down near the headstone and began sweeping the dry leaves from the grave like she always did.

"Hey, Randy Joe, it's me. I'm on my lunch hour, have a lot to tell you and not much time, so I'll get right to it. I'm making changes in my life, and part of it is letting go of you. I'm actually ashamed of how long I kept dragging you through my misery, but the truth is, I didn't know what to do with you. I know that sounds stupid, but I was only eighteen and teenagers aren't known for having all that much sense."

A siren suddenly sounded, but it wasn't a long, continuous whine. More like a short burst of "whup whup," which usually meant Lonnie was signaling someone to pull over. She supposed he was about to hand out a traffic ticket, then made herself focus again on the job at hand.

"So here's the deal, Randy Joe. I'm working on

making myself over. I want to belong to someone again and I know you understand, so this is good-bye. I'm sure it's fine with you. I'm the one who got trapped in the past. Anyway, I have my health and prospects. For a twenty-eight-year-old spinster, it's not a bad place to start."

She was all business as she got up to brush the dry grass from her slacks. That was a lot easier than she'd expected. She felt good about this as she started walking out—like she'd just centered her focus for the first time in years. She paused at the gates to look back. The silence was telling.

No one here had an opinion or an ax to grind about her decision. All the misery and confusion of life was left to the living. By the time she got back to work, she felt like a new person. What had once defined her was gone. What she would become was still an unknown, and that was where the excitement lay.

Chapter 9

MIKE WAS AT ODDS WITH HIMSELF. HE WAS STILL smarting from the chewing-out his dad had given him. Yes, he probably should have tried to woo LilyAnn years ago, but they'd settled so easily into the friendship, and he loved her so much that he was afraid if he told her how he really felt, it would ruin the little bit of connection with her that he had.

Today was Tuesday. Lily's mom and stepfather would arrive sometime tomorrow. He had to figure out a way to mingle congenially throughout Thanksgiving dinner without making a scene.

His dad had dropped him off at the fitness center over an hour ago and wouldn't be back for a while, which was fine with Mike because he had somewhere to go.

"Hey, Stewart, I'm going to The Curl Up and Dye. If Dad shows up, tell him where I'm at."

"Will do," Stewart said.

The day was gray and chilly, looking like it might rain. Mike buttoned his coat as he started up the street. Even though he was feeling stronger every day, he was in no shape to pick a fight.

There wasn't an empty parking place on the block where the salon was located. It didn't bode well for a walk-in, but the least he could do was ask.

As usual, the bell jingled when he opened the door,

and as usual, a half-dozen people turned to look at who was coming in. He recognized a couple of women from church with their hair in various stages of disarray, but no one was in Ruby's chair, and she was on the phone. He moved to the counter as she hung up.

"Hey, Mike. You look better every time I see you," Ruby said.

"Thanks, Sister. I feel better every day."

"Are you here for a haircut again?" she asked.

"Actually, I would appreciate it if you would trim up my eyebrows and anything else that needs trimming, if you know what I mean?"

Ruby grinned. "I don't have anyone for thirty minutes and can do it right now if you're ready."

"I'm ready," Mike said.

He hung his coat on the coat rack and then followed her back.

Ruby was considering the best way to interfere in Mike and LilyAnn's business again. It made her crazy when people didn't just come out and say what was on their minds, and sometimes the only way to make good things happen was for someone to stir the pot.

She got him in the styling chair before broaching the subject of LilyAnn again.

She got her little trimming shears and began cleaning up his thick, dark brows. "Y'all still having Thanksgiving at LilyAnn's?"

"Yes. My mom and dad are excited. They haven't seen LilyAnn's mom in years, and they've never met her husband."

Ruby continued to comb and trim, purposefully lulling him into a comfortable state of being as they talked.

"Is LilyAnn doing okay? I mean, after finding Mr. Gerty dead like that, and all?"

"I think so," Mike said.

"That's good. I sure like that girl. She's on quite a mission, isn't she?"

Mike's eyes narrowed. "What do you mean?"

"Oh, you know…all that walking back and forth to work every day and eating healthier. I swear, every time I see her she's on the run. The weight must be melting off, because I can sure tell a difference in her clothes. Not that she didn't look sweet as can be before, but she's getting some pride back in herself, don't you think?"

"Doing it for the new boyfriend, I guess."

Ruby paused to pick up a tiny pair of clippers for trimming ear and nose hairs. "LilyAnn has a new boyfriend? That's strange. She's never mentioned a thing like that to me. Have you met him yet?"

"No," Mike said.

Ruby laughed. "I'll bet she brings him by for you to vet, you being like a brother to her and all."

"I never thought of myself as her brother," Mike muttered.

"Really? Since you guys were always doing stuff together, and because you grew up next door, I just assumed that was probably the relationship you shared."

"Nope."

"Well, I'll bet that's how she sees it, because you treat her like your sister."

She turned on the clippers, which sounded to Mike like a bee had flown in his ear, leaving him to think about what she'd just said.

Mike wished she'd shut the hell up because she was sounding like his father, and he'd heard all this before.

Fine. So it was his fault LilyAnn didn't know he loved her.

Great. It was his fault that he'd let her get interested in someone new without stating his own case first.

Whoop-de-fucking-do. Everyone was an armchair psychiatrist and he was a dumb-ass.

"Girls are funny," Ruby said. "Sometimes they don't know what they want until they realize they can't have it."

Mike's eyes narrowed. "What do you mean?"

Ruby made a final cut and then picked up the blow-dryer.

"If I was a girl, and some guy I really liked, but only thought of as a friend, suddenly appeared to have a new girlfriend, it might make me see him in a different light. Just a thought. So give me a couple of minutes to blow this dry, then you'll be good to go."

Mike's head was spinning. Really? If he wanted LilyAnn to fall in love with him, he had to get himself another girl? Seriously? Lord. No wonder he was such a loser when it came to women. He would never have thought of such a crazy scheme.

He was at the counter paying when LilyAnn walked in. For a second he thought Ruby had engineered this meeting, but when Ruby spoke, he realized LilyAnn had an appointment.

"Hey, LilyAnn, go on back to the shampoo station. Soon as I take Mike's money, I'll be right with you."

Lily nodded. "Hey, Mike."

"Hi," he said, but she was already walking away.

Ruby shrugged at Mike, as if to say, see what I mean?

"You have a good Thanksgiving, honey, and take it easy."

"You too," Mike said, grabbing his coat on the way out.

He paused outside and glanced back through the window. LilyAnn was taking off her coat and talking to someone in an animated fashion, and as she turned, he could see the weight loss Ruby had been talking about. Funny. He hadn't noticed the loss any more than he'd noticed the gain. LilyAnn was still in his heart, no matter what she looked like.

He hunched his shoulders against the cold and had started walking when someone honked. He turned to see his dad pulling up to the curb. He stopped and got in.

"Ready to go home?" Don asked.

"Yep," Mike said.

While everyone else was planning Thanksgiving festivities, he was trying to figure out who the hell he could rope into pretending to be his girlfriend to make Lily jealous.

———

Ruby was scrubbing LilyAnn's scalp a little harder than usual because she knew it was the way Lily liked it. What the girl needed was a full-body massage. Either that or get laid, but she'd probably never go for it. She wanted to know who the guy was that LilyAnn had her eye on, and then she'd go from there.

"So, you're having Thanksgiving at your house, right?"

"Right," Lily said. "Mama will get here sometime tomorrow to help. It will be great to have her home again, even if it's only for a couple of nights."

"Have you started baking yet?" Ruby asked.

"I made two pecan pies last night and put them in the refrigerator," Lily said. "I'll make the cornbread tonight so it will be ready to make dressing on Thursday morning. Mama always says that fresh cornbread doesn't make good dressing. It needs to be a day or two old to do it right."

"I agree with your mama," Ruby said, then began to rinse the soap out of Lily's hair. "You do know you're looking fabulous, don't you? I swear girl, what have you lost, ten…fifteen pounds already?"

Lily smiled. It felt good for her progress to finally show.

"A little over fifteen, but part of that I attributed to the scare of Mike's accident. I've never been as afraid as I was when he passed out in the car on the way to the hospital."

Ruby nodded. "I can only imagine. He's like a brother to you, isn't he?"

Lily frowned. She'd never really put a tag to their relationship. Mike was just Mike and always there.

"I guess."

Ruby squirted some conditioner on LilyAnn's hair and began massaging it into the scalp.

"Oh my gosh, that feels so good," Lily said.

Ruby smiled. "I love to make my clients look and feel good, and you're looking mighty fine. I hear you have a new beau. When are we going to get to meet him?"

Lily frowned. "Where did you hear that?"

Ruby shrugged. "I was thinking Mike mentioned it, but I could be wrong. Maybe I just assumed it when you decided to make the big lifestyle change."

"Oh."

"So, who is he?" Ruby asked, and then leaned close so that no one else could hear. "I won't tell. I swear."

"I don't have anyone special in mind. I just want to look really good before I put myself back out there, so to speak."

"But honey, waiting isn't going to make a difference. Besides, if a man is worth his salt, he shouldn't care what you look like, and everyone in town has known you all your life."

LilyAnn shrugged.

Ruby laughed. "So we're being secretive, huh? Oh well, I've snooped enough. Let's get you over to the chair and make you gorgeous. Okay?"

"You can try," Lily said, and then she laughed, too, because it felt good to be positive about something.

Ruby grabbed the blow-dryer and the round vent brush and set to work.

"Mike was telling me that he and his folks are having dinner with y'all on Thursday. Said his mother was really excited to see Grace again."

"I'm sure she is," Lily said. "They lived side by side while they were young wives and then mothers raising their babies."

"That must be a great thing," Ruby said. "Maybe one day soon Mike will marry his girl, and you'll marry your guy. Then you two can live side by side and raise your children together like your mothers used to do."

Lily's eyes widened. "Mike's girl?"

Ruby nodded. "He never mentioned a name, but I definitely got the impression there was one. Oh well, I'm sure you'll meet her soon enough, you and Mike being such good friends and all. Now, I need to stop talking and get you finished so you won't be late getting back to work."

Lily smiled in agreement, but she was still mulling over Ruby's comment as she walked back to work. So Mike had a girlfriend? She couldn't help but wonder who it was. Probably someone who went to the fitness center.

When she walked past, she slowed down to look in, eyeing the people inside, but didn't see anyone she knew who was unattached.

"Hey, LilyAnn, looking fine," Mitchell said when she walked back in the pharmacy. He was trying to put up a display for a hand lotion special, but it kept leaning to the right.

"Thanks. Give me a sec to hang up my stuff, and I'll be right back to help you."

By the time quitting time rolled around, Lily was exhausted and wishing she didn't have to walk home. On any other day, she could have hitched a ride home with Mike. His absence made her realize how much she'd depended on him. Well, she'd just have to get over that if he had a girlfriend.

Her stride was long, her steps hurried, as she headed for home. There was a lot to do before Mama and Eddie arrived.

~~~

While LilyAnn was walking home, Rachel Goodhope was in her kitchen and up to her elbows in flour. They had three couples staying at their bed-and-breakfast who were in town to spend Thanksgiving with local families, and one more couple was expected later tonight, which would have them at full capacity. That's the way she and Bud liked it, yet Rachel was smarting under the pressure. She'd enjoyed her little interlude with T. J. very much and wanted a repeat performance while the mood was still hot, so to speak.

Bud was tiptoeing around her, afraid to even raise his voice since his outburst the other day. Everything that had happened after she had sex with T. J. seemed preordained to help her cover up the interlude. In a way, it felt like permission from God to cheat, even though she knew thinking like that was blasphemy.

She wondered what T. J. was doing for Thanksgiving. Too bad she didn't have a good excuse to invite him to their house. It would be a kick to sit at the table with both her husband and her lover, but that would be pushing things too far.

She stirred the last ingredient into her cheesecake batter, then poured it into the springform pan and popped it in the oven just as Bud came in from outside.

"It's getting colder."

Rachel didn't comment.

"I heard Patty June Clymer did a slide presentation at the Rose Garden Club on her trip to Italy," Bud added.

Rachel paused. "Really? I'll bet she's got some stories to tell, spending all that time in Italy. I'd like to travel like that someday."

"Well, it took wrecking her marriage to make it happen," Bud muttered.

Rachel bristled. "Patty June didn't wreck her marriage. Her cheating-ass husband Conrad did, and don't you forget it."

"I know. I didn't mean it like that," he muttered.

"Well, yes you did, but whatever," Rachel said.

Bud frowned. Ever since he'd stuck his foot in his mouth by getting all jealous, Rachel had been on her high horse and he was getting tired of it. They'd been shopping a couple of times for a new car, but she hadn't liked a one. He had a feeling it was going to take an upgrade to put a smile back on her face.

***

LilyAnn was freezing by the time she got home. If it stayed this cold, she was going to start driving to work again, at least through winter. She changed quickly and went to the kitchen to make her supper and cornbread for tomorrow's dressing.

The phone rang while she was grilling chicken. She answered absently while keeping an eye on the stove.

"Hello."

"Hey, Lilybug, it's me."

"Mama!"

Grace laughed. "I miss being called Mama. I should call you more just to hear you say that word."

"I second that," Lily said. "What's going on?"

"Just checking in to make sure it's still okay for us to come."

"Of course it's okay, and guess what? Don and Carol Dalton will be here, too."

Grace squealed. "I am thrilled to hear this. I haven't seen them in ages. How do they look?"

"The same, but it's because of Mike that they're even here. He fell in the shower a couple of weeks ago, ruptured his spleen, and nearly bled to death."

"Oh dear God!" Grace cried. "Is he okay now?"

"Yes, getting stronger, anyway. He's home. They'll

stay with him until after Thanksgiving for sure, maybe longer. It's been great to have them next door again. Almost like old times."

"Yes, like old times," Grace said, and Lily knew her mama was thinking about her daddy's passing. All of their lives changed after he died.

"So, you'll be at work tomorrow, right?"

"Until 5:00 p.m. You know where the extra key is kept if you get here before I get off work. I love you, Mama, and I can't wait to see you."

"Love you, too," Grace said.

Lily hung up the phone. Her chicken looked done, and the cornbread was in the oven. It was time to eat.

———∿———

It was just after 3:00 p.m. the next day when Mike saw Grace and Eddie Gleason pull up in LilyAnn's drive. He moved to the window for a closer look at Eddie. Ever since he learned Eddie had taken verbal potshots at LilyAnn, the urge to confront him had been huge. But he didn't have the right to interfere on LilyAnn's behalf, and that ate at him, too.

Grace was a shorter, older version of LilyAnn. She was still a blond and always stylish. Eddie Gleason was about six feet tall, with a head full of thick gray hair and a bit of a paunch. He reminded Mike of Alex Trebek, the TV host on *Jeopardy*.

He watched Eddie saunter toward the house with their suitcases while Grace retrieved the spare key and opened the door.

Moments later, Mike saw his mom and dad running across his front yard. The meeting between the old friends was heartfelt. He could hear the laughter and chatter, even from where he was standing.

He sighed. And so it began.

-~~-

LilyAnn left the pharmacy on the dot of five and drove home without making any extra stops. She was as prepared as she could be for the holiday meal, and whatever she'd forgotten, they would never miss.

When she saw her mother's car in the driveway, she giggled. Mama was home, a simple fact that had a huge impact on her world.

She didn't know Mike was watching from the window when she parked and got out, and probably wouldn't have acknowledged him if she had. She didn't want to play nice with Mike Dalton. He'd hurt her feelings. His apology had sucked eggs, and as far as she was concerned, he could go boss the new girlfriend around instead of her. That's what Mike Dalton could do.

She ran into the house, yelling as she went.

"Mama! I'm home!"

And just like the old days, Grace came out of the kitchen with an apron over her shirt and slacks and a smile on her face.

"LilyAnn! Oh child, how I have missed you," Grace cried.

Lily wrapped her arms around her mother's neck and held on because she could and because it felt so right.

Then she felt someone patting her on the back and looked over her shoulder.

Eddie.

"Hey, don't I get a hug, too?" he asked.

Grace was beaming, thrilled that he was showing her daughter affection.

Lily smiled grimly, her eyes narrowing as Eddie started to hug her.

"Great to see you," she said, gave him a hit-and-run hug, and then spun out of his grasp. "Mama, did the chicken cacciatore get done in the Crock-Pot?"

"Yes, and it tastes wonderful," Grace said. "You're turning into a great cook."

Lily beamed. "Give me a couple of minutes to change out of my work clothes, and I'll help set the table."

"Eddie can do that," Grace said. "As soon as you get back, we're ready to eat."

"Great," Lily said, and bolted out of the room.

She changed clothes quickly, anxious to get to the kitchen. But the jeans she'd laid out were so loose they wouldn't stay up, so she dug in the back of the closet for some of her older clothes that had been too small. Not only did they pull up over her hips, but they also zipped comfortably. She looked at herself in the full-length mirror and then grinned and patted her butt.

"Way to go, missy," she muttered, then put on a long-sleeved T-shirt, slipped into some soft-soled shoes, and headed back to the kitchen.

Eddie was the first one who saw her entrance, and his eyes widened perceptibly.

"Dang, girl, you're not nearly as big as you were last time we were here."

Grace's mouth dropped. The shock on her face was painfully visible.

"Eddie Gleason! I cannot believe that just came out of your mouth. I'm sorry, LilyAnn. I have yet to meet a man who could breathe and make sense at the same time, and it is obvious my husband isn't one of them."

The shock on Eddie's face was obvious, and Lily doubted her mother did much disagreeing with him. She laughed. It was the best thing that had happened under this roof in years.

"No biggie, Mama. He stated a true fact. I'm a little over fifteen pounds lighter, and I'm hungry. Did you find the rice to heat up?"

"You look amazing," Grace said, giving Eddie another hard look. "And yes, I found the rice. Let's eat while everything is hot."

The silence that ensued was awkward, but it slowly passed as Lily guided the conversation toward Carol and Don.

<center>~~~</center>

It was almost dark when LilyAnn heard a car engine revving over and over, and thought it was in her driveway. But when she went out on the porch to see who it was, she got a jolt of reality.

Between the glow from the streetlight and the beam from Mike's porch light, she had a very good view of the red sports car in Mike's driveway. There was a cute little redhead leaning against it, engaged in animated conversation with Mike. He had his hand on her arm in a possessive manner, and the look on his face was shocking. She'd never seen that expression and didn't quite know how to interpret it. It was something between a look of lust and longing. She shifted focus to the woman, trying to figure out who the hell she was.

If this was Mike's new girlfriend, she could already

tell she wasn't going to like her. Not only was she about a foot shorter than Lily, but she was younger and cuter, to boot. Lily stomped back in the house.

Whatever!

Chapter 10

THANKSGIVING MORNING DAWNED EARLY FOR LilyAnn. By 5:00 a.m. she was in the kitchen putting the turkey in the oven. It gave her a sense of familial continuity, remembering her grandmother doing this every holiday until her passing. Her mother had taken over and hosted the family meals until she remarried and moved away. After that, the tradition had stopped.

This was the first time since her mother moved away that she and Eddie had been back for Thanksgiving, and Lily was the one putting the turkey in the oven. It was a fact of Southern tradition that women who amounted to anything had to have an affinity with their kitchens and the food they made in them.

She had a breakfast quiche already baked and ready to reheat when her mom and Eddie woke up. In the meantime, she had the kitchen to herself.

About an hour later, her mother walked in yawning, still wearing her robe and nightgown.

"Morning, Mama," Lily said. "There's coffee made and quiche when you get hungry. Just heat it in the microwave and it's good to go."

Grace poured coffee and sat down, sipping carefully while watching Lily going from task to task.

"What's going on with you?" Grace finally asked.

"What do you mean?" Lily asked.

"Seeing you like this now, so vibrant and happy. It's

like you woke up, honey. I used to worry about you and how you seemed to be living in the past, but it wasn't my place to put an expiration date on grief. So whatever has caused this change, it is a godsend and I'm happy for you."

Lily smiled. "I did wake up, Mama. I want to get my figure back and start dating again."

Grace frowned. "Date who? What about Mike?"

Lily's stomach knotted. "What about Mike?"

"I don't know. I guess I always hoped you two would—"

Lily rolled her eyes. "Mike? Mother! Seriously?"

Grace shrugged. "Never mind. So do you have someone in mind you would like to date?"

LilyAnn thought of Lachlan, but she was no longer as intrigued as she'd first been.

"No, there's no one, really, but I'm not getting any younger. People are dying all the time around here, and I don't want to be an old maid when it happens to me."

Grace frowned. "Who died?"

"Lots of people have died in the years since you left town, Mama. Just this year two ladies from the nursing home have passed. The high school basketball coach died in a car wreck, Mr. Bissell passed away, and a little over a week ago I found Mr. Gerty sitting on the bench in the cemetery. He was dead. That was a shock, I can tell you."

Grace gasped. "*You* found him?"

Lily nodded. "I thought he'd fallen asleep. He's always in the cemetery visiting Ina's grave. But when I sat down to talk to him, I realized he was…he was gone."

Grace was stunned. "You still go out to the cemetery to visit Randy Joe's grave?"

"Hardly ever," Lily said. "I only went that day to tell Randy Joe I was moving on, and I found Mr. Gerty instead."

"Good Lord," Grace muttered.

At that point, Eddie walked in, bleary-eyed and silent. He went straight for the coffee and then sat down beside Grace to finish waking up.

"Would you two like a piece of breakfast quiche? Dinner probably won't be ready until around 1:00 p.m. That's a long time to go without eating."

"I'll have some," Grace said.

"Me too," Eddie said, and when Grace kicked him under the table, he winced and added, "Uh, LilyAnn, about yesterday. I'm sorry about what I said. What I was thinking was that you were looking nice and trim, and it came out wrong."

"It's already forgotten," Lily said. "Sit tight and I'll get that quiche warmed up."

As soon as they began to eat, she went back to work. She still had the celery and onions to sauté before she could begin the dressing—so many things to do and so little time.

It wasn't until breakfast was over and Grace and Eddie had gone to get dressed that Lily stopped long enough to eat a bite. She'd skipped the buttery quiche for a bowl of cereal with a banana and was chewing the last bite when the phone rang. She swallowed quickly, washing it down with a drink of water, and then answered.

"Happy Thanksgiving."

It was Mike. "Happy Thanksgiving to you, too. Mom wants me to remind you she's making candied sweet potatoes and deviled eggs, and I'm asking you if it's all right if I bring a guest. I have a friend who's going to be alone for Thanksgiving otherwise."

"Sure, it's fine with me whoever you bring," Lily said. "So, what's his name?"

"Oh, it's not a he, it's a she. Her name is Honey Andrews, that masseuse I was telling you about. Anyway, thanks. I'm sure you two will hit it off. See you later."

Lily's mouth was agape, her thoughts in freefall. What the hell just happened?

Grace walked in.

"What can I do to help?" she asked.

"Set another place. Mike's bringing his girlfriend," LilyAnn snapped.

Grace's eyes widened, but she had the good sense to keep her mouth shut as she went to lay another place at the table.

T. J. had the day all planned out. He was going to eat dinner at Granny's Country Kitchen, stock up on beer to get through a day of nonstop football on TV, and if he was lucky, find someone to fuck before the night was over.

He had options in the fuck department, but it all depended on who was still in town for the holiday and who was willing. If he had his druthers, he'd pick wild-ass Rachel Goodhope, but he doubted she could pull off a disappearing act on a family holiday, which left him with either the waitress at the Eight Ball pool hall or the carhop at Charlie's Barbecue. Whatever worked out was fine with him.

And there was that big blond at the pharmacy. He

didn't know what it was about her, but she interested him. Maybe because she didn't fall all over herself every time she saw him. He liked it when they played hard to get. The pharmacy was probably closed, but he'd cruise town a bit before heading home for the day. Who knows? He might get lucky.

~~~

The guests began arriving a little before eleven. Grace moved into hostess mode as if she'd never been gone, taking the pressure off LilyAnn, although Carol and Don didn't need entertaining. This house was as familiar to them as the one they'd left to Mike. As soon as they hung up their coats, they headed to the kitchen to say hello to LilyAnn.

"Hey, gorgeous! It sure smells good in here," Don said.

He kissed Lily's cheek and swiped an olive from an open jar on the cabinet while Carol stowed her deviled eggs in the refrigerator.

Lily laughed. "You only said that so you could steal food. Appetizers are in the fridge, and there's hard lemonade and a pitcher of iced tea in the living room in Daddy's old wet bar."

"Carol, you get the food. I'll play bartender," Don said, and backtracked to the living room.

Carol slid a hand along LilyAnn's arm. "The candied sweet potatoes are on the sideboard. Are you okay?"

LilyAnn beamed. "I sure am! Why wouldn't I be?"

Carol blinked. "Well then, I'll get the appetizers and get out of your way."

"You're never in the way. If you run out, there's always more."

"We don't need more, or we will be too full to enjoy all this food you're making." Then she paused. "Mike said he invited his friend to dinner. I hope you're okay with that."

Lily threw back her head and laughed. "Look at all this! There's food for even ten more of Mike's friends. One little bitty redhead won't make a dent in all this… bless her heart."

Carol's eyes widened. She bit her lip and then held her breath.

Lord, Lord, Mike has gone and put his foot in it this time.

Without saying a word, she took the appetizers to the living room, then grabbed Grace's arm.

"We have to talk," she hissed.

Grace gasped. "What's wrong?"

Carol shook her head and pulled her by the arm down the hall and into Grace's bedroom.

Grace was frowning. "Carol, what on earth is the matter with you?"

"Mike invited the woman who works for him at the fitness center to dinner today."

Grace's heart sank. "Really? Oh, well, I'm sure it will be fine with LilyAnn. She seems to be fixated on anyone *but* Mike."

Carol sighed. "I don't know what she told you, but I know what she just told me about Mike's guest. When I expressed concern, she laughed, said one little bitty red-head wouldn't put a dent in all the food she had made, and then she said, 'Bless her heart.'"

Grace grinned. "Did she really?"

Carol nodded.

Grace sat down on the side of the bed. "She said, 'Bless her heart'?"

Carol nodded again. "Southern code for everything from 'you're a bitch' to 'kiss my ass.' She's mad, Grace."

Grace's smile widened. "Then that means she's jealous. She may not know it yet, but she is, which means there's still hope for us yet."

Carol sighed. "We did everything we knew how to do to throw them together when they were growing up, which, now that I look back, was probably wrong. Familiarity breeds contempt, and all that. She sees him as family, not someone to be in love with."

Grace patted Carol's hand. "Be happy that Mike's happy with a new girl."

Carol snorted. "Mike will never be happy without LilyAnn. I don't know what he's up to, but he's playing with fire right now. Lord, Lord, what a Thanksgiving dinner this is turning out to be."

They heard the doorbell. Grace frowned. "Who might that be?"

"Mike?" Carol asked.

Grace shook her head. "He doesn't ring the doorbell."

Carol went to the door to listen. "Well, he did today because I hear his voice."

Grace rolled her eyes. "Let's get back. I'm thinking referees might be needed."

They reached the living room just as Mike was beginning introductions.

"Mom! Grace! Just in time. This is Honey Andrews. She's the masseuse at the fitness center. Honey, this is my mother, Carol, and the pretty lady in blue is Grace

Gleason, Eddie's wife. Grace is LilyAnn's mother and like a second mother to me."

Honey Andrews flashed smiles at both women, revealing dimples and snow-white teeth. Her dark red sweater made a statement against the copper red of her hair, and black slacks fit her curvy body like a second skin. When she walked, the heels of her black pumps clicked on the hardwood floor.

"It's a pleasure to meet both of you," Honey said. "Thank you so much for allowing me to share your holiday meal."

"Well, hi, y'all. I thought I heard other voices in here."

LilyAnn strode across the room with a smile on her face stretched from ear to ear and immediately thrust her hand forward.

"You must be Homey. I'm LilyAnn Bronte, the absent hostess, and it's my home in which you will be dining, so welcome, welcome."

Mike glared at LilyAnn, but she was ignoring him.

"My name is Honey," Honey repeated, still smiling, still working the dimples.

Lily giggled. "Well, silly me. When Mike asked if he could bring you to dinner, I would have sworn he said Homey. I do apologize. Whatever must you think of me?"

Honey shook her head. "That's fine. We all make mistakes."

"Bless your heart. You are a sweetheart," LilyAnn said, and then waved a hand at Mike as if he'd just committed the biggest faux pas. "Mike, for goodness sake. Get your honey Honey something to drink."

Then LilyAnn giggled again. "Your honey, Honey…

oh my goodness, I'll bet people play with your name like that a lot. Well, so nice to meet you. Enjoy yourselves. If y'all get bored with all the man talk, feel free to join me in the kitchen. I promise not to make you work."

She wiggled her fingers in a darling little bye-bye motion and strode out of the room with a toss of her head and her backside swinging.

Mike didn't know what to think. She'd been so damn nice, and he'd been hoping for at least a frown. He glanced at Honey, who was already engaged in conversation with his dad at the wet bar. When he looked at his mom and Grace, they were grinning. He glared at the both of them. He didn't know what the hell was funny and wished this day was already over.

On the other side of the room, Carol moaned.

"She said 'bless her heart' again."

Grace sighed. "Temper does run in the family. LilyAnn's great-great-grandma Delia once shot the hat off a Yankee general for pushing his way into her house on the plantation without taking it off first. At least Mike had the good sense to ask if he could bring a guest before he showed up with her."

Carol's eyes widened. "I need a drink."

"Sweet tea or hard lemonade?" Grace asked.

"I believe I could do with a little hard lemonade. My nerves are shot. Oh. Lord. Poor choice of words. Not shot, but I do believe my nerves are a bit raggedy."

Grace chuckled.

Lily was furious. The bitch was pretty, and her teeth looked like a billboard ad for chlorine bleach.

"Probably glow in the dark," Lily muttered. "I could ask Mike. No telling what else on her glows in the dark."

She was slamming lids and stirring sauces with all the vehemence she could muster. The extra heat in the kitchen had put roses on her cheeks and a damp sheen on her peaches-and-cream skin. When she heard footsteps behind her, she turned around, the knife she was holding aimed straight at Mike's belly.

"What?" she snapped.

He eyed the knife and blinked. "Uh…your mom sent me in here to get more ice."

She waved the knife toward the deep freeze in the utility room and turned her back on him.

Mike frowned. "Are you mad?"

Her eyes were flashing as she spun around again. "Mad? As in mad as a hatter? Or mad, as in off my fucking rocker? Why, no! Why on earth would you think that?"

Mike's stomach knotted. She was mad, as in off-her-fucking-rocker mad. He made a beeline for the deep freeze, refilled the ice bucket, and darted out of the kitchen.

He paused in the doorway, eyeing the assembly in the living room. Honey was having herself a ball, chatting up all the men and flashing winning smiles at the women. What they didn't know was that if Honey was inclined to flirt, it would probably be with LilyAnn, because that's how Honey Andrews rolled.

He caught his mother's eye. She came to relieve him of the ice bucket.

"Are you feeling okay?" she asked.

"Yes, I'm fine."

"Good. Your Honey seems sweet," Carol said.

Mike nodded. "Yes, she is."

Carol elbowed him. "LilyAnn is mad, isn't she?"

Mike's eyes widened, surprised she knew that. "As a wet hen."

"Jealousy will do that to a woman," she said, and walked away.

At that moment, it felt like all the breath had just left Mike's belly. Jealous? LilyAnn was jealous of Honey? Son of a gun. Ruby Dye had been right. All of a sudden, the day had taken a sharp turn to the good. He took off for the wet bar.

"Hey, Dad, hand me a couple of bottles of that hard lemonade."

Don pointed across the room at Honey.

"Honey's drinking tea."

"One is for LilyAnn. I was just in the kitchen, and she looked hot enough to spontaneously combust. I thought I'd cool her off a bit."

"Ah, good thinking," Don said.

Mike picked up the frosty bottles and made a return trip to the kitchen. Again, LilyAnn bristled at his approach, but he was ready for her this time.

"I know you're busy, but I hated to think of you in here by yourself while we're out there enjoying the fruits of your labor. I brought something to cool you off."

She sputtered a bit, wanting to argue, but manners won out as she took a quick sip.

"Thank you. That does hit the spot. I appreciate you being so thoughtful."

He shrugged. "I owe you my life."

Her eyes narrowed. "In some cultures, that means you owe me forever."

Mike smiled. "I guess it does. Well, let me know when you're ready for me to pay up. In the meantime, I'll get out of your hair."

He strolled out with a grin on his face, leaving Lily not only hot, but also confused. She took another drink of the lemonade and then sighed as it slid down her throat. The warmth it left afterward was nice, and before she knew it, she'd emptied the bottle.

It was just past 12:30 when LilyAnn took off her apron and went to the bathroom in the utility room to wash up and fix the hair that had come down from her clip.

She refreshed her lipstick, sprayed her hair with a little hair spray, started to pinch her cheeks, then stopped. They were already pink enough. The lemonade had left her feeling easier about the whole day, which was good, because they still had an entire dinner plus dessert to get through before Mike took Miss Honey-Ass Andrews home.

After one last look at her appearance, Lily headed for the dining room. Everything was in place, including the turkey that was ready for Eddy to carve. She had to admit that the table looked amazing. There was only one thing left to do. She moved toward the living room with her shoulders back and her chin up.

"Hey, y'all. I hope you've saved some of your appetite. Dinner is served."

They filed into the dining room, still talking.

"This looks amazing," Honey said as Mike seated her

between him and his mother. "I can't cook worth a darn. If it wasn't for Granny's Kitchen across the street from work, I'd be eating out of cans."

LilyAnn smiled. Strike one against the bitch. She couldn't cook.

"Don, would you mind giving the blessing? And Eddie, I would appreciate it if you would carve the turkey," Lily said.

Eddie beamed. Turkey carving was a status given to the head of the family, and he'd been feeling a bit left out with all these people talking about old times and memories he had not shared.

Grace glanced at her daughter and mouthed a "thank you." LilyAnn smiled. She'd do whatever it took to make her mama happy.

Then her gaze slid to the redhead on Mike's right and her eyes narrowed thoughtfully.

Mike saw the look and didn't know whether to be concerned or elated. Either way, he'd definitely stirred the pot of their relationship.

"Let us pray," his dad said, and bowed his head.

Lily listened absently as Don blessed the food, the cook, the family members who were missing from the table, the ones who were sitting at the table with him—and he was about to launch into a whole new prayer group when Carol nudged him under the table. He quickly brought the prayer to an end.

Eddie stood up and, with a grand flourish of the slicing knife, began carving the turkey, complying with requests for white meat or dark, while Grace held the plates that were passed.

LilyAnn leaned back in her chair, smiling in

satisfaction. Except for Honey Andrews, the people she loved most were sitting at this table. And the moment she thought that, her heart skipped a beat.

Loved most?

As in family, she meant. Not as in love, love.

Plates began to fill and conversation waned as they dug into the food. Lily fielded praise for the food she'd prepared with all the grace of a Peachy-Keen Queen. But the longer she sat, the louder her inner self was yelling.

You said it, and you know you said it! The people you love most are here, and lying to yourself about what you meant is stupid, LilyAnn. You can't lie to yourself. Just face it. Mike might mean more to you than you ever considered. And it's your own fault for missing the signs. He wasn't the one prowling All Saints Cemetery for the past eleven years. That was you. And, it's your own fault that he's finally interested in something besides wiping the tears off your dumb face.

"LilyAnn! LilyAnn!"

She blinked and looked up from her plate. "Huh? What?"

Her mother was frowning. "Honey is speaking to you."

Lily blinked and pasted a big smile on her face. "Oh my stars! Forgive me! I think I went into my own little world there for a minute. Chalk it up to good food and tired feet. So what's on your mind, sugar?"

Honey smiled. "I was telling Mikey that I'd never eaten dressing quite like this. It's very tasty. Just different from what we eat back home."

LilyAnn bristled. Different meant less than perfect, which she took as a slight, but she hid it with a smile.

"Really? What do y'all put in your cornbread dressing?" she asked.

Honey frowned. "Oh, we don't do cornbread at all. It's torn-up bits of bread with different herbs and, of course, the clams. Can't have dressing without the clams."

Lily's eyes widened. "Clams? Well, I'll say. Where are you from?"

"Boston," Honey said.

"Ah, that explains it," LilyAnn muttered.

"Explains what?" Honey asked.

LilyAnn flashed Honey another hundred-watt smile with just the teeniest dart of venom.

"You're a Yankee, sugar. Welcome to Thanksgiving in the South."

Honey felt LilyAnn's fury as if it was physical. She knew she was supposed to be making this woman jealous, but she didn't want to get her so pissed she caused harm. Honey was real fond of her face and all that went with it.

"Yes, I suppose you're right. When in Rome, and all that," Honey said.

Lily's voice went up an octave.

"Speaking of Rome. I heard Patty June Clymer has an amazing slide-show presentation of her tour of Italy."

"Patty June went to Italy? Where was Conrad?" Grace asked.

Mike groaned. He already knew where this was going but didn't know how to stop it.

"Oh, Mama, you wouldn't believe! It was the biggest scandal a few months back," Lily said. "She found out Conrad was having an affair with Bobbette Paulson, and when she and Bobbette accidentally wound up in The Curl Up and Dye on the same day, she lost it. Took Vesta Conklin's hair clippers right off her station, walked up behind Bobbette, grabbed a handful of her long red hair, and shoved her facedown on the manicure table, breaking her nose.

"Blood was spurting everywhere as Patty June proceeded to shave off a strip of hair right down the middle of Bobbette's head wide enough to park a car on. Symbolically speaking, of course." Then she giggled. "No disrespect meant to your red hair, Honey. It's... eye-catching."

Both Carol and Grace were in shock. "The preacher was having an affair with Bobbette? I assume he got fired."

"And then some," Mike said, and tried to steer the conversation to another topic. "Speaking of red, I heard Santa Claus is going to make a surprise appearance in Blessings on December first to launch the holiday season. I think that was Sue Beamon's brainchild. Ever since she wound up on the Chamber of Commerce she's been full of ideas."

But the women weren't done with the preacher's affair and ignored Mike's attempt to change the conversation.

"So what happened to Bobbette?" Grace asked.

Lily put her elbows on the table and leaned forward. "She picked up those clippers and finished shaving herself bald because she said it all needed to match, wrapped a towel around her head, stuffed another one under her bloody nose, and called her mama. You know how it is. You can act like a slut all over the place, but when you're down and out, there's only one person you trust to have your back, and that's your mama."

Carol shook her head in disbelief. "Good Lord! Being close to our grandchildren is why we moved to Denver, but I'm thinking we're missing out on a whole lot of life by not living here in Blessings."

"Oh, don't worry," LilyAnn said, fixing Mike and Honey with a sweet-as-sugar smile. "I'm sure Mike will furnish you with some more grandchildren soon enough."

Honey looked a little nonplussed, and Mike was speechless.

At that point, LilyAnn stood up from the table.

"Dessert, anyone? And y'all better not tell me no. I have pecan pie and pumpkin pie with whipped cream. If you'll pass your plates to me, I'll carry them out."

"I'll help," Grace said.

"And me," Carol added.

LilyAnn beamed. "Isn't this fun? I think this just might be my best Thanksgiving ever."

And with that, she set sail from the room with a toss of her head and her hips swaying. As her granny used to say, it felt good to be pissed now and then. It set the juices to flowing.

Chapter 11

DON DALTON LEANED BACK WITH A GROAN, PATTING his belly.

"You outdid yourself, LilyAnn. That food could not have been better."

"I second that," Eddie said.

Lily smiled, accepting the praise as her due.

"Not only was the food delicious, but I am grateful for being invited to share it," Honey said, and leaned against Mike in a suggestive manner. "Thank you for bringing me, Mikey."

Mike slid an arm around her shoulders and gave her a hug.

"You're welcome on so many levels," he said softly.

Honey giggled.

LilyAnn stood up so fast the dishes rattled on the table.

"Please feel free to take your coffee into the living room. I know you men are ready to settle in for some football."

"I like football, too," Honey said, and snuggled under Mike's shoulder.

The woman was getting on LilyAnn's last nerve. "And that's fine, too," she muttered.

Grace and Carol were already stacking dishes.

"You did all the cooking, Lilybug. We're cleaning up. Why don't you go put your feet up for a bit?" Grace said.

Lily didn't hesitate. "Thanks, Mama. I believe I'll

take a little walk around the block. I need to walk off some of my dinner and get a breath of fresh air."

She grabbed a coat out of the hall closet and the last bottle of hard lemonade from the wet bar and headed for the front door.

Mike didn't notice she was leaving until the door was already open.

"Hey, where are you going?" he asked.

She took a swig of the hard lemonade and shut the door behind her without answering.

Mike got up and walked to the window.

"She'll be fine," Grace said.

"I was just checking to see which direction she went," he said.

Grace sighed. "Ah. You mean you were looking to see if she went to the cemetery."

He shrugged.

"I think that's in the past, Mike. Don't worry about her."

"Right. No worries," he said, and sat back down.

———

LilyAnn took a deep breath of the cool November air, then a drink of the hard lemonade. Both were cleansing and calming. Even though she had intended to walk toward the park, she turned the corner at the block instead and headed toward Blessings High School. It was an unconscious choice, but to a familiar destination.

There was a trio of boys tossing a football in the front yard of a house as she passed. They saw her and waved.

She waved back and kept walking, sipping her drink as the chilly breeze continued to play havoc with her hair.

As she approached the local Catholic church, she saw Father Benton wrestling with the manger to the church's outdoor Nativity scene. She smiled and waved.

He waved back.

For the kids in Blessings, the appearance of the Nativity scene at the church seemed to signify the beginning of the holiday season. And, every year before the season was over, someone always absconded with the Baby Jesus, then brought it back under cover of darkness the next night dressed in something besides the swaddling clothes.

One year it came back dressed in long johns and wearing earmuffs. Another year someone put it in a baby onesie with the insignia of the local football mascot on it. Another year, a tiara, and the list went on.

In the beginning, that had horrified the devout and sent shockwaves through the religious communities. But, over the years, passions had cooled and, to their knowledge, no one had yet gone to hell for the act. Now it was just part of tradition in Blessings: wondering what Baby Jesus would come back wearing next.

"Hey, Father Benton. Are you going to put up a security camera this year?" she called out.

The old priest smiled and shook his head. "No. I think Baby Jesus can take care of Himself. Every year I am reminded that walking on church property to dress up the infant might be the closest the prankster will ever come to God, so we don't want to ruin the start of a good thing, now, do we?"

"Good point," LilyAnn said. "Happy Thanksgiving."

"And to you, my child," he said.

Lily lengthened her stride as she approached the high

school. She finished off her drink and tossed the bottle into a trash can on her way past. The school building looked different, smaller. She wondered if all the alumni felt that way after a few years had gone by.

She glanced at her watch, noting it was almost 3:00 p.m. Mike would probably be leaving to take his "honey bear" home about now, which was fine with Lily. She'd had all of the red hair and cheesy smiles she could stomach for one day. It was rude not to be there to see them off, but she didn't care. She'd used up all of her manners and restraint, and it was best for all concerned if she stayed out until they were gone. Besides, her mom and Eddie were there. They could play nice in her place.

She kept on walking, slowly angling her way back home, and was less than five blocks from her house when she heard the sound of a hot-rod engine on the street behind her. Her heart skipped a beat. There was no reason to assume the man would even notice her, but for whatever reason she felt uneasy. She ducked her head into the wind and walked faster.

And then he racked the pipes and she almost jumped out of her skin.

———

T. J. had turkey and dressing at Granny's Kitchen, played poker in the back room of the Eight Ball with the Wilder brothers, and had struck out all the way around when it came to taking a bed partner home for the night.

Both of the waitresses he'd expected to see were off duty, and after driving by the Goodhope Bed-and-Breakfast and seeing the parking lot full of cars, he'd completely given up on the idea of contacting Rachel.

He could always jack off, but he liked it better with a partner.

He was bored and cruising neighborhoods, because that's what predators did, when he saw a tall, blond woman striding down the sidewalk a distance ahead.

Both the build and the stride were familiar, but it took him a few moments to place her as the woman from the pharmacy, the one who had ignored him.

"Bingo!" he said softly, and racked the pipes on his truck, which he liked to think of as his mechanical wolf whistle.

He knew she heard him, but when she didn't break stride or look back, he frowned and did it again.

"Hey, blondie! I'm talking to you," he muttered.

When she still didn't stop, he rethought his options, tapped the brakes on his truck to slow down, then followed a half block behind her for the next three blocks, just to see what she would do next.

The dishes were done, the kitchen had been put back to rights, and the old friends were back in the living room.

Mike had already taken Honey home and returned, expecting to face LilyAnn and her bad attitude, only she wasn't home. It made him uneasy, but he seemed to be the only one concerned. When he mentioned her absence, both women pooh-poohed the notion and that was that.

He watched the clock as time continued to pass, and when he heard a driver out in the street suddenly rack the pipes on a hot rod, he frowned. That sounded like the truck Gene Bissell's nephew was driving around. He glanced up, expecting to see it go past the window at any moment. But it didn't. When the pipes rattled again, he got up and moved to the window.

At that point, his heart sank. It was Gene Bissell's nephew all right, but he was following LilyAnn in an obvious attempt to get her attention. The only positive in the whole blessed scene was that LilyAnn seemed to be ignoring him.

Then he saw her suddenly break stride and bolt across her neighbor's yard and into hers. There was a moment when their gazes connected. He saw her frown at him and realized it probably appeared like he was spying on her. But before he could react, the driver sped past to cut her off and she quickly spun around.

Shocked by the abruptness of the move, he headed for the door. But by the time he got it open, LilyAnn was standing in the yard with her feet planted and a hand on her hip. It was high school revisited, and the nightmare of Randy Joe had just come back to haunt him all over again.

Rage, coupled with defeat, washed over him. He stepped back and slammed the door so hard the windows rattled.

His mother looked up, frowning.

"Good Lord, Michael, I thought I—"

He walked right past her, through the kitchen, and out the door without looking back. It had been years since he'd gone over the fence between their yards, and it wasn't the smartest thing to do considering the remaining restrictions from his surgery, but he wasn't in a sane frame of mind.

He vaulted the fence and went in through the kitchen

door, slamming it just as hard. This was it. He was done. It was time to face the fact that she didn't have a single brain in her head when it came to picking men.

LilyAnn was not happy. She'd wanted to look better to garner male attention, but not like this. The man didn't even know who she was, and yet he was following her in a very threatening manner, like a wolf on the prowl. It bordered on stalking, which made her realize that anything she'd ever thought about entertaining his advances had been based on fantasies, not facts.

She was less than three houses from home and had lengthened her stride to just short of running. And still he followed. When she suddenly cut across her next-door neighbor's yard to get to her porch, he raced past her and then parked at an angle against the curb. Before she knew it, he was out of the truck and waving her down.

"Hey! Hey, honey! Do you have a minute?"

She caught a glimpse of Mike's face in the window: disapproving, even judging her. It pissed her off to no end. At that point, her good sense went into the house on its own and left LilyAnn standing out in the yard.

She turned on one heel to face her stalker instead of ignoring him and, as she did, heard her front door open, but she was so focused on taking the pervert down that it never occurred to her what Mike would do.

Suddenly, the door slammed behind her so hard that she expected to hear glass break. She turned to look, but the door was still on its hinges and the windows were whole. Her heart was pounding; her head felt like it was going to explode. She shouldn't have downed that last bottle of hard lemonade, and she shouldn't have stopped in the yard. Her mama had warned her not to talk to strangers. And this one was still talking.

"Hey, honey. Can we talk?"

She sighed. Why did she ever think she wanted to get a man's attention? They were nothing but trouble. All of a sudden she heard another door slam and realized it was the back door at Mike's house. Her eyes widened. He'd gone over the fence just so he wouldn't have to look at her again? What had she done that was so wrong? He showed up with a girlfriend out of the blue, and that was okay, but this wasn't?

Angry with men in general, she lit into Lachlan.

"Who are you, and what do you think you're doing?"

T. J. blinked. "Uh, I'm T. J. Lachlan, Gene Bissell's nephew, and I was just trying to say hello."

"Well, I didn't know that. I don't know you. From my standpoint, a stranger was following me and just so you know…it felt like I was being stalked. You need to get in your truck and go away now because whatever you're selling, I'm not interested."

Now T. J. was pissed. Women didn't talk to him like this. Ever.

"Look, lady, I was just—"

"Whatever your intent, it missed. You scared me, and I'm not interested. Go away."

He took off his hat and flashed a grin.

"I'm sorry I frightened you. Can we start over?"

"No," Lily said. "I've already told you to leave, and you're still standing in my yard. I've got a lot of family in the house behind me. Do I need to get someone to come show you the way out of town?"

"You don't need to do anything, bitch," T. J. snapped. "I was just trying to be friendly."

"Well, you have a strange way of showing it and it didn't work. I want you to leave, and don't ever talk to me again."

She turned on her heel and strode into her house, and once more, the door at the Bronte house rattled on its hinges.

T. J. felt like he'd just had his nose shoved in the dirt, and he didn't like it. It made him feel too much like he'd felt the night he'd come home from work and found Laverne's good-bye note. He stomped back to his truck and laid rubber all the way to the end of the block.

Lily was still fuming when she turned and locked the door behind her.

"Who was the guy you were talking to?" Grace asked.

"Oh…Mr. Bissell's nephew. He's a creep. I thought I wanted to get back into the dating game, but I must have been out of my mind. Men are nuts! All of them! Nuts!"

The shock on their faces was evident. She shuddered as the adrenaline of all that rage and indignation began to crash.

"I'm so sorry for making a scene," she said. "I wanted this day to be perfect. You're all the family I have, and you mean the world to me."

They gathered around her, patting and hugging her.

"Don't be silly, Lilybug," Grace said. "This day was perfect, and you didn't ruin a thing."

"But I did," she said, as tears began rolling down her face. "Mike has a girlfriend, which means I just lost my best friend. He's just as dead to me as Daddy and Randy

Joe. The only difference this time is that I don't have to bury him."

Her shoulders slumped as she went to her bedroom and locked herself in. She didn't want to talk to anyone about Mike. She didn't want to hear his name or see his face. And she hoped he and the redhead with the hundred-watt smile would be very happy—bless their hearts.

———

LilyAnn cried herself to sleep that night and, as a result, woke up the next morning with a headache of massive proportions. She washed some painkillers down with coffee and toast as her mom and Eddie were carrying their things out to the car.

Grace hated to leave when Lily was this upset, but she knew her presence wasn't going to change the outcome. Either Mike and LilyAnn would figure it out, or they wouldn't.

"Are you going to be all right?" Grace asked, as she hugged LilyAnn good-bye.

LilyAnn rolled her eyes. "Of course I'll be all right. I have passed the stage of dwelling on my sorrows and accepted that life kicks you in the teeth now and then to remind you that you're never in charge."

Grace smiled. "You do have a way with words, honey."

Eddie gave her a hug. "Hang in there, kiddo. Stay tough and don't change whatever it is you've been doing, because you look amazing."

"Thanks, Eddie. Y'all drive safe, okay? And tell your daughter I said congratulations."

"We'll do that," he said, and headed out the door, leaving Grace and Lily alone.

Grace cupped her daughter's face. "Yesterday was amazing. Thank you for such a wonderful dinner and for surprising me with Carol and Don's presence. It was the best surprise ever."

Lily shrugged. "I had nothing to do with their presence. I just invited them to dinner after they arrived in town."

"However it happened, it was the best. Thank you. I love you. And call me if you just want to talk. I'm still your mama. I care what happens to you."

Now Lily was struggling with tears. "I know. I'll be fine. Go on now. Eddie's waiting."

Moments later, Grace was out the door.

Lily stood on the porch, waving as they drove away, and then the moment they were gone, went back inside to get her coat and car keys. It was time to go to work, and with a sky threatening rain, this wasn't a day for walking.

Mike's parents left the day after the doctor released him to drive. The silence in the house mirrored the emptiness he was feeling.

LilyAnn was confronted daily by T. J., who had turned into a real-life stalker. He never spoke, but the looks he gave her said volumes.

All of this and it was only the second week in December.

The next day Baby Jesus turned up missing from the manger at the Catholic church, which turned into the topic of conversation at The Curl Up and Dye.

Ruby started a pool that day for anyone who wanted to play. For a dollar, they were to guess how the Baby Jesus would be dressed when it showed back up, and the one closest to the truth got the money, which would then be given to Father Benton for the poor box.

Once word got around, people from all over town stopped by to add their selection to the pool. It was all in fun and all for a good cause, and the business was good for the shop.

Sue Beamon had just paid her dollar and guessed the baby would come back dressed as Honey Boo Boo, a little girl from a TV reality show.

Ruby thought it was a ridiculous choice considering Baby Jesus was a boy, not a girl, but Sue was oblivious. She thought Honey Boo Boo was cute, and that was the end of that.

When Patty June Clymer came in the shop for her appointment decked out in designer clothes straight from the designers' own shops in Milan, the pool for Baby Jesus took a momentary lull.

Patty June was still sporting the black hair and the short, spiky style Ruby had given her after her husband's betrayal. She looked ten years younger and a lot less uptight than she had when she left.

She sat down in Ruby's styling chair for a trim and immediately began fielding questions about her trip to Italy.

"Were the men good-looking?" Vesta asked.

"Did you make friends with anyone while you were there?" Vera countered.

Patty June rolled her eyes. "I didn't meet anyone I care to see again, and I cannot describe how pretty Italian men are. I mean it, y'all. Black curly hair, beautiful faces, sexy eyes, and they love the women. I wouldn't trust one as far as I could throw him, but they sure are pretty to look at."

Laughter ricocheted through the salon, and that's what LilyAnn heard as she opened the door. She saw Patty June and sauntered to the back to say hello.

"Hey, Patty June. I heard you and your slide show were a big hit at the Rose Garden Club meeting. It's good to see you again."

Patty June's eyes widened. "LilyAnn? My stars, girl! You look amazing!"

"Thanks," Lily said.

Ruby's eyes narrowed. She'd heard through the grapevine that Mike had a new girlfriend, which meant Mike had taken her advice on trying to make Lily jealous. What she didn't know was if it was working. She eyed Lily closely but couldn't tell anything. LilyAnn had crawled back into her old quiet self with that emotionless mask.

"Did you come to play the pool?" Ruby asked.

Lily nodded. "Here's my dollar."

"Go write your name up on the chart on the wall along with your guess. If you win, you get to present Father Benton with the money."

"Cool idea, Sister," Lily said.

She dropped her dollar in the money jar and wrote her name and guess on the chart, then walked out without looking back.

Mabel Jean was doing Rachel's nails. "Hey! What did she write?"

Vera went over to look, then burst out laughing.

"Santa's elf. That's a good one."

Patty June continued to regale them with stories of her trip, while Lily began the walk back to the pharmacy.

She was at the intersection as the light for traffic turned red, which gave her the right of way to cross. She was about to step off the curb when she heard T. J.'s truck and cringed. She kept remembering one of her grandma's sayings about being careful of what you wish for.

Disgusted with him and the situation in general, she started across the crosswalk. As she did, he revved the engine and let the truck jump forward just enough to make her think he might run over her. She stopped in the middle of the crosswalk and flipped him off, then kept on going.

T. J. was livid. No matter what he did, she didn't respond in the way he expected. It was her defiance and her lack of fear that continued to surprise him. His reaction to her continued rejection was visceral. He watched her hips swaying and her arms swinging and wished he had her flat on her back beneath him, begging for mercy.

Someone honked behind him. He jumped as he realized the light had turned green and accelerated too fast through the intersection just as a cop drove by. He cursed when he saw the cop do a quick U-turn and flip on his lights. On top of everything else, he was about to get a ticket. It was the bitch's fault for putting him in such a foul mood.

Baby Jesus showed up in the manger the next day dressed as Yoda from *Star Wars*. The picture was on the front page of the local paper.

Myra Franklin from the flower shop, Pots and Posies, won the pool at The Curl Up and Dye because she guessed Darth Vader. Since her guess had been from the *Star Wars* cast, she was named the winner. That evening, she presented Father Benton with over two hundred dollars. A photographer from the local paper came and took their picture at the manger, with the Baby Jesus in his green robes and pointy ears lying between them.

It was a good ending to a weird week.

Chapter 12

THE NEXT WEEK PASSED IN A FLURRY OF CHRISTMAS shoppers and an outbreak of flu in Blessings, which made the pharmacy one of the busiest businesses on Main Street. Mr. Phillips had already hired two extra clerks for the holiday season, taking some of the pressure off LilyAnn and Mitchell, but since the weather was no longer conducive to walking to work, Lily wasn't getting in enough exercise to continue her weight-loss program.

Her only option was to go back to the fitness center. It would be miserable for her, and she knew Mike would hate it, which was why she finally decided to do it. She didn't understand why the jerk was mad at her when he should be concentrating on his girlfriend, and if her presence ticked him off, then so much the better. Once that decision had been made, she began using her lunch hour for workouts. Mike might hate her guts, but Stewart considered her a hero for saving Mike's life and she'd happily settle for one smiling face.

Today, as she started to leave the pharmacy, the rain that had been threatening all morning began to come down. She backtracked to her locker for an umbrella, then made a run for it.

———

When Mike saw her come in, his heart told him to go talk to her, but his stubborn streak won as he went into his office and shut the door. He was still so mad he couldn't look at her without wanting to shake her senseless.

Lily saw him bolt and ignored the spurt of pain as she approached the front counter.

Stewart had also seen her come in and was ready for her with a towel and a locker key.

"Hey there, LilyAnn. It's sure coming down outside, isn't it?"

She nodded and headed for the women's lockers to change her clothes and shoes. A few minutes later she was on the treadmill listening to Alvin and the Chipmunks singing "Rockin' Around the Christmas Tree" on her iPod. It was far from inspiring, but it had the right rhythm for her workout. Her head was down, her back to the spa area, as she concentrated on her stride, so she missed seeing Honey Andrews at the counter writing a ticket for the massage she'd just given.

However, Honey saw LilyAnn and was immediately torn between confronting her and staying out of their business.

Ever since Thanksgiving, Mike had become a bear to work for. His one attempt at making LilyAnn jealous seemed to have backfired, but Honey didn't know why.

"Do you feel better?" Honey asked, as Rachel Goodhope gave Honey her bank card to scan.

Rachel smiled. "Lord yes, and thank you for that. Ever since I had the wreck, my neck and back have been in knots. This is a busy time of year at the bed-and-breakfast, with so many people traveling home for the holidays, and I can't be all in a kink and unable to work."

"Any time you begin hurting like that again, give me a call. I can even come to your house," Honey said.

Rachel waved good-bye and was starting toward the door when she saw LilyAnn on the treadmill and went the other way. She was still pissed at the woman for intervening in her attempt to visit Mike in the hospital.

The rain was really coming down when Rachel got outside. She made a dash for her new car and breathed a sigh of relief as she got inside. She shivered from the cold, then took a deep breath and briefly closed her eyes.

"I love the smell of a new car in the morning," she drawled, paraphrasing the famous line from *Apocalypse Now*.

As she was backing out, she saw T. J. Lachlan's truck parked in front of Richards' Realty. She knew his uncle's house was now up for sale, which gave her a perfectly good reason to visit him again. The house was far larger and grander than theirs was, and since it was only a little over a mile out of town, it would make a great venue for a bed-and-breakfast. Instead of going home, she drove up the street to the Realtor's office.

She came in with the wind, laughing and shaking the droplets from her hair, well aware that she looked as good without makeup as she did with it.

"My goodness, this day is a mess, isn't it?" she said, smiling at Ann Richards, the owner's wife, who manned the front desk.

"Yes it is," Ann said. "What on earth brings you out in such nasty weather?"

"I heard the Bissell place is for sale. Bud and I might be interested in viewing it. It's far larger than our place and would be a great location for a bed-and-breakfast."

Sensing the possibility of a sale, Ann quickly agreed. "That's a marvelous idea, and as luck would have it, the owner is in a meeting with Hank right now. Have a seat and I'll see if we can set up a time to view."

"Sure thing," Rachel said as Ann went into her husband's office.

She could hear the murmur of voices and recognized T. J.'s voice, as well. The excitement of another interlude made her squirm in her seat, although she wasn't sure how she could make that happen without one of the Realtors trailing along. Moments later, Ann stepped out and waved her in.

Rachel sashayed into the office. Hank was on his feet and introducing her to T. J. as she sat. She flashed a wide smile.

"I've already had the pleasure of meeting Mr. Lachlan. He's the gentleman who stopped at the site of my accident and took me to the emergency room." Then she shifted her smile to T. J. "Mr. Lachlan, it's good to see you again."

T. J. wanted to sell the house and get the hell out of Blessings, and he was guessing the only thing Rachel Goodhope was really interested in was another free fuck, not buying his property. It made his bad mood worse. Still, he had to respond.

"Mrs. Goodhope. It's good to see you have recovered."

"Mostly," she said, and then angled her question toward Hank. "So when would be a good time to check out the property?"

"I'm showing other property this afternoon," Hank said, "which means Ann will have to man the office. Do you have any time free tomorrow?"

Rachel sensed fate was about to hand her what she wanted and made a face and then sighed. "No, sorry. We have guests coming in, so I'll be tied up for the rest of the week, maybe all the way through Christmas. This is our busy time, you know."

Hank knew what happened when prospective buyers had to wait. They often cooled off on the idea and the sale was lost. He looked toward T. J. for assistance.

T. J. was trapped, and Rachel knew it. He could see it on her face.

"I guess I can show it, if it's not against the Realtor rules," he said.

Ann laughed. "Not really, if the prospective buyer agrees."

"It's fine with me," Rachel said. "I need to give Bud a call. When do you want to do this?"

"I'm ready anytime," T. J. said.

Rachel smiled, remembering the state of his impressive erection.

"How about now?" she asked.

T. J. glanced at Hank. "Are we through?"

Hank cautioned Rachel. "You understand that any offers you make on the property need to go through us. This visit is just to give you an idea of the extent of the property."

"Of course," Rachel said.

"I'm going home now, Mrs. Goodhope, so come at your leisure," T. J. said.

She smiled again. Sex was something to be enjoyed, not rushed. She always came at her leisure.

"Then I'll see you soon," she said. "Thank you, Hank. Nice to see you, Ann. Happy holidays to the both of you."

She was still smiling when she got in the car and was

calling Bud when T. J. walked out. He gave her a brief glance, then got in his truck and left.

The phone rang several times before Bud answered.

"Goodhope Bed-and-Breakfast."

"It's me," Rachel said. "What are you doing?" As if she didn't already know.

"Playing cards with a couple of the guys."

"Seriously? Are you guys betting with real money?" The silence was telling.

"Bud Goodhope, you better not be losing all the profit we just made during Thanksgiving."

"It's not like we're going broke. Chill out. What did you want, anyway?"

"I wanted you to go out with me to look at the Bissell place as a possible location for a new business site. It's for sale now. I was just talking to Hank Richards about it."

Bud sighed. This was a subject they'd talked about before, and he was fine with the idea, but not with the timing.

"I can't go now and leave the guys in the middle of the game. Why don't you go check it out and see if it would work? If it has possibilities, we can go back together."

"Oh, okay, whatever you say. I'll be home later."

"Drive safely."

"And you don't lose all our money."

She heard a snort as he disconnected.

"Like taking candy from a baby," she muttered. She put the car in gear and drove out of town.

Lily's lunch hour was almost over when she turned off the treadmill. She wiped the sweat from her face on the way to the locker room and was getting dressed when Honey Andrews walked in.

"Hi, LilyAnn. Good to see you again," she said.

"You too," Lily muttered, as she pulled her sweater over her head and then reached for the hairbrush to fix her hair.

"You've got a good workout regimen going. Are you eating healthy? Drinking lots of water?" Honey asked.

"I'm fine," Lily said, as she put her hair back up in a ponytail and sat down to put on her work shoes.

Honey sat down beside her. "Can I talk to you, woman to woman?"

Lily tensed. "I'd rather not have this conversation."

Honey sighed. "I think you need to hear it, anyway."

Lily started to get up, but Honey stopped her.

"What's going on with you and Mike? Did you have a fight or something? He's mad at everyone all the time, and it's making work a drag."

Lily couldn't believe what she was hearing. "You two have to work out your own issues. They are not my concern."

Honey lowered her voice. "That's just the deal. We don't have issues to work out because we're not a couple."

It was the last thing Lily expected her to say.

"What do you mean?"

"Mike used me to make you jealous. Oh, don't get me wrong. I agreed. I mean, I like Mike, but I don't swing that way," she said and grinned.

Lily was trying to absorb the fact that Honey Andrews was gay and Mike wanted to make her jealous when she realized Honey was waiting for a comment.

"Why would he do that? We don't feel like that about each other," Lily said.

Honey shook her head. "And that is obviously your opinion only, because he wanted to make you jealous. You might not like him like that, but if you think he doesn't like you, you are as blind as you are tall. I knew the first day I went to work for him that he was attached to someone. I just didn't know who it was until I saw him with you. So what's the deal with not liking him?"

Lily felt like she'd just been sideswiped. "I never thought of Mike like that. I never thought of anybody like that after Randy Joe died. I sort of shut down, and everyone let me do it."

Honey patted her knee. "Well, woman to woman, I thought it only fair that you know where you stand. Men are okay in their place, but God love 'em, they don't have the sense God gave a goose. Women on the other hand…if we have a gripe, someone's gonna know about it before the sun goes down. Know what I mean?"

Lily nodded, while her heart was racing.

"I have a client due, so I'm going back to work. Do what you want with what I told you, and just so you know, I have no intention of telling Mike I spilled the beans."

"Okay, and Honey…"

"Yeah?"

"I'm sorry I was so rude to you at dinner."

Honey frowned. "But you weren't. You were sweet as can be."

Lily sighed. "No, I wasn't, and just so you know, when a Southern girl smiles at you real sweet and says 'Bless your heart,' she's pretty much telling you to go to hell."

Honey's eyes widened, and then she threw back her

head and laughed and laughed until tears were rolling down her face.

"Oh my God, that's the best thing I've learned since I came to Georgia, and just for the record, if you ever get fed up with men and wanna give a girl a try, look me up. I think we'd hit it off just fine."

Lily grinned. "Well, that's not likely to happen, but I could definitely use a friend."

"Deal," Honey said. "Hang in there, girl. Anything worth having is worth fighting for."

~~~

Rachel's cockiness ended the moment T. J. opened the door. He grabbed her arm, shoved her up against the wall, and began tearing off her clothes.

"Hey, hey, wait a minute," Rachel said, trying to laugh it off.

"Not in the mood for it," T. J. muttered. "Did you come to buy my house?"

She stuttered. "Well, we've thought about—"

His eyes narrowed angrily. "That's what I thought. You know why you're here, and I don't like being used. This time I'm the one in charge."

Rachel's heartbeat kicked out of rhythm as his fingers curled around the collar of her blouse.

"Do not tear my clothes," she said sharply. "You fuck with me and cause me to explain stuff to my husband I don't want to explain, and you'll be looking down the barrel of a rape charge. Do we understand each other?"

He froze. Once again, he'd been sideswiped by a female calling all the shots and something inside him just snapped.

"Then strip, bitch," he said softly.

Rachel's hands were trembling as she came out of her clothes.

"Aren't you going to take yours off, too?" she asked.

He undid his belt and let his jeans drop down around his knees.

"I don't need to. Nothing personal, Mrs. Goodhope, but this is what you came for."

She was stunned by the sight of the condom already on his erection and realized he'd planned this welcome, even as she had been driving out to meet him. She was in over her head and knew it. The only way to get out was to get through it.

He shoved his knee between her legs and took her standing up, punishing Rachel for her rich-bitch assumption that all he was good for was a fuck, and then doing it all over again for LilyAnn Bronte's put-down.

Tears were running down Rachel's cheeks when he finally climaxed. He withdrew abruptly, ripped off the condom, and dropped it in a wastebasket, then readjusted his clothes without even looking at her.

Rachel was shivering, her arms crossed against her breasts. A trickle of blood was running down the inside of her thigh.

Then he swung back around. "Get your clothes on and get the hell out, and don't come back. I got my eyes on younger meat."

Rachel was trembling, but there was a look in his eyes that scared her beyond the rape. She began grabbing her clothes, putting them on as fast as she could, desperate to get out before he silenced her for good.

She was dressed in all but her shoes when she saw

him double up his fist. She picked them up and ran bare-foot through the rain to her car. Her fingers were shaking so hard that she couldn't get the key in the ignition, and all the while, she could see him from the corner of her eye, still standing in the doorway, watching.

When the key finally went in, she started the engine and accelerated so fast that she slung mud all the way to the porch and up onto the legs of T. J.'s jeans.

His eyes narrowed angrily. "Motherfucker," he muttered, and went back inside, slamming and locking the door behind him.

Rachel drove until she was out of sight of the house, then pulled over onto the shoulder of the road, laid her head down on the steering wheel, and sobbed.

By the time she got home, she had regained her composure, thankful she was still alive.

The poker game was still in progress, because she recognized the cars in the parking lot. Since they would be playing in the library, she went in the back door, then to her bedroom, and locked the door. She scrubbed the blood out of her panties in the bathroom sink, then got in the shower and scrubbed her body until it was pink, washed the massage oil and the rain from her hair, and proceeded to put herself back together again.

By the time she was finished, she'd come to a conclusion. She'd gotten herself into that mess, and the only way to make sure it never happened again was to quit cheating. Bud wasn't the best apple in the barrel, but he was hers, and so was his money. It was enough.

That night, she told Bud she didn't think the Bissell house was right for them, then she called Hank Richards and told him the same thing. With that decision made, her foray into fucking outside the bonds of marriage was over.

———

Mike saw the lights come on in Lily's house while he was in the kitchen peeling potatoes. Fine. She was home safe. He didn't want anything bad to happen to her. He just didn't want to be in her world anymore. His heart hurt, and his vision was blurry, but he kept peeling the potato and telling himself if he said it enough times to himself, it would surely become fact.

———

Lily, on the other hand, had the opposite wish. She'd been the center of Mike Dalton's world and never knew it, and now that he'd cast her out, she felt lost. She wanted him back but didn't know how to make it happen.

She had just stepped out of the shower when her phone rang. She answered absently, still caught up in the drama of her life.

"Hello."

"Hey, honey, it's me, Mama."

Lily heard the voice and before she knew it, she was crying.

Grace felt helpless. She was too far away to comfort her baby's broken heart.

"Talk to me, Lilybug. What's wrong?"

Lily stifled a sob. "Mike loved me. I didn't know it. Now he hates me, and I want him to love me again."

Grace rolled her eyes. Her daughter had finally seen the light, but as usual, a day late and a dollar short.

"Then find a way, LilyAnn. If he matters that much to you, find a way. Don't quit on him like you quit on life. He was there for eleven years for you. You owe him some time to get over whatever it was you did."

"Well, that's just it. I didn't *do* anything."

"You did something," Grace said. "The whole time you were gone on your walk, he was uneasy, pacing the house, looking out the windows, waiting for you to come back. Right before you walked in, he was standing at the windows. Then all of a sudden he ran to the door, and whatever he saw or heard outside must have been the last straw. So think. And then fix it. I would dearly love for him to be my son-in-law, okay?"

"Okay," Lily said. "I'm glad you called."

"Me too," Grace said. "Stay in touch."

"I will. Love you."

"Love you more, Lilybug."

Lily disconnected, then went to the front door and opened it. If Mike had been standing in the doorway, he would have had a clear view of T. J. and the truck, and he would have seen her, but only her back, so what the hell had she been doing?

Then it hit her. Right before all that happened, she'd seen him watching her from the window like he was spying, and it had made her mad. After that, she'd heard the front door open. That's when she turned her back to the house. She closed her eyes, remembering that she'd shifted her stance and put a hand on her hip. It had been a challenging stance for Lachlan, but from behind, it could have looked different to Mike. And since he was convinced she had another boyfriend, he had to assume that was the guy.

She groaned as she shut the door. She'd been all about making a change in her life, but if he'd been in love with her through Randy Joe and the eleven ensuing years without ever having his feelings reciprocated, seeing her pick yet another man over him would most likely have been his "last straw."

What on earth had she done?

Ruby Dye had changed her hair color from Audacious Red to Chocolate Sin. The color was a warm, rich brown with auburn highlights and was the start of the conversation when Vesta and Vera got to work.

"Ooh, Sister! I love that," Vesta said.

"Me too," Vera said. "That color really makes your eyes pop."

Vesta frowned at her twin. "Vera, you know I hate that phrase. Pop. Pop. Pop. 'A pop of color.' 'Makes it pop.' What the hell is that supposed to mean? Balloons pop. Popcorn pops. We drink pop. But color doesn't pop."

Vera frowned. "Well, for the love of God, Vesta. I was bragging on Sister's hair, not begging for a slap-down."

Vesta sighed. "You're right, Vera. Sorry, Sister."

Ruby was used to their banter and mostly ignored it.

At that point Mabel Jean came in sporting a new manicure. In an attempt to do some PR of her own, she'd painted a tiny Christmas icon on each of her fingernails and was wearing little red bell earrings that actually jingled when she moved.

"Now that's cute," Ruby said, pointing to the fingernails.

Mabel Jean beamed and tossed her head, which made the earrings jingle.

"Oh my God," Vera cried. "If I had to hear that jingle in my ears all day, I'd be crazy by quitting time."

"Ever since the doctor took you off the hormones, you've been crazy by quitting time anyway," Vesta said.

Vera giggled. "It's true. I don't know whether to claw my eyes out or get new batteries for my vibrator."

Ruby rolled her eyes. "TMI, TMI… Seriously, too much information."

They all burst into laughter and the day began.

Chapter 13

LILYANN'S FRIDAY HAIR APPOINTMENT WITH RUBY coincided with Rachel Goodhope's appointment with Vesta. They walked in within moments of each other, then squared off and turned their backs as they hung up their coats, refusing to acknowledge the other one's presence.

Rachel felt uneasy and guilty. She'd fostered the ill will that was between her and LilyAnn by her behavior. All she could do was behave better and hope she eventually lived it down. She gave LilyAnn a quick glance and then sighed. The woman wouldn't even look at her.

Ruby noticed the tension between them and, without knowing the reason for it, remembered ignoring Patty June's antagonism toward Bobbette Paulson and the chaos that had ensued. She decided the wiser thing to do was to separate the two women ASAP.

"Hi, LilyAnn. I'm ready for you. Come on back," Ruby called out, and waved her to the shampoo station.

Vesta moved to the second chair and waved at Rachel.

"Rachel Goodhope! Come on down."

Everyone in the shop laughed at the *Price Is Right* shout-out.

Rachel smiled. "Do I have to guess the right price to win my hairdo?"

Vesta laughed as she put a cape around Rachel's

neck. "We haven't changed prices here in over five years, so you get a pass."

The comment set off a conversation about favorite daytime television shows, which LilyAnn immediately tuned out. She hadn't watched daytime television in so long she had no idea of the programming. She also didn't want anything to do with a conversation involving Rachel Goodhope and began counting ceiling tiles instead.

Rachel, on the other hand, saw daytime television on a daily basis because it was always playing in the background of her kitchen.

As Vesta began to wash Rachel's hair, Rachel closed her eyes and, the minute she did, flashed on the expression on T. J. Lachlan's face while he was raping her. It was so startling that she gasped, making Vesta think she'd hurt her.

"Oh honey, I'm sorry. Did I pull?"

Rachel's fingers curled tightly on the arms of the chair as she made herself smile.

"No, no, it's fine."

"I'll be more careful," Vesta said.

Ruby didn't know what was going on, but the tension between these two women was palpable. It wasn't as if they'd ever been best friends, but they'd never behaved like this before. They hadn't spoken or looked at each other since they sat down. And knowing Rachel's propensity for flirting, Ruby couldn't help but wonder what might have sparked this.

As soon as the women went to their hairstylists' respective stations, the energy lightened, which confirmed Ruby's suspicions even more. She glanced at the shuttered expression in LilyAnn's eyes.

"Hey, honey, have you heard from your mama and Eddie since they left?"

Lily winced as Ruby's comb caught on a tangle. "Yes. She called just the other night."

Ruby smiled. "I would have liked to be a fly on the wall at your house Thanksgiving Day. I'll bet Grace and Carol had some tall tales to tell about their good old days."

Lily thought about the day and tried not to cry.

"It was something, all right," she muttered.

Ruby frowned and asked a different but related question, trying to work her way around to what she really wanted to know, which was whether Mike managed to make LilyAnn jealous.

"How is Mike feeling these days?"

"The doctor released him to drive, which I'm sure you know because he's driving all over town now."

"That's good," Ruby said, and combed out some more tangles. "What are you guys doing for Christmas?"

"I have no idea what he's doing. He's not talking to me."

Ruby frowned. *What in the world? I suggested he make LilyAnn jealous, not get mad at her and clam up.*

"That's too bad. What happened?"

LilyAnn shrugged. "It's complicated."

Ruby had snooped enough. If she wanted to know more, she would have to ask Mike.

"Do you want to do anything different with your hairstyle?" Ruby asked.

LilyAnn looked at her face and frowned. "Just dry it. After that, I couldn't care less."

Ruby was worried. She didn't want to see LilyAnn slip back into her old rut.

"You really don't care?" Ruby asked.

Lily blinked back tears and tried not to cry. "I don't care if you shave it all off."

"Oh honey, what's wrong?" Ruby whispered.

"I messed up," she said.

"I'm sorry. Did your dream guy turn you down?"

Tears rolled down Lily's face. "I can't get rid of one I didn't want, and I can't get the one I ignored half my life to even talk to me anymore."

"This calls for drastic measures," Ruby said. "How attached are you to this hair hanging halfway down your back?"

"Not at all…at least not anymore."

"No need to go bald, but I think we need to bring you into the present with your hairstyle. Do you trust me?"

"Surprise me," Lily said, and closed her eyes.

Ruby grinned. She had wanted to do this for years. She put the blow-dryer down and picked up her scissors.

It didn't take long for everyone in the shop to realize an event was in progress. LilyAnn Bronte had always had long blond hair. Who would she be without it?

Even Rachel became mesmerized by the lengths piling up on the floor beneath Ruby's feet, and couldn't help but wonder what had prompted this drastic change. Maybe it was part of the diet-makeover process LilyAnn was on. If it was, she should be pleased when she saw herself again.

Lily could feel the weight coming off her head, but she was too numb to care. When Ruby finally quit cutting, LilyAnn smelled styling gel and then Ruby shoved her fingers through LilyAnn's hair and worked it in.

When she finally turned on the blow-dryer, she finished the styling in half the time it normally took.

Ruby was giggling with delight.

The Conklin twins kept saying "How pretty, how pretty" over and over, and Mabel Jean was agreeing.

"Now you can look," Ruby said, as she turned the chair back to the mirror.

Lily opened her eyes and was so shocked by the transformation that, for a second, she didn't recognize her own face.

"Oh my Lord!" she whispered, fingering the side sweep of bangs and the shoulder-length hair Ruby had layered. "I look… I look…"

"Beautiful," Ruby said, as she gave Lily's shoulders a quick squeeze. "You need to hurry or you'll be late getting back to work."

"It'll be okay," Lily said and then impulsively pulled out her phone. "Take my picture. I want to send it to Mama."

"I'll do it," Vesta said, as she put the phone on camera function and aimed and clicked. "Oooh, look at yourself, honey! The LilyAnn from your past is gone."

"It's about damn time," Lily muttered. "What do I owe you?" she asked and, when Ruby told her, began writing out the check.

"Thank you so much," she said, as she got up, then turned around and gave Ruby a quick hug. "You are a good friend, Sister. Thank you for everything."

She sent the picture to her mother's phone, then put on her coat, slung the strap of her purse over her shoulder, and took off out the door.

Rachel stifled the twinge of jealousy as she watched her go. She had too much penance to pay to start that crap again.

—⁓—

T. J. had just walked out of Richards' Realty and was about to get in his truck when he saw a woman walking toward him down the street. The thought went through his mind that he'd never seen her before, and then all of a sudden he realized who it was. He was so stunned by the transformation that she was all the way past him before he realized he'd missed his chance to harass her.

Lily was so caught up in thinking about how she was going to make amends with Mike that she didn't see Lachlan. But when she walked past the fitness center, she paused to wave through the window at Stewart. She saw the confusion, then recognition in his eyes and laughed.

When she got back to the pharmacy, she headed toward the door marked *Employees Only* to go put up her things. As she began to enter, Mr. Phillips actually called out for her to stop.

"It's just me, Mr. Phillips," Lily said.

He was still staring in disbelief as she went in to stow her things.

Mitchell gave her a big thumbs-up when he saw her, and every patron she checked out for the rest of the day had to comment. By the time she was ready to go home, she knew her new haircut was a hit.

Mike drove into his driveway at almost the same time Lily pulled into hers. She knew he was there, but he'd rebuffed her so many times that she didn't want to be hurt again. She got out of the car and went inside without breaking stride.

Mike saw the woman get out and for a few moments

didn't recognize her. Then when he did, he was so shocked he could do nothing but stare. The LilyAnn he'd known all his life—the one he'd fallen in love with—had disappeared, leaving another woman in her place.

Within moments of her disappearance, he heard T. J. Lachlan's pickup coming down the street. Heartsick, he didn't want to see how she greeted him—if she hugged him, if they kissed—and went into his house.

He heard Lachlan rack his pipes as he shut the door, and in spite of his determination not to look, he did it anyway.

Lachlan was sitting in his truck with the engine idling. Mike heard him rev it again, which made the pipes rattle, but still no LilyAnn. As the minutes passed, Lachlan didn't move. He just kept gunning the engine. Mike was about to go run his ass out of the neighborhood for being a noise nuisance when he saw a police cruiser turn the corner and come down the street.

As the cop came closer, Lachlan put the truck in gear and drove away, with the cop car following right behind him. His eyes narrowed as he looked over at LilyAnn's house.

What the hell was that all about? Had she called the police, or was it another neighbor who had done that?

He didn't want to care, but he'd spent too many years worrying about her to quit cold turkey. Just because he didn't love her anymore didn't mean he wanted her in trouble.

LilyAnn waited at the window, peering through a crack in the curtains while her anxiety grew. She had

called the police the moment she'd heard him, and
when she finally saw the cruiser, she breathed a sigh
of relief. Lachlan drove off with Lonnie Pittman following him.

She had no idea how Lachlan would view what she'd
done, but she needed backup, and Mike was no longer
available. Frustrated and just the least bit worried, she
went to her room to change.

As she stripped off her clothes, she paused at the
mirror to look at her body in a subjective manner and,
as she stared, slowly came to a new decision.

She was done with diets. She wasn't as small as she
used to be, but she no longer strived to get that look
back. She didn't want to look like a girl again, but rather
like the woman she had become. And if that meant she
had rounder hips and more meat on her bones, then so
be it. She felt good. She liked how she looked, and that
was all that mattered.

She went into the bathroom, then stopped again, this
time to look at her hairstyle, marveling at the change
it had made in her appearance. She kept running her
fingers through the strands and fluffing the layers,
delighted with the feel.

She took a quick shower, then put on a pair of old
sweats and a matching shirt, and was brushing her hair
when her doorbell rang. She ran to answer, still in her
bare feet, and saw the cop car parked in her driveway.
When she opened the door, she grinned at the shock on
Lonnie Pittman's face.

"It's still me," she said.

Lonnie blinked. "My goodness, LilyAnn, you look
great!" Then the moment he said it, he flushed. "I

apologize. I did not mean to get personal. I came to ask you a couple of questions about T. J. Lachlan."

She nodded. "Come in. Have a seat."

"Thank you. I just have a couple of questions. You called the police about Lachlan, right?"

"Yes."

"Is this the first time he harassed you?"

"No. He's been doing it since Thanksgiving Day."

Lonnie frowned as he began to make notes. "Why didn't you report it sooner?"

"And say what, Lonnie? He hasn't done anything to me. He just turns up everywhere I go. It's gone beyond coincidence, leaving me to believe he's stalking me. And frankly, he's a little scary."

"Do you want to press charges?"

"For what? He hasn't come on my property or touched me in any way."

Lonnie frowned. "I understand. Still, don't hesitate to call again if you feel uneasy."

"I won't," she said.

"Okay then. Have a nice night," he said.

She shut and locked the door behind him, then went back to get her house shoes. Moments later she was on her way to the kitchen to make herself some supper.

As she began digging food out of the refrigerator and heating up a skillet to scramble some eggs, she could almost hear her mama's voice, telling her to fix whatever was wrong between her and Mike.

Being the dutiful daughter that she was, she turned around and headed for the phone.

Mike had kicked back on the sofa, nursing a beer and watching TV. He'd ordered a pizza and was waiting for it to be delivered when his phone rang. He answered without checking caller ID.

"Hello?"

"Mike, it's me, LilyAnn."

He closed his eyes. "What do you want?"

Lily winced. "I was about to make myself some supper and wondered if you wanted to come over and—"

"No."

She took a deep breath and tried again. "What about eating dinner with me Christmas day? I'll be—"

"No. Call your boyfriend and invite him. I'm busy."

He hung up before he weakened, then felt like a heel. It was behavior unbecoming of a Southern gentleman.

Across the drive, LilyAnn blinked away tears and then hung up the phone and began to make her own meal. She ate her scrambled eggs without tasting them, put a little jelly on what was left of her toast, and called it supper.

As soon as the kitchen was clean, she called Ruby Dye. Ruby had been in charge of organizing workers for the Salvation Army Christmas dinner for the past few years, and LilyAnn wasn't about to spend the day alone feeling sorry for herself.

Ruby answered on the third ring.

"Hello."

"Hey, Sister, it's me, LilyAnn."

Ruby curled her feet up beneath her as she settled in for a chat.

"Well, hi, honey! Are you still happy with your haircut or did you call to gripe at me?"

LilyAnn smiled. "No, I'm not mad, and yes, I love it. The reason I'm calling is about the Salvation Army dinner. Are you still in charge of organizing servers?"

"I sure am. Are you volunteering?"

"Yes, ma'am. I suddenly find myself alone on Christmas Day, and you know how the song goes, I better not pout and I better not cry, or Santa won't leave me a present."

Ruby laughed. "That's the attitude, and this is wonderful. I always need servers."

"So what do I do?"

"Show up at the community center about nine o'clock Christmas morning. We start by decorating tables and go from there."

"I'll be there, and thank you for letting me in at this late date."

"On the contrary, it's I who should be thanking you. So I'll see you Tuesday morning, okay?"

"Oh, wait! What do I wear?" Lily asked.

"Something festive, and be as quirky as you want. Lots of the servers wear little headbands with reindeer antlers, or Santa hats…anything like that."

"Will do," LilyAnn said. "And thanks again."

"You're welcome."

Lily smiled as she disconnected, already thinking about the day. This was what her grandma would have referred to as putting on her big-girl panties. So, tomorrow being Sunday, and only two days before Christmas, she was going shopping in Savannah. Her clothes no longer fit right, and she wanted something fun to wear at the dinner.

By the time she went to bed, she'd set her disappointment

aside. As long as there was a tomorrow, there was still hope to make things right.

———◊———

Mike stood in the dark, watching out his bedroom window until he saw the light go out in hers, and then went to bed, but he couldn't sleep. He kept thinking about LilyAnn all alone on Christmas Day. No tree, no presents, no family. Then he rolled over angrily and punched his pillow.

When he woke up the next morning, it was almost 9:00 a.m. When he went out to get the paper, he noticed her car was gone and assumed she'd gone to church.

When noon came and went and she still wasn't home, he told himself it didn't matter. She was a grown woman and not his responsibility.

———◊———

LilyAnn's arms were full of sacks and packages as she made her way back to the mall parking lot. It was almost 2:00 p.m. Her feet hurt from walking, but she felt better than she had in years. Even if she was alone—even if Mike hated her guts—at the moment, she was happy.

She dumped her stuff in the trunk and then sighed with relief as she slid behind the wheel. She had an hour-and-a-half drive to get home, and would be there long before dark, which was her only concern.

She'd skipped lunch and now she was starving, but she'd thought of that before she left the mall food court. She dug out her veggie sandwich from Subway, unscrewed the top on her cold drink, and then took a big bite. She ate until her appetite had been satisfied, wrapped up what was left, and headed home.

—⁓—

Mike was bordering on all-out panic. On the one hand, he refused to call her and let her know he was worried. On the other hand, he didn't know what he would do if he called and she didn't answer. So he did neither as his fears increased with leaps and bounds.

One minute he'd looked out the window to the empty driveway, and the next time he looked, her car was in the drive and she was nowhere in sight.

Relief washed through him so fast that his legs went out from under him as he dropped onto the sofa.

"Thank you, Jesus," he said softly, and buried his face in his hands.

But the longer he sat, the more disgusted he became with himself. He could talk big and act tough, but he was never going to get over loving her and he knew it.

Chapter 14

PHILLIPS' PHARMACY OPENED AT 8:00 A.M. ON Christmas Eve, and LilyAnn stood at the register checking people out nonstop until her time for break finally came. She was already tired when she headed for the bathroom, and the day was a long way from over. It felt like every man in Blessings had waited until the last minute to do his Christmas shopping, and now, because other things were so picked over in retail stores, they all had come through the pharmacy in panic mode, hoping there were bottles of perfume or boxed sets of bath powders and lotions left for sale. Once those sold out, the shoppers opted for foot massagers and Yankee candles, and when those were gone, they emptied the racks of gel insoles, socks for diabetics, and K-Y Jelly. Sometimes it was difficult to keep a straight face as she checked them out.

One little boy had come in with three dollars to buy his mama a present. He bypassed a display of nail polish and a bin of mini-tubes of hand lotion, opting for a box of SpongeBob Band-Aids. He looked so pleased with his purchase that she couldn't help but envy the woman who would open that gift.

When 5:00 p.m. came, LilyAnn was exhausted. She drove home in something of a daze, oblivious to the pickup following two cars behind her. She parked in her driveway and was already inside before the truck passed her house. She never saw it or the driver.

But Mike did.

He came around the corner just as the truck drove past LilyAnn's house, and he knew who it was. Although they met in the middle of the block, Lachlan wasn't looking at Mike. His full attention was on the house where Lily's car was parked.

When Mike saw the expression on Lachlan's face, the hair stood up on the back of his neck. That wasn't lust, it was rage.

What the hell?

Mike watched him in his rearview mirror, and when Lachlan reached the intersection, he took a hard right. Mike accelerated, pulled in his driveway, and hurried into his house, then raced to a window and peered through a crack between the curtains.

Sure enough, Lachlan was making a return pass. He did it two more times before he finally left the neighborhood.

Mike was beginning to think Lachlan was not the boyfriend he'd imagined him to be.

So if not a suitor, he was her stalker, which explained why she'd called the police the other day.

Son of a bitch.

He went straight to the phone to call the police, and then stopped. What could he say? That he saw Lachlan circle the block four times? That wasn't against the law, and he'd made no threatening moves toward her, so they couldn't arrest him for assault. Mike was beginning to understand how hard it would be for a woman to prove she was being stalked, and how useless the law really was when this was happening.

And while he was deciding what to do about making

his peace with Lily, she got in her car and, once again, was gone before he knew it.

———~~~———

LilyAnn had been going to Christmas Eve services at her church for as long as she could remember. She wasn't spending the holiday with her family, and she wasn't spending it with Mike, but that didn't prevent her from spending the holiday with God.

She pulled into the church parking lot and, as she was parking, saw children going into the church dressed as angels and shepherds, and even one little boy in what looked like a donkey costume and another, a sheep. At that point, all the exhaustion she'd been feeling melted away.

She took a seat on the aisle near the middle of the room just as a little angel came running from the altar. His halo was hanging lopsided on his head, and his harried mother was right behind him, which sent a titter of laughter throughout the congregation.

By the time the service started, Lily was at peace. She couldn't control what was happening around her, but she could control how she received it.

Much later, after the program and the singing, they had refreshments in the dining hall of the church, and once again, Lily was reminded of all the years she and Mike had been thrown together as kids, seated side by side with a cup of punch and a sugar cookie apiece, with a caution not to make a mess.

She ate a cookie and drank some punch for old times' sake and, when she got home, found a FedEx package on her front porch from her mama and Eddie.

She didn't have a tree, but she had a present and her mama's love, and that was enough.

———

It had taken Mike exactly five minutes to calm down and realize where LilyAnn had probably gone, and after a quick trip past the church parking lot where he saw her car, he knew he was right. He thought about going in, but didn't—partly because he didn't want to carry their antagonism into a house of God, but mostly because he didn't know how to face her.

He went home in a calmer frame of mind, and when she came home a couple of hours later, he was at peace. He didn't know if she would ever forgive him, but he would willingly eat crow for the rest of his life if he could just have her back as his best friend.

———

The phone rang as LilyAnn was styling her hair to accommodate the halo she planned to wear at the Salvation Army dinner. She dropped the brush and ran to answer, plopping down on the bed as she put the receiver to her ear.

"Merry Christmas!"

Grace laughed. "Merry Christmas, LilyAnn! Did you get your present?"

LilyAnn smiled. "Yes, but I waited to open it this morning so it would be official. Thank you, Mama, and thank Eddie for me, too. The sweater is beautiful. You know blue is my favorite color, and it fits me perfectly!"

"That's great! And thank you for our present, as well. You know me so well, darling. This flower-a-month thing is amazing. We got the first delivery day before yesterday, and after we enjoy it blooming in the house, we can plant the bulbs out in our garden. Every time we see them blooming, we will think of you."

LilyAnn beamed. "I'm glad you liked it, Mama."

"Oh, and speaking of like, I *love* your hair. It turned you into a rather gorgeous woman."

Lily's smile widened. "Not that you're prejudiced or anything, but thanks."

"I am not prejudiced, at least not much. So what are you doing today? Have you and Mike made up?"

"I'm trying, but he's not having any of it. I won't give up, but so far, nothing has changed."

"I'm so sorry. It kills me that you're going to be alone today. I wish you had come here to be with us."

"Oh, I'm not going to be alone! I'm helping serve at the Salvation Army dinner. I bought a green sweatshirt with a Christmas tree on the front and back, and the little lights on the tree really light up and twinkle. And I have a halo to wear with it. I can't wait to put it all on."

Grace smiled. She could hear the excitement in her daughter's voice and was amazed at the transformation she'd made.

"Good for you. That's a perfect way to mark the season. So, have a good time, and tell me all about it next time we talk."

"I will. I love you, Mama."

"I love you, too, honey."

Lily was smiling as she disconnected. She glanced at the clock, then headed to the kitchen. She had no idea if the people who worked the dinner ate dinner there, too.

So, just to be on the safe side, she made herself some
food and ate with an eye on the time so she wouldn't
be late.

T. J. Lachlan had been carrying around the ticket he'd
gotten for disturbing the peace, but he was tired of looking at it. When he got home, he got out of the truck,
set the ticket on fire, and dropped it in the yard. The
grass tried to catch with it, but he stomped it out. He
stood for a moment, staring intently at the house he'd
inherited. He'd had his fill of this place, in more ways
than one. He refused to consider he'd brought his cur-
rent troubles on himself. He didn't get this kind of grief
back in Tennessee, he thought as he strode angrily inside
with a fifth of Jim Beam in one hand and some takeout
ribs from Charlie's Barbecue in the other.

The house smelled like fresh paint and varnish. The
fading sunlight shone weakly through the windows he'd
washed days earlier. It looked like a home and felt like
a jail. It would have made his life a whole lot simpler if
this had been money in his pocket, not a remodel job he
had yet to flip.

His footsteps echoed in the house as he walked
through to the kitchen. He'd been here for weeks, repair-
ing, painting, fixing wiring and windows, and it still felt
foreign, almost as if the house itself rejected his presence. He'd brought it back to its former glory, but he'd
done more harm in this house with a single act of rape
than his uncle Gene had ever thought about in the sixty-
seven years he'd lived there.

He dropped the ribs onto the table and opened the

whiskey, chugging down enough to set his belly on fire before he sat down with a thump.

"Sorry-ass bitch called the cops on me," he muttered, and tore into the ribs like a starving dog.

He ate ribs and fries until there was nothing left but bones, then took the whiskey with him to the living room. He kicked back in the recliner, turned on the TV, and took another swig.

By midnight, he was passed out in the chair, the empty bottle on the floor, the remote in his lap, while QVC kept selling laptops with a frantic promise to deliver by Christmas.

He woke up the next morning with a hangover of massive proportions and a growing grudge against the tall blond bitch. He wanted her to pay. He wanted to see that disdain replaced with fear. He wanted to hear her scream and beg for mercy.

—∿—

By the time the first diners arrived at the community center, LilyAnn was in full holiday mode. The tables had been covered with white paper and decorated with little red sleighs filled with candy and artificial poinsettias. The Christmas tree had been set up in a corner of the room, and the presents beneath wrapped in red gift paper for little boys, green gift paper for little girls, gold gift paper for teens, and sturdy tote bags of canned goods and fruit for the adults.

Her sweatshirt was a hit, as was the glittering halo on her head. The Christmas tree image on her shirt mirrored the one in the corner, right down to the colored blinking lights. Her slacks were winter white, and her flats metallic gold.

The reporter from the *Blessings Bugle* took her picture as she was carrying plates of food for a woman with children, but she didn't know it and wouldn't have cared whether they took one or not. This was the best she'd felt in years, and it was because the last person she was thinking about was herself.

Both Vesta and Vera Conklin were also helping serve and had come decked out in brown sweaters and slacks with little antler headbands and red noses. Twin versions of a female Rudolph. The kids loved it and the sisters were playing it to the hilt.

Ruby's homage to the festivities of the day was elf ears and a little green elf hat.

Mabel Jean was set up in a corner of the room with a tray of face paint, dressed in red and white stripes and doing her part to entertain the children.

About an hour into it, LilyAnn paused to take in the sight. The tables were full of people eating and talking. It reminded her of what a family reunion was like. The ones where you know some of the people very well, while a few more look familiar, and the others are people you've never seen before.

What she couldn't get over was that every one of these people lived in Blessings and had qualified for this meal because they lived at or below the poverty line. She suddenly felt very grateful for her life, no matter how screwed up it had become.

Ruby came up behind her and gave her a quick hug.

"I can't thank you enough for coming to help."

"Oh, Sister, you have no idea how grateful I am to be here."

"I love your Christmas tree sweatshirt, but with that

halo, you look like the angel topper on it, for sure. Oh…
hey, I see that table on the far side needs drinks refilled.
Can you go do that for me?"

"Absolutely," LilyAnn said. She grabbed two pitch-
ers of sweet tea and took off.

What LilyAnn didn't know was that Ruby wasn't
through meddling in her and Mike's lives.

About an hour after LilyAnn had called asking to
volunteer, the man scheduled to be Ruby's Santa Claus
called to say he had been taken ill, leaving Ruby without
a Santa for the dinner.

And the moment she realized LilyAnn was on her
own, she guessed Mike Dalton would be, as well. And
he was. After a quick selling job on how disappointed
the kids would all be, he agreed. It was Ruby's little
secret, and yet one more event in which he and LilyAnn
would be thrown together. And maybe, just maybe, this
time they would get it right.

⚬⚬⚬

The community center was packed, and people were
visiting among themselves when they began hearing the
sound of bells jingling, and then there was a great big
thump on the roof, and then a loud, hearty voice saying,
"Ho, ho, ho."

The kids who had been running amok were suddenly motionless, their mouths agape, their eyes wide
with expectation. Someone pointed to the hall at the
back of the room as the doors began to open, and then
a big, fat Santa Claus came through the door, laughing
as he walked.

LilyAnn was in shock. The moment she heard that

laugh, she knew it was Mike. Even before she saw him—even beneath that full white beard and the wig and hat, even beneath the big fat belly and the red fuzzy suit—she knew it was him.

She sat down in the nearest empty chair with her heart in her throat, watching as Ruby seated him beside the tree. And then she remembered that the servers would also be Santa's helpers, which meant she was not going to be able to keep her distance.

And sure enough, the moment Santa was seated, Ruby signaled for them to come up.

"God give me strength," Lily muttered, and headed for the front of the room.

Mike was actually having fun with this. As he was waiting for all the servers to reach the front of the room, he noticed one woman wearing a halo, but he could only see her silhouette, backlit by the light from the windows behind her. When she walked out of the backlight and he got a better view, his gut knotted.

LilyAnn. Well, hell, of course it would be her. I cannot escape her because I am not supposed to. I get it, God. I get it.

He refused to meet her gaze because he'd never get through the task ahead without total concentration, but when he saw the lights flashing on her sweatshirt, he stifled a smile.

Then the first child slipped up and put a hand on his knee, and he got down to business.

Mike looked down, saw the awe in the little boy's eyes, and realized the importance of what he was doing. He picked the boy up and set him on his knee.

"Ho, ho, ho. Hello, young man. What's your name?"

The little boy frowned. "It's me, Billy! Don't you recognize me?"

Oops, nearly blew that one. "Well, Billy, you've grown so much I didn't recognize you."

The little boy's expression lightened. "Oh yeah, that's what Grandma said, too."

Mike patted him on the back. "So, have you been a good boy this year?"

Billy rolled his eyes. "Most of the time."

"Good for you," Mike said, and took the present Vesta handed him and gave it to Billy. "Merry Christmas, Billy."

"Merry Christmas, Santa Claus!"

Billy was all smiles as the photographer took his picture. Then he hopped down from Mike's lap and ran toward his mother as another child took his place.

As the time went on, the children were so charming in their innocence that LilyAnn forgot it was Mike beneath the beard and got lost in their stories.

By the time a second child had wet on Mike's pant legs, LilyAnn was struggling not to laugh. If it hadn't been for the swift action of one mother, another would have thrown up in his lap. The photographer had whipped cream on the back of his pants after a little boy who'd been eating pie with his fingers used the man's pants for a napkin, and Vesta gave up her reindeer antlers to a little girl with curly brown hair, just so she would sit in Santa's lap long enough for a picture.

After two hours of kids, presents, and pictures, it was finally over, and LilyAnn was convinced that— even though the only present she opened had been in a FedEx box, even though the only food she'd eaten had been a mini-ham sandwich made with a cold dinner roll and a scrap of ham at home—she'd never had a better Christmas in her life. And, despite his best intentions, she'd still spent it with Mike.

She'd already said her good-byes and was on her way out the back when she heard someone calling her name. She turned to see Santa Claus lumbering down the hall.

"LilyAnn! Wait!"

She stopped, uncertain what to expect and unwilling for this to be another bad experience because she didn't want to ruin this day.

Mike was puffing when he finally reached her.

"I have to take this off, and I need to talk to you. Will you come with me?"

"Are you going to be mad at me? Because if you are, I don't want to hear it. This has been a nearly perfect day, and I don't want it ruined."

The tremor in her voice was nearly Mike's undoing. He poked her halo just enough to make it sway, then shook his head.

"No, I won't be mad, and I won't ruin your day."

"Then okay," she said, and followed him into the office.

He began peeling off the Santa suit one piece at a time.

"Wow, it is hot and itchy under all that," he said, scrubbing his hands against his face, then shedding the rest of the suit until he was left in gym shorts and a T-shirt.

LilyAnn had seen him in this getup all her life, but all of a sudden she was hit with the intimacy of watching him undress and took herself to a chair on the other side of the room and sat down. He put a tracksuit on over the shorts and tee, then changed back into his tennis shoes.

Once he was dressed, he pulled up a chair in front of her and sat down.

"I have a question to ask you," he said.

"So ask," Lily said.

"Is T. J. Lachlan stalking you?"

She sighed. "Pretty much."

"Since when?"

"Well, you saw it. Since Thanksgiving Day."

"Did you two have a fight or something? Is that why he's acting like that?"

LilyAnn frowned. "A fight? We've never even been introduced! I've waited on him in the pharmacy and never even exchanged a hello. Yes, I knew who he was, and yes, we've all seen and heard that hot rod he drives, but I don't know him. And what I do know, I don't like."

"Son of a bitch," Mike mumbled. "So, I owe you this huge apology because I got the idea you liked him and…"

All of a sudden LilyAnn stood up. She didn't want to have this conversation in the office at the local community center because she didn't know where it was going to go. She needed the privacy of her own home if the need became necessary to cry…or if she was lucky…to get a hug and a kiss.

"So, now the mystery is solved. Now you know I don't like him."

Mike panicked. She was about to bolt and he'd barely begun.

"Wait! Where are you going?"

"Home. I haven't really eaten, and I have gravy in my shoe. I'll repeat the invitation I offered the other night. Do you want to have Christmas dinner with me?"

Mike's heart skipped a beat as he smiled.

"Yes, I would like to have dinner with you."

LilyAnn sighed. "Good. It's your own fault it will be scrambled eggs and toast."

"I like scrambled eggs and toast."

And just like that, her world was once again intact.

"So, I'm going home now. See you in a few minutes?"

He wanted to kiss her. Instead, he settled for cupping her cheek.

"Yep. See you soon. I'm going to drop this suit off at the mayor's house. His grandchildren are due in tonight and unfortunately for him, he has to play Santa Claus for them in the morning in a suit that smells like pee. I'll be right there afterward. It'll give you time to get the gravy out of your shoe."

LilyAnn laughed, and as she did, the halo bounced from side to side, sprinkling just the tiniest bits of glitter down into her hair.

Mike was certain he'd never seen anything quite as beautiful, but he couldn't say it for the lump in his throat. She waved good-bye and then went out the door, leaving him to pack up the suit.

LilyAnn's heart was as light as her steps as she ran across the parking lot to her car. It was just after 4:15. If she hurried, she could get biscuits in the oven before Mike arrived. And maybe fry some bacon and make a little gravy. By the time she pulled into the driveway at her house, she had a whole meal of breakfast for supper prepared in her mind. All she had to do was make it happen.

‒‒∿‿‿‿∿‒‒

T. J. Lachlan had come to a Christmas Eve conclusion that it was time to get out of Blessings. He'd already had a conversation with Hank Richards, his Realtor, about going back to his home in Tennessee. He didn't like being the outsider, or treated like some damn pariah. Every time he thought about LilyAnn Bronte, she brought Laverne to mind, which set his teeth on edge. They both had acted like high-falutin' bitches who needed to be taken down a notch, and while he hadn't been able to enact any kind of revenge on Buddy and Laverne, he could and would set a new course for the Bronte woman before he left, and he would make sure she would, by God, never forget his name.

When Christmas morning came, he began to pack. It was nearly noon when he left a key to the house underneath a rock near the back door and loaded his bags into his truck. He wanted to go home, but had to dismantle LilyAnn and her high and mighty attitude first.

He knew he was taking a risk, but he'd lived his whole life on the edge and gotten away with it. He had no reason to assume his luck would fail him now. The only uncertainty he still had, as he took a back road into Blessings, was if she would be home. If she was, he *was* going to take her off that high horse she liked to ride and take her down in a most humiliating manner, just like she'd done to him.

He cruised by her neighborhood and smiled when he saw her car gone, as was the car in the drive next to hers. He whipped his truck into the alley, thankful for the six-foot-high privacy fences on both sides, and parked at the gate leading into her backyard.

He went through it without caution, picked a lock on

her back door, and went inside like he owned the place. He walked all through her house, looking for the perfect hiding place. Once he found it, he unscrewed the light-bulb, then went back into the living room and settled in to watch for her return.

He'd been waiting for less than an hour when he saw her car turn a corner up the street. He waited until she was pulling into her driveway before he left the living room on the run, quickly settling into his hiding place.

Biscuits and Mike were on Lily's mind as she unlocked her door and went inside. The first thing she did was drop off her shoes in the utility room and hang the halo on a coat hook. She'd get some spot remover for the gravy later.

She ran barefoot through the house, anxious to change and get to work. She didn't know where the conversation with Mike would go, but just the fact that he was no longer mad at her was enough.

She flipped the lights on in her bedroom and then headed for the walk-in closet, but when she opened the door, it was in darkness. Thinking that the bulb had burned out, she was already turning around when she was hit from behind in a flying tackle.

Her heart was pounding with sudden terror, but she didn't have the breath to scream as the weight of her attacker pressed her into the carpet.

"What's the matter, bitch? Cat got your tongue?"

She recognized the voice at the same time she recognized the danger. With Mike on the other side of town, there was no one to save her but herself.

She threw her head back as hard as she could and

heard him grunt when it hit his nose, then she bucked him off and heard his head hit the footboard of her bed. With only seconds to get out, she scrambled to her feet and bolted out of the door.

He caught her in the hallway, slamming her up against the wall and slapping her face so hard blood spurted on the inside of her mouth.

Now she was screaming as she constantly struggled to get free, but she'd bloodied his nose with her head-butt, and in his rage he continued to overwhelm her, pinning her arms above her head and ramming his knee between her legs.

LilyAnn was on autopilot, fighting him with every ounce of strength that she had, and yet he kept pushing harder and harder against her until she was pinned so tightly between him and the wall that she was all but motionless.

He was laughing when he put his cheek against hers, then turned just enough to lick the side of her face from her jaw to the side of her nose.

The fear in LilyAnn was crippling until she felt his wet tongue against her skin. It was like having water thrown in her face. She turned her head just enough to bite down on his ear. Blood spurted in her mouth as the flesh separated. She spit it out in his face.

His scream was deafening, but now she had room to maneuver.

T. J. didn't know his earlobe was gone, but he did know the blood on her face and shirt was his and that he had seriously underestimated his prey.

He doubled up his fist and swung, but as she ducked beneath the blow, he ran his fist through the Sheetrock instead. She came back up in front of him as he was trying to pull his hand out of the wall and stabbed her fingernails into his face, raking deep gouges into the skin and leaving raw, bloody tracks.

The pain on T. J.'s face was crippling; he was nearly blinded by his own tears.

"Bitch! I'll kill you! I'll kill you," he kept screaming.

But she was still on the attack, which had taken him off guard.

He took a step back in an effort to get out of her reach, but not soon enough, as she jammed her knee into his groin and, when he shrieked from the pain, drew up her foot and kicked what was hanging between his legs with such impact that she heard a pop.

He staggered backward, bent double from the pain and gagging from a sudden wave of nausea.

Lily ran and didn't look back—out of the hall and into the living room, heading for the front door. She couldn't believe it when she heard his footsteps again! He was still mobile.

Then she happened to glance out her front window, and like an answer to a prayer, she caught a glimpse of Mike's car in her driveway, then Mike himself, walking toward the house.

She screamed his name at the top of her lungs, her fingers curling around the knob.

The adrenaline urge to kill was so strong that Lachlan was oblivious to body pain. He caught her just as the door came open, slammed it in her face, and choked off her scream. Then he grabbed her arm and threw her against the wall, knocking the breath out of her body and rendering her momentarily senseless.

Lily moaned and was struggling with her equilibrium when she saw him coming at her with a knife.

When Mike heard the scream, it was so shocking that he froze, trying to locate the source. Then he saw the front door to LilyAnn's house begin to open, caught a glimpse of the blood and terror on her face just before the door slammed shut, and then he bolted.

LilyAnn had a brief glimpse of the door flying inward and then a man in motion sailing past her, hitting Lachlan chest high. They went down in a tangle of arms and legs, fighting for control of the knife.

LilyAnn kept screaming for help, hoping her neighbors would hear as she dived for the phone and dialed 911.

"911. What is your emergency?"

She could hardly breathe because of her welling panic and spit out the information in short, choppy sentences. "LilyAnn Bronte. 1704 Willow Drive. Man in my house. Trying to kill me. My neighbor is fighting. Send help. We need help."

"Is he armed?" the dispatcher asked.

"Knife. He has a knife! Hurry!" she screamed, as Lachlan swung the knife at Mike, barely missing his face.

"Ma'am, wait on the phone with me," the dispatcher said, but Lily couldn't.

One moment Mike had the upper hand, and then Lachlan rolled and pinned Mike to the floor.

"No!" LilyAnn screamed, and even as the dispatcher was telling her to stay on the phone, she grabbed her grandma's lead crystal vase and swung it against T. J.'s head like a ball bat.

The ensuing crack sounded like a gunshot as T. J. went limp. Mike pushed out from under him, crawling to his knees to check Lachlan's pulse.

"He's still breathing," he gasped, trying to catch his breath.

"Well, damn. Then I didn't hit him hard enough," LilyAnn said, and then broke into sobs.

As Mike looked up at her from the floor, he got his first clear view of her condition, and his heart nearly stopped.

She was covered in blood.

"Oh my God, oh my God."

He scrambled to his feet and grabbed her shoulders, frantically running his hands up and down her body, checking for wounds. "Where are you hurt? Where did he cut you? Talk to me, sweetheart! What the hell did he do?"

Chapter 15

LILYANN PUSHED HIS HANDS AWAY AND THREW HER arms around Mike's neck.

"You saved me! You saved me!" she sobbed. "I thought I was dead."

Mike was shaking. In the distance, he could hear sirens, and he caught a glimpse of their neighbor through the open door, running across the street toward Lily's house.

"LilyAnn, look at me," Mike shouted.

She felt like she was going into freefall. Everything was beginning to echo, and Mike's face kept going in and out of focus.

"There's blood all over you. Where are you hurt?" he asked.

She swayed on her feet. "It's all his," she mumbled, and passed out in his arms.

He caught her as she fell and was laying her down on the sofa as Thomas Thane ran into the house.

"Dear God! What happened?"

"The man was trying to kill her. I heard her screaming as I drove up."

Thomas toed T. J. with his shoe. "Is he dead?"

Mike took a breath. "No, but she damn sure tried to make that happen."

All of a sudden, he was too shaky to stand. He sat down on the floor beside the sofa and laid his head against her arm. His belly was hurting, and he was going to be pissed beyond words if the sorry bastard busted anything loose.

The first police car slid to a stop at the curb, with an ambulance half a block behind it. Mike saw Lonnie Pittman running toward the house with his gun drawn and then saw two other cruisers pull up, as well.

Lonnie came through the door with his gun aimed and saw T. J. Lachlan out on the floor and LilyAnn unconscious and bloody on the sofa. He was almost afraid to ask.

"Is she alive?"

Mike nodded. "She fainted."

Lonnie knelt to check Lachlan's pulse. "He's still alive."

Mike sighed. "She has already apologized for that oversight."

Lonnie managed a sideways grin. "She's damn sure bloody. Are you sure she's not wounded?"

"She said it was all his, and I am inclined to believe her."

At that point, two other officers came in, followed by the first wave of EMTs. One stopped by Lachlan, and the other went to LilyAnn.

Mike watched him checking her vitals, checking for wounds, feeling for obvious broken bones, but after a thorough check of her body and blood pressure, he rocked back on his heels.

"How is she?" Mike asked.

"She has a good pulse and no visible wounds other than bruising. Blood pressure is 140/85, which is a little high, but under the circumstances, I think she's good."

The other EMT's comments were vastly different.

"This one is not. His blood pressure is low, and his breathing is labored. There's a deep gash in the back of his head and I suspect concussion, possibly a skull fracture."

"That would be from where LilyAnn took him out with her grandma's vase." Mike pointed to the shards of broken glass.

Lonnie was counting off the obvious wounds that he could see as the EMT turned Lachlan over.

"He's missing part of an ear, and the gashes on his face look like they went into some of the facial muscles."

The EMT beside LilyAnn picked up her hand. "Part of his face is under her fingernails," he said.

The other one was still checking out Lachlan's condition. "I've got teeth marks here...and lipstick on his ear?"

All of a sudden they all turned and stared at LilyAnn.

"Well, shit," Lonnie muttered. "She bit off his ear."

Mike tried to laugh, but it made his belly hurt. He grabbed it and doubled over.

Seconds later they had him on his back.

"You have a new surgery scar," the EMT said.

"Yeah, I had an accident about six weeks ago. They took out my spleen."

The EMT picked up his radio as Mike pushed himself up to a sitting position.

"This is Beau. We need a third bus at the address. I've got three down."

He popped smelling salts beneath LilyAnn's nose. She came to with a gasp, reaching for Mike.

"I'm here, honey," he said, and grabbed her hand.

She was shaking as she pushed herself up, then saw Lachlan facedown on her floor.

"Is he *still* breathing?"

Lonnie grinned. "Yes, ma'am, he is. Can you tell me how he got in?"

"I don't know. I went to my room to change clothes. The light was out in the closet, and when I turned around to go get a bulb, he tackled me facedown to the floor."

Mike was shaking. He couldn't wrap his head around how close he'd come to losing her.

Lonnie continued to take notes as the second set of EMTs came in the house.

"How did you get away?" he asked.

"I threw my head back and busted his nose, then bucked him off my back and ran. He caught me again in the hall. He took a swing at my head and missed. You can see where he rammed his hand through the Sheetrock. I scratched his face, kneed him in the dangly bits, and ran again."

Lonnie grinned. He'd never heard a man's balls referred to in quite such a manner.

LilyAnn felt light-headed as she looked down at the red blood on her white pants and the Christmas tree on her sweatshirt. After all that had happened, the lights were still flashing. She shoved her hands through her hair and thought it was a good thing she'd taken off her halo before this happened, because she'd been anything but an angel tonight.

Lonnie was still writing. "Then what happened, LilyAnn?"

"I was almost out the door when he caught me again, and that time he had pulled a knife. If it wasn't for Mike, I would be dead."

Lonnie's eyes narrowed. "Yes, ma'am, Mike arrived at the right time for sure. It appears you're gonna have yourself a black eye, but I'm giving this round to you. Lachlan's missing a piece of an ear, parts of his face, and I'm betting you fractured his skull with that vase."

"Who's up?" the EMT asked, as they rolled a second gurney into the house.

"Take this one," Lonnie said, pointing to Mike. "He's recently out of surgery. I want to make sure we don't have some internal bleeding here."

LilyAnn suddenly realized Mike was on the floor for a reason. She bolted to her feet.

"Oh my God! Are you saying he hurt Mike?"

Before they knew it, she was swinging a fist at Lachlan's head as they were trying to lift him onto the gurney.

Lonnie caught her before she connected and pulled her back.

"Leave something for the law," he chided.

Mike crawled to his feet and put himself on the other gurney.

"You're next, little lady," the medic said.

"I'm fine," she argued.

"Ma'am, if you could see yourself, you wouldn't say that." He gently pushed her down onto the last gurney and rolled her out.

"Lonnie, lock my door," she called back.

"Don't worry about your house, LilyAnn. Once everyone hears what you did to Lachlan, there isn't a crook within a hundred miles who would take you on again."

—◆◆◆—

Before nightfall, the news of the attack on LilyAnn, and Mike's heroic rescue on her behalf, had spread throughout Blessings, putting something of a damper on the holiday festivities.

When Rachel Goodhope heard what had happened, she shut herself in the bathroom and cried until her throat was raw. The guilt of not reporting her rape would weigh heavily on her soul. If she had reported it, there was every reason to assume this would never have happened to LilyAnn.

Mike was back in the hospital under observation, as was Lily, in a room down the hall. The last she'd heard, T. J. Lachlan was under guard and handcuffed to his hospital bed on the floor below.

He had a skull fracture and his ear had been repaired to seal the wound, but there were no immediate plans to address the wounds on his face. The theory was that if he survived, it wouldn't matter how pretty he was in prison.

The photographer who'd taken pictures of LilyAnn at the Salvation Army dinner only hours earlier was on his way out of the hospital with a follow-up shot of her in a wheelchair.

By morning, LilyAnn Bronte would, once again, be the topic of conversation in Blessings, just as she had been when she won the title of the Peachy-Keen Queen and when she'd lost her almost-fiancé in the war. But notoriety was no longer on her radar. All she wanted was to find Mike.

She waited until the nurse who'd been checking her vitals left her room, and then she slipped out of bed, wincing from the amount of growing aches and bruises, and headed for the door.

With nothing on under her gown and the opening in the back a little too airy for public viewing, she snagged another hospital gown from inside the bathroom and put it on like a shirt, tying it in the front beneath her chin. It wasn't much of a bathrobe, but it covered her bare backside, which was all that mattered. She already knew Mike's room number, so she waited until the hall was clear and made a run for it.

She burst in Mike's room with long legs flying, and her bare feet making little slapping noises on the tiles. Her eye was already several shades of purple, her bottom lip was swollen and puffy, and Mike thought she was beautiful.

"Do they know where you are?" he asked.

"Not yet they don't."

She wanted to crawl in bed with him. Instead, she fiddled with the ties on the hospital gown and tried to pretend she wasn't naked beneath it.

"What did the doctor tell you?" she asked.

"That I'm bruised, but nothing broken or pulled loose."

She kept looking at him, remembering what a relief she'd felt when she'd seen him in her yard. Instead of saying what was on her heart, she addressed food.

"I didn't get to make you eggs."

He leaned back against his pillows and patted the side of his bed.

"Come sit by me."

She scooted up onto the side of the mattress as Mike reached for her hand.

"We've had a rough couple of weeks, haven't we?"

She nodded.

"This feels like high school. Misunderstandings that could easily be explained but weren't because two people acted like dumb-ass teenagers." Her pulse was racing. She wanted to hear him say he cared.

"So you said you wanted to talk to me. What did you want to say?"

His fingers tightened. The lump in his throat was so big that he felt like he would choke if he opened his mouth, but he'd waited eleven long years to say this.

All of a sudden the door flew open. A nurse peeked in, then turned around and yelled down the hall.

"I found her!"

She crooked her finger at LilyAnn and frowned.

"You said I could move around," LilyAnn said.

The nurse arched an eyebrow. "I did not mean in *his* bed."

Mike grinned at LilyAnn.

"Busted."

Lily frowned at the nurse. "I needed to talk to him."

He gave her fingers another squeeze. "We have lived next door to each other all our lives. I'm not going anywhere."

LilyAnn sighed. "Thank you for saving me."

"Just repaying the favor, honey."

She slid off the bed and went out the door with the nurse right behind her.

He felt as frustrated as she looked, but it was still better than how he'd felt last night, even with a sore belly.

After the doctor made rounds later, he left orders at the nurses' station that, if they stayed stable through the night, Lily and Mike were to be released the next morning.

Lily went back to her room in dejection. She couldn't talk to Mike, but she still had to call her mama. Grace needed to hear what happened from LilyAnn's lips before she heard what happened through the Blessings grapevine.

She made the call, waiting for someone to pick up, and knowing the news was going to put a huge damper on her mother and Eddie's holiday spirit. Still, it would be far better news than if Lonnie was calling to tell them she was dead.

Then she heard her mama's voice.

"Hello?"

"Hey, Mama."

Lily could hear the delight in her mother's voice.

"LilyAnn, hi, honey. Did you have a good day at the Salvation Army dinner?"

"Yes, the whole event was great. I had a lot of fun, and Mike was the Santa Claus."

There was a little silence. "Uh…so are you saying you two aren't fighting anymore?"

"We're not fighting, Mama, but that's not why I called. Something happened after I got home, and I wanted to tell you before you heard it from someone else."

Grace's voice tensed. "What happened, baby? Where are you? Are you okay?"

"I'm in the hospital, but—"

"Oh dear God! Lily! What happened? Wait! I need to get Eddie! Eddie! Get on the other phone."

LilyAnn pinched the bridge of her nose to keep from crying as she waited for her stepfather's voice.

"I'm here, sugar! What happened?"

"T. J. Lachlan has been stalking me."

"Oh dear God!" Grace cried.

"Hear me out, Mama. I already told you I'm okay."

Grace was crying. Lily could hear her, but she had to get it said or she would cry, too.

"When I came home this evening, he was hiding in

the house. He attacked me, and I fought back. The house is a bloody mess. Mike arrived in the nick of time and saved me, okay? I have no injuries other than some sore muscles, bruises, and a black eye. Mike is here under observation, mostly because of his recent surgery and the fight."

"What about Lachlan?" Eddie asked. "Please tell me he is in jail."

"Ummm, not yet. He's actually in critical condition here in the hospital, but he's handcuffed to the bed and under guard."

"Good. Mike must have really clobbered him. What did he do?" Grace asked.

"Lachlan had a knife when Mike took him down. I called 911 as they were fighting, and then I grabbed Grandma's lead crystal vase and swung it like a bat at T. J.'s head."

"Ooh shit," Eddie said, and then chuckled. "So he's got a concussion. Way to go, honey."

Grace knew her daughter better than Eddie. She could tell LilyAnn was skirting around the whole truth.

"Just spit it out, girl. What else?" Grace asked.

"I bit off a piece of his ear, dug tracks down the front of his face with my fingernails deep enough to plant corn, sent his testicles into orbit, and then fractured his skull with Grandma's vase."

Eddie gasped.

Grace groaned and then chuckled.

"Sweet Jesus, daughter. You've got more of Delia Bronte in you than any of us knew."

"Yes, ma'am," Lily said. "And I have to say, it felt good. The sorry bastard."

"LilyAnn!"

"Mama. Seriously! He tried to kill me, and he is a bastard."

"I'm sure he is, but that is so not ladylike."

Lily laughed. "Neither was what I did to him, Mama. For God's sake! Cut me some slack here."

Eddie chuckled. "It's easier for your mama to scold you for cursing than it is to admit her baby nearly died tonight. You call the asshole anything you want and say it's from me. I'm proud of you, girl."

Lily could remember when she thought she didn't like Eddie. Now, she was beginning to wonder if it was herself she really hadn't liked, and she'd just blamed it on him.

"Eddie's right, LilyAnn. What you just told us is a parent's worst nightmare, and I thank God and Michael that you are still with us."

"I know, Mama."

"I can be there by tomorrow."

"No, Mama. There's no need. Really."

"You don't need us?"

"Not at all. We'll both be released tomorrow, and I'll be back at work the day after. Mike will take care of me, and I'll take care of him."

Grace sighed. "That's how it's supposed to be, baby. Has Mike called Don and Carol?"

"I don't know."

"Well, I'm going to. She'd be angry with me if I didn't."

"Just make sure she knows Mike is fine. I'm sure he'll call."

"I will, and just so you know it, God was with you tonight."

"I know that, Mama. And it's all good. Merry Christmas."

The connection ended, and LilyAnn leaned against her pillows and closed her eyes. It might be a little late to ask, but all she wanted for Christmas was her life back.

Down the hall, Mike was in a similar mode.

He'd called home, only to learn his mom was at his sister's house, and wound up talking to his dad, which was just as well.

Don Dalton wasn't the kind to panic. Once he found out Mike and LilyAnn were fine and the intruder was under arrest, in his mind, the situation was resolved.

And then Mike told him what LilyAnn had done, and Don whistled softly beneath his breath.

"Damn, son. I have a question. Are you two still at odds?"

"No, we're good," Mike said.

"Then I have one piece of advice. Whatever you do, don't make her mad."

Mike grinned. "Oh, I already knew that a long time ago. When we were in the fourth grade, she laid Bobby Gene Pettit out cold because he said she wasn't a lady."

Don laughed. "Yeah, yeah, she did do that. I'd forgotten. So, at least you're not flying blind in this."

Mike sighed. "No, Dad. I've known where I was going with her for what seems like forever."

"Then Godspeed," Don said.

"Thanks, Dad."

Mike hung up, satisfied and exhausted. He rolled over onto his side and closed his eyes, and when he woke up, it was morning.

Ruby Dye opened up The Curl Up and Dye bright and early Wednesday morning. Christmas might be over, but their holiday business was still in full swing. Office parties and family get-togethers were still happening all the way through New Year's Eve, which meant the need for fancy hairdos and manicures was still in force. She appreciated the vanity of women because it kept her shop in the black.

The town was still reeling over the news about what had happened to LilyAnn, and the stories about what she'd done to Bissell's nephew continued to grow.

Some versions had her biting the nose off his face, while others claimed she'd taken away his knife and castrated him with his pants still on. Ruby knew it was bullshit, but that's how gossip went in small Southern towns.

When the Conklin twins came in to work, they were carrying a plate of decorated sugar cookies and both talking at once.

"Sister, can you believe what—"

"Oooh, did you hear that T. J. Lachlan even—"

Vera said, "And to think we—"

Vesta rolled her eyes. "When he was in here, I knew—"

Vera fired back. "Vesta even flirted—"

"And Vera cut his hair." Then they both giggled as Vesta ended the conversation.

"She should have cut off his balls instead and saved LilyAnn the trouble."

Ruby frowned. "It just proves a pretty face means nothing."

"Well, Lachlan won't have to worry about that misunderstanding ever happening again. I hear his face looks like a wildcat got hold of him, so that face isn't so pretty anymore."

"No more than he deserves," Ruby muttered.

Mabel Jean came in the back door with a Tupperware bowl of leftover fudge.

"Happy day after Christmas!" she said.

"Oh Lord, not more sweets," Vesta groaned.

Vera giggled. "Vesta busted a zipper in her good blue pants this morning."

Vesta frowned. "Well, thanks for blabbing my shame all over the place."

"Time to get to work," Ruby said. "Let's just hope there's no more excitement in Blessings for a while."

Chapter 16

MIKE AND LILYANN HELD HANDS IN THE TAXI ALL the way home from the hospital. Despite what they felt for each other, the gesture was purely moral support. The silence between them was telling. But for timing and the grace of God, LilyAnn would be dead.

She was wearing hospital scrubs, and Mike had turned his sweatshirt wrong side out to hide the blood. Out of deference for their lack of winter clothing, the cabbie, Melvin Wells, had turned the heater up for their comfort.

He spent most of his day driving people around Blessings while conversing with them from the rearview mirror, and these two were no exception.

"Are you warm enough, ma'am?" Melvin asked, eyeing the pretty blond with the black eye.

Lily smiled. "Yes, thank you."

He nodded. Everyone knew about what she'd done and that Mike Dalton had saved her life.

"So, Mike, after your recent surgery, I hope you didn't hurt yourself fighting that scumbag."

"Nothing injured, Melvin. I'm just a little sore. We're both fine, and thank you for asking," Mike said, rubbing his thumb across the top of her hand.

Melvin nodded. He was satisfied with the conversation. Now he had firsthand info from the victims.

"Here we are," he said, as he pulled in the driveway at LilyAnn's house.

Mike handed him a ten-dollar bill to cover the five-dollar ride, but Melvin waved it off.

"No, no charge. I'm happy you two are okay. Merry Christmas."

Mike smiled. "Thanks, Melvin, we appreciate it."

"Yes, thank you very much, Melvin."

They got out of the cab and then, despite the cold, stopped in the front yard of her house.

"I don't know if I can face this," LilyAnn said.

Mike frowned. "Face what?"

"Blood everywhere, the hole in the wall, all the broken stuff."

She shuddered.

Mike frowned. "It's your home, damn it. What you're talking about is superficial. Looks don't matter, LilyAnn. It is always what's beneath that matters, and you're not facing it alone."

LilyAnn sighed. The fact that he'd just said that explained why he had loved her when she hadn't loved herself.

She nodded. "You're right. So let's get this over with."

They were starting toward the house when their neighbor, Thomas Thane, called out to them from his porch.

"Hey, wait a minute. I have your house key," he said, and came running. He was breathless and patting his belly when he reached them. "Too much turkey yesterday. I'm supposed to tell you that Officer Pittman locked up and here's your key."

"Thank you," LilyAnn said.

Thomas grinned sheepishly. "I hope you aren't mad, but the Ladies Aide from your church contacted the police last night, who put them in touch with me. I think they went in and cleaned up for you. They were there until almost dawn."

LilyAnn was stunned. "Oh my. That's wonderful. I was dreading going back to face all that mess."

"I think you'll be surprised," he said. "Really good to see the both of you upright and smiling. Now get in out of the cold."

He ran back across the street as they headed for the porch. When they opened the door, they were met by the smell of pine-scented cleanser, lemon oil, and fresh paint.

The house was sparkling. Every piece of furniture was in place, the hole in the wall had been patched and painted, the broken glass all swept up. When she went into her bedroom, there was no sign whatsoever that T. J. Lachlan had ever been inside. The only thing missing from before was the lead-crystal vase.

LilyAnn's vision blurred. The Christmas spirit had been alive and well last night.

"I love this town."

Mike took a deep breath. This was it.

He slipped his arms around her, tilting her chin until she had to meet his gaze.

"And I love you, whether you like it or not...whether you return the feelings or not. All I could think about last night was how close I'd come to losing you, and how pissed I would have been at myself for never telling you what was in my heart."

Her fingers fisted in the fabric of his shirt, a subconscious urge to hold on to this feeling. Her voice was shaking, but she'd never been more certain of how she felt.

"Oh, Michael, I love you, too. I didn't realize how much until I thought I had lost you. It was all I could do Thanksgiving Day not to scratch out Honey Andrews's eyes."

"God bless The Curl Up and Dye," Mike muttered.

"What?"

"It's nothing. Just a reference to a piece of advice someone gave me."

LilyAnn's heart was hammering so hard she could barely breathe. Finally, the universe was through punishing her for taking too much for granted.

"Mike, I know you're very sore…"

His eyes narrowed as his pulse began to race.

"Not that sore."

Lily touched the puffy side of her mouth, then traced the shades of bruising around her eye.

"And I don't know what you think about making love to a woman with a face like this."

"Purple is my new favorite color," he said softly.

"Did you lock the front door?"

He exhaled softly, as his life suddenly made perfect sense.

"Yes."

"Am I going to have to beg?" she whispered.

"Only when you want me to stop," Mike said, as he pulled his sweatshirt over his head and dropped it on the floor.

LilyAnn gasped at the sight of the bruises on his torso.

"Oh my God! I don't think—"

He put a finger over her lips. "And I *can't* think, so that makes two of us. Take off your clothes, LilyAnn, or your first experience with me will be in hospital scrubs."

LilyAnn was shaking when she started to undress, then paused, suddenly reminded of body image and the possibility of rejection. But when she saw the love in Mike's eyes and the tremble in his hands, she knew it was going to be all right.

"Oh Jesus," Mike whispered, as the last stitch of clothing fell to the floor at Lily's feet. "You are even more beautiful than I ever imagined."

LilyAnn started to cry. "I'm sorry I went and died on you, Mike."

"No, honey, you didn't die. You just got stuck in time. Come to bed with me, LilyAnn."

She threw back the covers and stretched her long, leggy length upon the sheets.

Mike slid in beside her, raised himself up on one elbow, and very, very gently kissed her mouth. Not like he wanted to, but enough to get the message past her puffy lower lip that she was never going to be lonely again.

"Your skin is like satin," he whispered, as he cupped the heavy fall of her breasts, then mapped the contours of her body.

"Woman," he said softly, and kissed the side of her cheek. "Beautiful, *sexy* woman."

LilyAnn's heart was pounding. It felt like she'd been waiting for this moment all her life.

She looked up at the light fixture above the bed. The last cognizant thought she had was of a spiderweb strung from one globe to another and that the spider was gonna fry. After that, time lost all meaning.

When all was finally said and done, Mike came apart in her arms. He couldn't think. He couldn't speak. His strength was spent. He thought his love for LilyAnn had been perfect, but he'd been wrong. Nothing had prepared him for all this. He buried her face against the curve of his neck and held her close, his muscles trembling, his heart full of an emotion without the words to express it.

And then Lily's telephone rang.

Mike rose up. "Do you want to answer?"

"Lord, no. I couldn't make sense if I tried."

Mike grinned. "So, I was that good?"

LilyAnn sighed. "You were that good."

His eyes narrowed. "Would you say that, right now, I pretty much have you under my spell?"

Her mouth tilted upward at one corner. "Pretty much. Why?"

"Hold that thought. I'll be right back."

She frowned, watching as he rolled out of bed and began pulling on his clothes.

"What on earth?"

He pointed. "No questions. Remember, you're under my spell."

She fell backward on the bed, grinning as he ran out of the room. She could hear his footsteps as he went down the hallway, then through her living room. When she heard the front door open and shut, she swung her legs off the bed and made a quick trip to the bathroom.

When she emerged, she started toward the closet for something to wear and then stopped, remembering what had happened the last time.

"But he's not here and I am," LilyAnn muttered.

Her hand was shaking as she opened the door. It was still dark inside, but she knew where her sweatpants were hanging. She grabbed a pair and a shirt to go with them and backed out.

She had the pants on and was pulling the sweatshirt over her head when she heard the front door slam again. She turned toward the doorway as Mike raced into the room, his eyes flashing and a wide smile on his face. He'd obviously changed into clean clothes and brushed his hair, but when he approached her, he stopped short of an embrace and then took a deep breath.

"Some might say this is rushing the issue, but not for me. I've waited most of my life for this moment."

He took a small black box out of his pocket and dropped to one knee to open it. The diamond inside was a solitaire, and it was huge.

Once again, Mike had left her speechless. All she could manage was a shaky, "Oh my, oh Mike, how long have you had this?"

"Nine years."

Tears were streaming down her face.

Mike had imagined how this moment would be for so long that the reality almost felt like a dream.

"I have loved you for as long as I can remember, and I will love you for as long as I live. Will you marry me, LilyAnn? Will you live with me…love me…will you be my wife?"

Now she was laughing through tears.

"Yes, yes, a million times, yes."

Mike stood as he slid the ring on her finger.

"It fits!" she cried. She threw her arms around his neck and kissed him soundly. First on the lips, then on both cheeks, then back on his lips again, while laughing through tears.

"I feel like I'm flying. Oh Mike, I didn't think I would ever be happy again."

"I had a couple of days like that myself," Mike said. He eyed her sad, puffy lip, wanting to kiss her so bad, but settling for a hug. "Merry Christmas, sweetheart."

Lily was almost bouncing as she hugged him, then held out her hand to eye the ring, then hugged him again.

"Merry Christmas, Mike! This is the best Christmas ever!"

"We should celebrate," he said.

"On New Year's Eve. We'll celebrate on New Year's Eve," Lily said.

"Yeah, great idea! One of my clients gave me two invitations to the New Year's Eve ball out at the country club. I wasn't going to go, but maybe now…would you like to go?"

"Oh yes! I've never been! Oh no! I don't have anything to wear!"

He rolled his eyes. "And why didn't I see that coming?"

She thought of Kitty Carlton's Unique Boutique on East Main and the racks of gowns she always carried this time of year. They couldn't all be gone.

"Don't worry. This I can handle," she said.

Mike smiled. "Honey, of that I have no doubt. It is my blessing that you are one of those women who can handle pretty much whatever life dishes out."

She hugged him, being careful not to squeeze where the bruises all were, then tilted her head just enough to see her own reflection in his eyes.

"Mike?"

"What, honey?"

"Uh…are you sore?"

He grinned. "Not that sore."

"If my face is too ugly to look at, you can always close your eyes."

He kissed the side of her cheek, then the tip of her nose.

"Hell no, I'm not closing my eyes," he growled. "I like raccoons, and besides, purple is my new favorite color, remember?"

She shivered.

Mike ran his finger down the side of her face as she stood there smiling…waiting.

"My beautiful, sweet, sexy woman, how many times are we going to do this before you remember you need to take off your clothes?"

Lily blinked. "Oh. Right." She peeled the sweatshirt over her head and dropped the sweatpants where she stood, then frowned at him.

"Well, this is a little awkward. What are *you* waiting for?"

"For my brain to quit misfiring."

She turned toward the bed as she heard his shoes hit the floor.

Ruby was covering up Sue Beamon's gray roots with a brown rinse when George, from the Pots and Posies flower shop, came into the salon with an enormous bouquet of fresh flowers.

"These are for you, Sister. Where would you like me to set them?" he asked.

"Anywhere you can find a spot. I'll move them later if I need to, and thanks!" Ruby said.

George waved as he exited the shop. At the same time, Vera was curious as to who they were from.

"Hey, Sister, want me to bring you the card?" Vera asked.

Ruby grinned. She knew Vera wasn't into being helpful so much as nosy, but what the heck.

"Yes, sure, that would be great," Ruby said, and then squeezed the last of the color onto Sue's hair, worked it into the roots, and put a little plastic cap on her head while the color was setting.

"Here you go," Vera said, and held the card out for Ruby to read. "You might want to read it out loud," she added.

Ruby stifled a chuckle. "Well, of course I want to," she said. "It reads… 'Thank you for the suggestion. Mike D.'"

Vera frowned. "Who's Mike D.?"

"Dalton. Mike Dalton," Ruby said, smiling to herself.

"What suggestion?" Vera asked.

"I'm sure all will be revealed in due time," Ruby said.

Mabel Jean frowned, which made the scar on her forehead wrinkle up to form the letter C. "Is it a secret?"

Ruby rolled her eyes. "What part of 'wait and see' don't you guys understand?"

"Well, you must have given him one heck of a suggestion," Vesta muttered, as she stuck a clip in the last roller on Mrs. Dawson's hair.

"Am I ready to get under the dryer?" Mrs. Dawson yelled.

Vesta nodded. "Yes, you're ready," she said, and helped the old woman to a dryer, handed her a couple of magazines, and set the timer before going back to her station to clean it up.

She glanced at Vera and then mumbled, "I swear to

goodness, I wish that woman would leave her hearing aids in her ears instead of carrying them in that pill bottle in her purse. They're not doing anyone a bit of good there."

The bell over the door jingled again. Ruby turned to look as LilyAnn walked in, resplendent in black slacks, a blue sweater, and a shiner in varying shades of lavender and purple.

Ruby peeled off her disposable gloves and dropped them in the trash, then went to meet her.

"Oh honey! It is the best thing ever to see you walk in here with that smile on your face, but your poor little eye! Does it hurt?" Ruby said.

"It's not so bad if I don't touch it," Lily said.

The moment LilyAnn's hand went toward her eye, Ruby saw the ring. She squealed, then grabbed Lily's hand and turned it to the light.

"Lord have mercy! Is that thing real?"

LilyAnn was grinning so wide it made her face hurt.

"Yes, ma'am, it is real, and so is my engagement to Mike."

Ruby laughed out loud. Now the bouquet and the cryptic message on Mike's card made sense.

Mabel Jean was gluing bits of bling onto Rachel Goodhope's new nail polish, but she was happy for LilyAnn and wanted in on the conversation.

"When's the wedding?" she asked.

"This coming Valentine's Day," LilyAnn said.

Vesta frowned. "My stars! That doesn't give you much time to make a big wedding happen."

"That's because we're not having a big wedding," LilyAnn said. "In fact, we're not getting married in Blessings at all."

"Why?" Vera asked.

"Because all of his family is in Colorado, and what's left of mine is in Florida. However, when we get back from the honeymoon, we're going to have an open reception for family and anyone in Blessings who wants to come."

"Okay then," Ruby said. "You have just redeemed yourself."

"Where are you going to get married?"

"Jamaica."

"Take me with you."

Everyone laughed at the woman sitting in Vesta's styling chair. It was no secret why Alma Button would want to run away from home. She had six boys who, on a daily basis, made her regret her decision at seventeen years of age to forego life in a nunnery, and she wasn't even Catholic.

"Sorry, Alma, but I intend to be the only female under Mike Dalton's radar," Lily said.

Although the shop was full of chatter and good wishes, Rachel Goodhope had stayed silent. From the moment LilyAnn walked in, and through the entire congratulatory process, she had felt out of place. She'd made a fool of herself about Mike, and LilyAnn knew it, and then there was that thing about T. J. Lachlan. That was a secret Rachel would carry to her grave.

When Mabel Jean finished Rachel's nails, Rachel laid cash on the manicure table, hoping she could slip out without notice. But when she turned to walk out, she found herself face-to-face with LilyAnn.

She made herself look up at the bruises on LilyAnn's

face, the puffy lower lip, and a black eye no amount of makeup could ever hide.

"Oh my," she said softly. Without thinking, she lifted her hand toward Lily's face, and then caught herself and stopped. "I am sorry…so, so sorry that happened to you," she whispered.

Then she ducked her head and hurried out of the shop.

"What was that all about?" Ruby asked.

LilyAnn frowned. "That was weird."

"How so?"

"Like everyone else, she just pointed to my face and said she was sorry. But it didn't feel like commiseration. It felt more like an apology."

"That *is* weird," Ruby said. "But what else is new? There's always something weird going on around here. So, did you come in for a special reason, or did you just come to show off your new ring?"

"Both," LilyAnn said. "I came to ask if you know anyone in town who does alterations."

"I know someone," Mabel Jean said. "Mrs. Ling. She does all kinds of sewing, including making the cheerleader outfits for the high school. She has a sign in her shop that says 'Alterations and Tailoring.'"

"Where does she live?" LilyAnn asked.

"Across the street from me. She has a little shop in what used to be her garage. Here, I'll write the address down for you."

"Thanks, Mabel Jean," LilyAnn said.

Ruby, being Ruby, wanted to know what was going on. "Are you going to have her make your wedding dress?"

"No, nothing like that. I have something I need altered for the New Year's Eve ball at the country club. Mike is taking me to celebrate our engagement, so I better hustle. I have to go back to work tomorrow and need to get all of this set in motion before I do."

Ruby frowned. "Should you be back at work?"

LilyAnn thought of the workout she and Mike had been giving her bed and smiled.

"Yes, ma'am. I think I'll be fine."

The bell jingled over the door as she left.

—⁓—

An hour later, LilyAnn left Mrs. Ling's house with a spring in her step, confident that her gown would be ready in plenty of time. She was on her way home when she remembered she needed some things from the grocery store and headed for the Piggly Wiggly.

—⁓—

T. J. Lachlan regained consciousness a little over twenty-four hours after LilyAnn clobbered him with the vase. Even before he opened his eyes, he guessed he was in a hospital, but he couldn't think why. The last thing he could remember was putting the house key under a rock at his uncle's house and driving away.

He hurt in so many places that he was convinced he had been in a wreck and, at the same time, wondered why his balls were so sore. He moved his leg just a little to accommodate the pressure and started to readjust them under the covers when something yanked hard against his wrist.

He opened his eyes, but everything was blurry. When he tried to move, he heard a man's raspy, cigarette voice.

"About time you woke up."

He turned toward the sound, blinking rapidly to clear his vision as a man's face came into focus.

"Are you my doctor?"

"Nope. I'm Harnett Easley, your court-appointed lawyer."

T. J.'s heart skipped a beat. All of a sudden his head was pounding so hard it was making him sick.

"My what?"

"Your court-appointed lawyer."

T. J. shifted his gaze from the man to the bed rails, and then to the handcuffs.

"What the hell?"

"Do you want to tell me your side of the story?"

"What story?" T. J. cried, and then moaned because the sound of his own voice made him ill.

"I don't want to put words in your mouth, but maybe a rundown of the wounds you suffered that put you in here might help you remember. You have a fractured skull, severely swollen and bruised testicles, you're missing a piece of your right ear, and your face looks like you tried to kiss a bobcat."

T. J. flashed on a face.

"The blond bitch did it."

"That's what I heard. What I need to hear is your side of the story of what you did to her, and you can start with why you broke into her house."

"I'm going to puke," T. J. whispered.

"I'll get a nurse," Easley said, and headed for the door.

T. J. was seriously fucked. He couldn't claim being drunk or high on drugs, because he figured they'd already run all the blood tests on him while he was dead to the world. And he couldn't claim a grudge or retaliation for something that had happened to him first. The fact that she wouldn't give him the time of day was not grounds for breaking and entering. And the fact that she had rebuked his advances and flipped him off in the middle of Main Street was not against the law. What was even more humiliating was that when he went after her to teach her who was boss, she pretty much whipped his ass.

He didn't need a mirror to know she'd put some scratches on his face, and he didn't need to see them to know she'd literally busted his balls. He remembered she'd bitten his ear, but he had not realized a piece of it was gone.

Shades of Mike Tyson, a little blond from Georgia had taken off a hunk of his ear, and he had barely lived to tell about it. On second thought, once they threw his ass in prison, and he knew that they would, he could never tell the truth about how he'd been maimed.

His daddy had always told him his temper was going to get him in trouble one day. He didn't like the old bastard, and admitting his daddy had been right was going to be a hard fact to swallow.

At that point, his gut lurched. Thanks to the handcuffs tying him to the bed, he couldn't sit up to reach for a bedpan, and he couldn't roll over to puke on the floor. There was nowhere for it to go but all over him. He was still retching when a male nurse walked in.

"Oh, hey…what a mess. Why didn't you buzz for a nurse?"

"'Cause I was jacking myself off," T. J. moaned, then rattled the handcuffs against the bed rail to emphasize the answer.

"Oh. Right! Well, hang on. We'll get you cleaned up," the nurse said, and headed back out the door.

Harnett Easley poked his head in the door, saw the state his client was in, and frowned.

"I'll be back later. You're not going anywhere."

Chapter 17

LILYANN WENT BACK TO WORK ON THURSDAY, enduring the stares, comments, and the occasional request for an autograph. It was almost like being the Peachy-Keen Queen all over again, except for the black eye and the fact that she had a three-carat diamond on her finger and not a crown on her head.

Her boss was in awe. He had never imagined—in all the years that she had worked for him in her quiet, unassuming manner—that she was capable of such ferocity.

Mitchell viewed her black eye with interest, wanting to know how she got it, and then asked the inevitable question: Did she really bite off Lachlan's ear?

"Just a piece of it," she said. "Do you want to shelve the aspirin or the Kotex?"

Mitchell flushed three shades of red and threw his arms up in the air.

"Like you had to ask!" he mumbled, and grabbed the carts with the boxes of aspirin and headed for the drug aisle.

"And that's how you end a conversation," LilyAnn said to herself, and finished restocking the shelves of feminine products.

She was getting ready to switch duties and man the register when she saw two teenage boys huddled up at the far end of Aisle 9. She watched as one grabbed several packets of condoms from a rack and stuffed them in his pocket, while the other one pocketed a bottle of massage oil from the shelf beside it.

She couldn't get Mr. Phillips' attention and knew if she moved, they would be gone. Considering their age and the pimples on their faces, she could pretty much guess at the reasoning behind the thefts. If no one knew they bought those items, then no one would know they were having sex. It was stupid, but taking into consideration that most boys of that age had no concept of cause and effect, and had the reasoning level of a newt, it made sense.

They were so intent on the thievery that she was behind them before they knew she was coming. She grabbed them by their elbows.

"Sorry, boys, but you need to come with me."

The taller one jumped and started to pull away, then saw her black eye and paused.

The other one was crestfallen, his head already hanging in shame.

"Move it," she said, pushing them toward Mr. Phillips's office, even though they were arguing with her and each other, and dragging their feet. At any moment, she expected one or both of them to break and run.

Mr. Phillips saw her and frowned.

"LilyAnn! Do you need me?"

She nodded. "We'll be in your office."

She pushed the boys inside, then shut the door, standing between them and freedom.

"Have a seat, boys," she ordered.

They sat. One of them whispered to the other, and LilyAnn frowned.

"Hey! No talking."

The taller one raised his hand for permission to

speak. She rolled her eyes. Nothing scarier than crooks in school mode.

"What?" she snapped.

"How did you get your black eye?"

She thought about brushing it off, and then realized maybe she could use this to deter an event of future stupidity.

"Someone hit me."

"What did you do to her?"

"It wasn't a her, it was a him. A guy hit me."

They looked at each other, as if confirming their suspicions.

"So what did you do to him?"

Although it hurt a little, she narrowed her eyes in what she hoped was a menacing expression.

"I hit him back."

"Are you her?"

LilyAnn sighed. She knew what they meant, but she wasn't going to make it easy on them.

"Her, who?"

"Her. That woman who bit off a guy's ear?"

"Yeah, that's me," she said, as her voice grew softer with each word she spoke. "Only it wasn't a whole ear. Just a piece of it. And I dug chunks of his face out with my fingernails, busted his balls, and fractured his skull. He broke the rules when he came in my house, and now he's going to prison for a long, long time."

Her voice was barely above a whisper by the time she finished. They were in tears, shivering in their seats. She stifled a grin.

My job is finished here.

Mr. Phillips walked into the office.

"LilyAnn?"

She pointed. "Don Juan here has a pocketful of condoms, and his partner stole some massage oils and Lord only knows what else. They loaded up so much stuff that I decided they were pimps. Have you called the cops?"

"No! No! We're not pimps!" they cried and began to bawl.

Mr. Phillips frowned. "Empty your pockets, boys."

They were sobbing loudly, begging Mr. Phillips not to call their parents.

Big Shot with the condoms was in an all-out panic.

"Don't call my dad. He'll kill me. The only reason we took them was so my parents wouldn't know we were having sex."

"Put your wallets on the desk," Phillips said. "The police will need to see your IDs."

"Did you already call the cops? Please don't call the cops. I don't want my parents to know."

LilyAnn rolled her eyes. *I rest my case.*

Someone knocked on the office door. Phillips got up to answer, and both boys cried out almost at the same time.

"Don't leave us alone with her."

Mr. Phillips's eyes widened.

"What did you say to them?"

She grinned. "I gave them a glimpse into their future."

The police took them down to the station, along with the loot they'd tried to shoplift. After they were gone, Mr. Phillips came looking for her.

"Good job, LilyAnn. I lose more of that inventory to kids than I do anything else in the store."

"I know. Kids are stupid. I was one once."

He rolled his eyes. "So was I."

She went back to work, and the next time she looked up, it was a quarter to twelve. Almost time for her to go to lunch. She had a date with Mike at Granny's Country Kitchen and was on her way to the back of the store to wash up when someone called her by name. She turned to see Honey Andrews waving her down.

"Oh, hi, Honey!"

Honey shook her head. "Don't 'Oh, hi, Honey' me. I heard all about what happened from the horse's mouth, so to speak. I had to see for myself that you were still in one piece, and you are, although I don't know how. Are you okay?"

LilyAnn shrugged. "As you can see, a little battered, but that's about it."

Honey shook her head. "You are one tough cookie. I have nothing but admiration for you. You did everything you had to do to survive, and there aren't many of us who could say the same. Way to go, LilyAnn. Way to go."

"Thanks. It was the scariest thing I've ever endured, for sure."

"Thank God, Mike showed up."

Lily smiled. "Yes, I've been thinking that a lot the past couple of days."

Honey grinned. "I heard about the ring. Can I see?"

LilyAnn held out her hand.

"Is that real?" Honey whispered.

LilyAnn giggled. "Yes. Pretty awesome, isn't it?"

"What is that…two carats' worth?"

"Three."

"Holy shit. Maybe I should have considered changing my gender preference after all."

LilyAnn threw back her head and laughed.

Honey grinned. "Well, maybe not, but you get what I mean. So, gotta get back to work. I have a client due in a few minutes. Take care of yourself, lady, and I love the look of that natural eye shadow. It might catch on."

LilyAnn was still smiling when she got her coat and headed across the street.

Mike was already there, waiting for her arrival, when he saw her come in. He stood up and waved, and as soon as she settled, he shoved a handful of pamphlets toward her.

"What is all this?" she asked.

"I stopped by Miller's Travel Agency. Willa Dean thought you'd like to see them. It's the location of your destination wedding, LilyAnn."

"Our wedding," she said softly.

Mike smiled. "You know what I mean. If it was left up to me, I'd marry you tomorrow down at the courthouse, but I want you to have all the best memories ever of the wedding and the honeymoon."

"And I will, as long as you're part of it."

"Then we're good to go," Mike said. "Here comes the waitress. Do you know what you want to eat?"

"It's Thursday, which means the meatloaf special at Granny's. I'll have that, but trade the mashed potatoes for coleslaw."

As he gave the waitress their order, friends and acquaintances kept coming by to talk. Between the attack on her life and Mike's subsequent proposal, they were big news in Blessings. When their table finally cleared, he leaned forward to catch her up on their news.

"Your mama called the house after you were gone," Mike said.

"Is everything all right?"

"She has gotten over the fact that you aren't having a church wedding but says she's planning the reception, so get over it."

LilyAnn laughed. "Well, that settles that, then. What about your mom? Is she irked with us, too?"

"No. She's so happy we're getting married that she won't care how it happens. Besides, she's been through all that stuff with Faith."

LilyAnn nodded, but when she went suddenly silent, Mike guessed there was something more.

"What?" he asked.

"I got a call from the district attorney while I was at work."

"What did he say?"

"They arraigned Lachlan. He pled guilty, waived his right to a trial, said he would accept the judge's sentence, but asked for leniency and understanding."

"What does that mean?" Mike asked.

"The DA said it was Judge Fitzwater who presided and that Lachlan won't see leniency or the light of day for a very long time."

"Good."

"In other news," she said, and then giggled, because it sounded like a newscaster's way to segue into a new story, "I caught two shoplifters this morning."

Mike's eyes widened. "No. Really? Did you know them?"

"Unfortunately, yes. One was Hank and Ann Richards's son. You know, the people who own the realty company. The other was the middle school principal's son. I predict they're both in hot water."

"Did the police arrest them?"

"They came and got them, but I'm guessing they'll call the parents instead of booking them. It was a first-time offense for both, and they weren't exactly stealing drugs."

"What did they steal?"

She leaned closer and lowered her voice. "Condoms and massage oils."

He grinned. "Figures. Let me guess. They took them because if they bought them, someone might know they were having sex."

"Pretty much, but I put the fear of God in them."

He leaned back, his smile widening. "What did you do?"

"They wanted to know if I was 'her.' So I told them." She told him about playing up her reprisal on Lachlan and that they were bawling by the time her boss got to the office.

Mike chuckled. "So, now I know when our kids act up, I'll be the good cop and you'll be the bad cop."

"No. We'll both be the bad cops," she said.

"Deal. So what other mischief have you been into?" he asked.

"I got my dress for the New Year's Eve ball," LilyAnn said.

Mike grinned. "What does it look like?"

"You'll see soon enough. Oh, good, here comes our waitress and I'm starving."

———※———

They made love that night in Mike's bed, to fulfill his last fantasy, he said. As they slept, a predicted storm front came through, bringing rain and a drop in temperature.

When they woke the next morning, the house was cold and they'd overslept, which meant no time for morning snuggles. Lily bolted out of bed, grabbing clothes as she went.

"Today's my hair day at The Curl Up and Dye, so I'll miss lunch."

"And I'll miss you," Mike said.

He looked so damn sexy sprawled in that big king-size bed that LilyAnn weakened. She dropped her clothes where she stood and crawled back into bed.

"Can we make this quick?" she asked.

He grinned. "The right question is can *you* do it quick? Men are always primed and ready to fire."

LilyAnn laughed as he pulled her into his arms. He kissed her once and then moved away from her mouth and began a foray down her body—from her chin to the hollow at the base of her neck, to the valley between her breasts, the dip of her navel, and then to the juncture of her thighs.

She was half out of her mind with shock, and the other half with lust. This was unexplored territory, and she wasn't sure how it worked.

"Oh Mike, I'm not sure—"

"Close your eyes and just feel it," he said softly.

So she did.

It was startling, then seductive, then like being shot from a cannon—like riding in Randy Joe's hot rod and going from zero to sixty in five seconds flat.

She was still shaking from her climax when he parted her legs with his knee and slid in. He was primed and ready to blow, and she was so hot and wet that it didn't take long to accelerate. Like going from zero to sixty in five seconds flat.

―⁘―

LilyAnn had to run to keep her Friday appointment and was breathless when she entered the salon. There was nothing unusual about the clientele or about the stylists working on them, but it still felt different. She chalked it up to her own anxiety at being late and slid into the shampoo chair with seconds to spare.

"Busy morning?" Ruby asked, as she quickly soaped LilyAnn's hair.

"Yes. I don't know what in the world was going on. Every time I started out the door, Mr. Phillips found another reason to call me back."

Ruby shook her head. "Complete lack of care for a woman's need to look pretty."

"I guess," Lily said, and closed her eyes, reveling in the mini head massage that came with the shampoo.

Ruby rushed her through the shampoo, then into the styling chair without much to say. It was unusual, but LilyAnn was so harried that she was actually glad for the chance for some peace and quiet.

Within a few minutes, Ruby had LilyAnn's hair dry and styled, and she was ready to leave.

LilyAnn glanced up at the clock.

"You just set a new record. You did my hair in under thirty minutes."

"It's that shorter length," Ruby said, but when LilyAnn started to get up, Ruby stopped her. "Wait a minute. You can't leave yet. Okay, everybody! She's ready!"

Vera and Vesta rolled a tea cart out of the break room filled with mini sandwiches and tea cakes as Mabel Jean pushed out another one with drinks. At the same time, the front door of The Curl Up and Dye began to jingle nonstop as people began pouring in.

"Surprise!" Ruby said, as her salon slowly filled up with familiar faces.

When she saw Mr. Phillips come in grinning, she realized he'd been in on this and had purposefully kept her busy until they were ready. She was laughing but confused.

"What's going on? It's not my birthday or anything."

"It was her idea," Ruby said, pointing to Rachel Goodhope. "She made all these goodies for us and donated her time and tea cart for the festivities."

LilyAnn locked gazes with Rachel and, once again, felt a connection she didn't understand.

"Thank you, Rachel, but why all the fuss?"

Rachel wasn't an emotional kind of woman, but these days, she was often struggling to hold back the tears.

"I suggested to the City Council and the Chamber of Commerce that we should set aside a day each year as Hero Day. People can be nominated all during the year for the distinction, and the winner will be, from this day forward, crowned on this date, the 28th of December. And, I suggested, and they agreed, that the first name on the plaque should be yours. You are more than a heroine, LilyAnn. Through your life here in Blessings you have proved to be a survivor, and you have made the women of Blessings proud."

The room erupted in applause as the mayor came from the back carrying a miniature of the big plaque that would hang on the wall at City Hall.

"She made me pretty proud, too," Mike said, as he came out of the crowd behind her.

She was stunned, remembering their fiery roll in the hay only this morning.

"Mike! You knew and didn't tell?"

Mike's eyes widened. "Oh crap. My daddy told me, after what she did to T. J. Lachlan, to never make her mad. If I swear on my life that this is the last time I ever keep a secret from you, then are we good, honey?"

Everyone burst into laughter, including Lily. She couldn't believe this was happening, then saw the mayor approaching and stood up as Mike slipped in beside her.

"Miss LilyAnn Bronte, it is my honor to present you with this plaque, in recognition of your heroism and bravery in the face of extraordinary circumstances. You will be the first honoree of Hero Day, and on behalf of all the men in Blessings, we are ashamed that one of us mistreated you in such a manner."

"Mistreated, my ass! The sucker tried to kill her!" Vesta muttered.

Mutters of agreement ran through the crowd as the mayor blushed. He handed LilyAnn the plaque, waited just long enough for the photographer to snap a couple of shots, then hurried off to another meeting.

Lily couldn't get over it. Once again, she was making news, although it was the kind she could have done without.

"This is overwhelming. I don't know what to say."

Ruby was next as she presented a small gift wrapped with silver paper and a silver bow. It looked most impressive, and she presented it with as much to-do as the mayor had done giving her the plaque.

"This is just a little something from the girls and me," Ruby said.

Lily sat back down in the styling chair and put the plaque in her lap so she could open the gift. She was smiling as she tore into it, revealing a brand new toothbrush, still in its packing, and an economy-size tube of toothpaste.

Vesta smirked. "It's to keep those pretty teeth of yours in good shape, should you ever need to bite on something hard and crunchy again."

The connection between Lachlan's ear and the toothbrush was immediate. Laughter bubbled up Lily's throat and came out in a belly laugh that spread through the crowd.

Ruby waved her hand. "The ceremony is over. Time to sample some of Rachel's tasty treats."

"Sit tight, baby," Mike said. "I know what you like."

As Mike walked away, Rachel slipped up beside her. "Congratulations, LilyAnn."

"Thank you for this," Lily said.

Rachel shrugged. "It's nothing you didn't deserve. You may never think of me as a friend, but I would like to think we are not enemies."

Again, LilyAnn felt a sadness in Rachel that made no sense. How she'd gone from hot to trot to just shy of reserved was both a mystery and a shock.

"You're not my enemy, Rachel. You never were." She hesitated, and then had to ask, "Are you okay?"

Rachel smiled. "I will be. Here comes Mike, and I see he chose some of my sausage rolls and cucumber and cream cheese sandwiches. I made them fresh this morning. I think you'll like them."

She patted Lily's arm and slipped into the crowd as Mike handed Lily a plate and napkin.

"All finger food, sugar. What were you and Rachel talking about?"

Lily shrugged. "Not much. Mostly girl stuff, I guess."

"That lets me out," Mike said, and stuffed two of the

sausage rolls into his mouth. "Oh wow, this is good. Rachel is a good cook, but she can't cook on your level. You're the best," he added.

"The perfect comment from the perfect man. No wonder I love you," LilyAnn said.

He grinned and pointed to her plate. "Are you gonna eat that?"

She laughed and popped her sausage roll into his mouth.

"Now, would you please get me one so I can at least taste it?"

"Good excuse for seconds," he muttered, and headed back to the cart.

By the time New Year's Eve rolled around, LilyAnn's life was beginning to make sense. She was going to marry the man who loved her. They were making plans for their wedding and had almost figured out a way to connect and remodel both their houses into one.

When evening finally rolled around and it was time to get dressed for the ball, LilyAnn wanted the element of surprise with her dress so she got ready for the New Year's Eve ball at her house and made Mike get dressed at his. The excitement over her dress was second only to going to the ball. It would be their first appearance at a public event as a couple, and it was the most prestigious event that happened in Blessings.

When she pulled the dress over her head and it slid down her body in silky folds, she had a moment of déjà vu, remembering all the years earlier in her life when ball gowns had their own closet in her house.

It had been so long since she'd worn a dress like this

that she'd forgotten how great it felt to be a girl, and Mrs. Ling had done exactly what Lily asked her to do to change the styling.

The fabric was soft and clung to her, the style long, black, and slinky. From the front, it was understated elegance with a cowl neck that dipped to just below her collarbone, resting lightly on the mounds of her breasts. The sleeves were long, and the hemline just brushed the tops of her feet. Her new silver heels had the tiniest bit of bling on the toes.

It wasn't until she turned around that the dress suddenly made sense as a statement piece. The back dipped past her waistline, and the slit in the back of her skirt stopped just short of getting her arrested.

It was the perfect little black dress: demure at first glance, drop-dead sex appeal from the back. With the three-carat diamond on her finger and her grandmother's diamond studs in her ears, she looked like she'd stepped out of a *Vogue* photo spread, only better. She was a woman with curves who'd learned to love what she looked like and who she was.

The doorbell rang.

She grinned.

Mike was going all out, waiting for her to let him in instead of using his key.

When she opened the door, she gasped. The last time she'd seen Mike Dalton in a tux had been at the senior prom, and it was nothing like this.

"James Bond, as I live and breathe. Please come in."

Mike smiled as he walked in, slid a hand around her waist to kiss her, then felt bare skin instead of fabric and froze.

She batted her eyes just enough to get his attention.

"Are you ready, sugar?"

He nodded.

"I'll just get my wrap," she said, and sauntered back to the sofa, giving him a front-row seat to what was showing, and leaving the rest of what was not to imagination.

When she turned around, the grin on his face was stretched from ear to ear.

"It is a damn good thing I got that ring on your finger before the rest of Blessings sees all this. I might have had to fight 'em off on the doorstep."

She smiled. "You approve?"

"If I had a gold seal of approval, I'd pin it on your ass. You are stunning, LilyAnn, and I seriously love you."

"Thank you, Mike. I seriously love you, too."

"After you," he said, then closed her door and locked it behind them before walking her to the car.

"This feels like a date," she said, as Mike got behind the wheel.

He paused, his hands on the wheel.

"You're right. It does feel like a date, sugar, so I guess it is. We definitely missed out on a lot, but I will not complain since it got us here."

"Agreed. I hope I don't make a social faux pas tonight. It has been ages since I've been out in polite society. I tried to cover up my black eye. Does it look okay?"

"You look perfect. Your face is perfect. Everything about you is perfect. Now quit fussing and let's go have a party."

The streets were still lit with Christmas lights, as were the trees and shrubs and the porches of the houses that they passed. The air was chilly, but the night was clear. It was a perfect night to ring in a new year.

The country club was lit up like the Fourth of July. Lights shone from every window of the three-story edifice, and the grandeur of the old Corinthian architecture lent itself to the ambiance of the night.

"This place is so pretty," LilyAnn said, as Mike wheeled into the parking lot. "The last time I was here I was crowned Miss Peachy-Keen Queen. Mama and Daddy were beside themselves with pride. I thought Daddy was going to bust a button. He took so many pictures that night."

"I remember. I'm sorry he's not here, LilyAnn. We lost him way too soon," Mike said.

She nodded, but there was something she needed to get off her chest.

"You know I said I didn't like Eddie."

"Yeah?"

"Well, I just wanted you to know that I think it wasn't Eddie I didn't like. I think it was me. He's good to me, Mike. He's a little rough around the edges, but that's nothing. I just wanted you to know that."

Mike patted her knee. "You have done a lot of growing up in the last two months," he said.

She rolled her eyes. "Don't you think it was about time?"

He chuckled. "Ah, here's a good spot, and not too far from the entrance."

He wheeled into the parking place and then got out and ran around the car to help her out.

She settled her wrap around her shoulders, thankful for the warmth, and slid her hand beneath the crook of Mike's arm.

"Lead the way, Prince Charming. I feel like tonight is going to be magic."

And she was right.

She checked her wrap at the door, making their entrance into the grand hall nothing short of dramatic as they approached the ballroom entrance. A uniformed footman stood at the top of the stairs, reading out each couple's name as they descended into the throng of guests below.

When Mike handed him their invitations, the footman scanned the names against the guest list, then loudly announced in the same sonorous voice:

"Mr. Michael Dalton and Miss LilyAnn Bronte."

The chatter below trailed off into a murmur and then into complete silence as they descended the stairs.

LilyAnn knew how to play the part. It was a little bit like walking the runway during a beauty contest, only easier, because here there were no interviews or trick questions at the end of the runway to separate her from the others, and no crown to fight over.

Her chin was up, her shoulders back, and she was smiling and whispering to Mike in little asides, just enough to put a smile on his face.

"Pretend I'm witty. Look at me like you can't take your eyes off me," she whispered.

Mike grinned. "I don't have to pretend, and I'm afraid to take my eyes off you, even for a second. Your dress is TNT with a fuse, and I'm scared to death someone is gonna strike a match."

LilyAnn giggled.

And all the crowd saw were two people with eyes only for each other, which was exactly the point.

Almost immediately, Niles Holland, the president of the country club, stepped forward and shook Mike's hand.

"Mr. Dalton. Miss Bronte. It is a pleasure to have you here. The champagne is flowing. The buffet is full to *over*flowing, and the music is about to start. Miss Bronte, if I may be so bold… May I be the first to ask if you would save me a dance?"

"Of course, Mr. Holland, but the first and last dances are reserved especially for my fiancé."

Niles's eyebrows rose. "Fiancé? I hadn't heard. Congratulations, Dalton. You are a lucky man."

LilyAnn flashed the ring. "On the contrary, sir. I believe I am the lucky one."

Niles Holland knew about futurities and the stock market, and he knew gems. When he saw the rock, his eyebrows arched.

"That is absolutely stunning." He eyed Mike with new appreciation.

"Thank you, sir."

LilyAnn flashed him a smile as they walked away.

All of a sudden they heard the sound of glass breaking.

"Keep walking," Mike said.

"What happened?" LilyAnn asked.

"Holland just dropped his champagne. I think he caught sight of the back of your dress."

"Then I have achieved success," she said softly, then leaned over and kissed the spot right beneath his ear, knowing it made him want her. "In more ways than one."

Mike groaned. It was going to be a long-ass night before he got her out of that dress and in his bed, but it was definitely something to look forward to.

Chapter 18

IT WAS FIFTEEN MINUTES UNTIL MIDNIGHT. THE countdown to going home was about to become a reality, and none too soon for LilyAnn. Her grandma used to say that the best way to tell if a party was a success was how bad your feet hurt and how loud your belly growled. According to Grandma, a lady didn't graze from the buffet table, she nibbled, and then never ate anything that could go bad. It was a Bronte rule, and one LilyAnn had conformed to from an early age. She'd guided Mike through the same rule all night, steering him away from the shrimp and smoked salmon appetizers, choosing bites of cheeses and savory crackers for him instead of pâté, treating him with petit fours and fruit tarts, in lieu of mini quiches with cream sauces.

She'd danced with Niles Holland, and then the mayor, and then the chief of police, who managed to whisper a quick aside about what a remarkably brave woman she was. She had thanked him kindly, while keeping an eye on all the pretty women who were hovering around Mike. After his heroic rescue, he had his own group of admirers, many of whom seemed to have him cornered.

The only thing that kept LilyAnn from getting green-eyed jealous was the ring on her finger and the looks he kept giving her. Tonight was a nice break from the reality of their lives. They were not quite in the same social structure as the movers and shakers of Blessings, but good enough to keep them respectable on this very special night.

As soon as the music stopped, LilyAnn smiled but waved away the next gentleman who'd walked up.

"I'm sorry, but my fiancé is looking far too comfortable in the midst of all those pretty ladies. I feel the need to remind them of their boundaries."

She flashed him a smile to soften the turn-down as she walked away. She heard a faint wolf whistle behind her and smiled. God bless Mrs. Ling for the masterpiece she was wearing.

Mike saw her coming and was again struck by the change in her. It had very little to do with the weight that she'd lost, and more to do with how she'd come alive from inside.

"Sorry, ladies, but I have come to claim my one and only," LilyAnn said.

They smiled and giggled and said all the right things, but LilyAnn knew women, and she knew when she walked away with Mike that they would not be admiring her dress so much as picking her apart at the seams, because it was what women did.

"You're tired," Mike said.

The smile she was wearing slipped, and her eyes got a little teary.

"But it's a good kind of tired. I want to dance with you, Michael. I want you to put your arms around me. You center my world. You make me feel safe."

A wave of emotions washed through him as he took her in his arms and swung into a waltz step.

LilyAnn let Mike's strength flow through her, filling

her heart and calming her soul, settling the chaos that came with memories of thinking she was going to die.

They circled the floor, over and over in a mindless daze, just happy to be here and with each other.

One moment they'd been moving in waltz time, and just as suddenly the music stopped.

LilyAnn glanced toward the clock at the top of the stairs. It was only seconds before midnight.

"I have always wanted to do this," Mike said.

"Do what?" she asked.

"Kiss the woman I love at the stroke of midnight."

She shivered with sudden longing.

"I've never done this either," she whispered.

"Not with—"

She pressed a finger to his lips. "Not ever."

A muscle jerked near his jaw.

She knew what that meant to him—being her first.

The crowd hushed, everyone's eyes on the second hand as the bandleader began a countdown.

"Ten. Nine. Eight."

The crowd was counting down with him now.

"Seven. Six. Five."

Mike cupped her face.

"Four. Three. Two."

The second hand swept past the one.

As the bandleader shouted "Happy New Year!" the crowd erupted.

The notes of "Auld Lang Syne" swelled within the room as balloons began to fall. Party horns were blowing, little poppers spewing bursts of confetti, and then streamers and even more confetti began to rain down from the ceiling.

But LilyAnn didn't see it. Her eyes were closed. Her

arms were around Mike's neck while she was held close in his embrace. Their kiss was a symbol of what they had laid to rest and of the years to come.

Someone bumped into them in the crowd, then mumbled a rather drunken "sorry" and staggered off.

Mike traced the shape of her cheek all the way to her chin, then tapped the center of her lower lip with his finger. It was still damp from his kiss.

"Happy New Year, my love."

"Happy New Year, Michael, and for all of our years to come."

They were still asleep when the first round of guests from the New Year's Eve ball hit the ER with full-blown symptoms of food poisoning. If they weren't throwing up, they were battling dysentery. It became obvious that there were nowhere near enough bathrooms in the hospital to accommodate the nearly one hundred victims in varying stages of distress.

Ruby Dye heard it straight from the banker's wife that the police chief's wife threw up in the mayor's lap and then passed out on the floor at his feet. She said the orderlies couldn't mop fast enough to keep up and that it was basically a fecal free-for-all.

When LilyAnn heard the news, she silently thanked her grandma's wisdom and took Mike's gratitude as her due.

The day in February when Mike and LilyAnn boarded the cruise ship for Jamaica, T. J. Lachlan was one of a bus full of prisoners unloading at the Georgia State Prison.

His hair was just beginning to grow back, although the scar on the side of his head would be a vivid reminder of a woman's wrath, as were the scars on both cheeks, running perpendicular from his eyes to his chin.

His ear had healed to a funny-shaped knot where the lobe used to be, and he walked with a slight limp. He had but a shadow of his former bravado and was far from ready for what lay ahead. Unfortunately for T. J., the facial scars he abhorred only added to his sex appeal for the men who still thought him pretty.

Karma was a bitch.

The good thing about being on an island teeming with tourists is that when you don't know another soul except your partner, it's the same thing as being in exile. You are as alone as you want to be—with no phones to answer, no demands to be met—and that is how Mike and LilyAnn were welcomed to Jamaica.

The sun was setting on their second day in Jamaica when Mike and LilyAnn walked onto the beach. Mike was in a loose shirt and matching pants, and LilyAnn in a sheer summer dress with an empire waistline and a long, flowing skirt, garments as white as the sand between their bare toes.

A garland of red orchids around Mike's neck hung midway down the front of his shirt.

LilyAnn had a matching orchid over her right ear and a bouquet of white ones in her hands.

They stood with a preacher before them, a photographer to his side, and their backs to the ocean as a bright yellow moon rose over their heads.

"Are you happy?" Mike whispered.

"Beyond measure," she said.

And then the minister began.

"We are gathered here together, in the eyes of God…"

LilyAnn's heart was pounding as she blinked away tears. Growing up, like every little girl, she had expected to be on her daddy's arm on this day as he walked her down the aisle. She'd always pictured him standing before the altar as he gave her away.

But he was long gone and LilyAnn had come close to missing out on everything. It had taken an emotional shock and a physical assault to set her feet on the right path. That it had led to this island and this night, with this man, was nothing short of a miracle.

Mike's fingers curled around her hand. She felt both strength and tenderness in the touch, and it was good. Then the minister commanded:

"Repeat after me. I, LilyAnn, take thee, Michael…"

Lily's throat swelled with tears as she turned to face Mike and repeated the vow, knowing that with every word she spoke, her heart and soul were binding to him forever.

"Michael, please repeat after me. I, Michael, take thee, LilyAnn…"

And he did, repeating the vow word for word while he watched the reflection of the moon rise in her eyes and knew he had been bewitched.

The ceremony was brief, the vows straightforward. When they exchanged the rings, LilyAnn's hands were as shaky as Mike's were sure.

The photographer was snapping pictures all the while, but Mike was waiting for the magic words that legally bound them together in the eyes of God and of man.

And finally, they came.

"I now pronounce you man and wife. You may kiss the bride."

With the path of moonlight across a dark ocean behind them and a big yellow ball of moonlight above them, he took her in his arms. He had a momentary flash on all the empty years they'd lost, and then let go of the regret. Good things come to those who wait.

He cupped her face with both hands and lowered his head.

LilyAnn lost track of everything but the kiss, letting her hand fall to her side, the bouquet of white orchids dangling loosely from her fingers.

And that's when the photographer snapped the shot.

They emailed the picture to the local paper in Blessings. It made front-page news.

Ruby was at home having breakfast when she opened the paper and saw the picture. It was so beautiful that it made her cry. She liked things to be in their proper places, and the Lord knew those two were meant to be together.

Later, as she was opening up the shop, she saw a young girl walking past pushing a baby carriage. Ruby paused, eyeing the sadness on the girl's face and the innocence of the child.

She knew the girl's story and that the baby's daddy was long gone. It was a shame how young men were these days: out for all the fun with none of the responsibilities.

Ruby watched until the girl turned the corner at the end of the block and walked out of sight. She glanced up at the clock. It was almost time to open.

The Conklin twins came in the back in their usual

dark mood, needing caffeine and sugar before they could be civil.

Mabel Jean was on their heels and talking to someone on the phone. She waved hello as she headed for her manicure table.

Ruby turned the Closed sign to Open, and unlocked the front door.

The Curl Up and Dye was open for business.

Read on for an excerpt from Sharon Sala's

i'll
stand
by
you

Available now from Sourcebooks Casablanca

Chapter 1

ADORABLE GRANT ROLLED OVER IN BED AND SHUT OFF the alarm as a familiar cramp rolled across her belly. The monthly miseries had arrived, and by the smell coming from the baby bed where her son, Luther Joe, was sleeping, the baby food jar of prunes she'd fed him last night may have been a mistake. Between her cramps and Luther's runs, it was not the optimum way to start a workday, but she had already learned the hard way what it was like to live on leftovers.

She made a mad dash down the hall to the bathroom and came out a few minutes later carrying a tube of ointment for Luther's diaper rash. There was nothing glamorous about being a seventeen-year-old unwed mother, but after giving birth, she had vowed never to complain about getting her period again.

She hastened her steps as she headed back to her bedroom. Luther was awake and beginning to whine, and she didn't want to wake Granddaddy until the very last minute.

"Hey, little man," she said softly as she hurried toward the crib.

Luther was big for his age and already pulling himself up and standing inside the baby bed. His little, fat hands were curled around the spindles, and he was chewing on the bed rail, probably trying to cut teeth, but it had yet to happen. As soon as he saw her, he smiled that toothless baby smile she loved while saliva dripped down onto his chin and points below. He clutched the bed rail and squealed as she approached.

Dori chuckled. "Shh, now! You're gonna wake Granddaddy."

The mere mention of his favorite male sent Luther's gaze straight toward the door.

Dori sniffed, then rolled her eyes.

"Ooowee, Luther Joe! You sure do stink. Here, lie down a minute and let Mama get you all cleaned up again."

She unsnapped the crotch of his pajamas and began to clean him up while making faces at him, then laughed as he tried to mimic the expressions she was making. It was a game they'd been playing for almost a week now, and she was convinced that he was going to be a genius. As soon as she finished, she picked him up out of the crib, settled him on her hip, and headed for the kitchen.

It was still dark outside, but Dori's job as a dishwasher at Granny's Country Kitchen began at six a.m., when they started serving breakfast. She settled him into his high chair, handed him a teething biscuit, and started making coffee and warming milk to put in his cereal as she glanced out the kitchen window. The sky was still dark, but she could see darker, heavy-looking clouds. May was always a rainy month and this May was no exception. Maybe if she hurried, she'd get to work before it began.

Within minutes, she had bacon frying and beaten eggs in a bowl ready to scramble. She was putting bread in the toaster when Luther let out a big squeal. She turned to see her grandfather entering the room. He was slightly

stooped from so many years as a roofer but still in fine
form for seventy-six.

"Mornin', Granddaddy."

"Morning, honey," Meeker Webb said and wiggled
his fingers at Luther, who squealed again and whacked
his teething biscuit on the tray of the high chair.

Meeker eyed his granddaughter closely as he kissed
the top of her head and swiped a piece of crispy bacon.
From the day she'd been born, he'd always thought she
was the prettiest thing in Blessings, Georgia, and still
did, although her blue eyes weren't as sparkly as they
used to be, and she didn't pay much attention to how
she looked anymore.

He'd given up trying to get her to tell him who
Luther's father was. He had already figured out that
she wasn't telling because of what she feared he'd do to
him. She wasn't a run-around girl, and she hadn't had a
boyfriend when she turned up pregnant. Meeker might
be old, but he wasn't stupid. Somebody had his way
with Dori and left her to suffer the consequences alone.

"Looks like rain," he said as he poured himself a cup
of coffee.

Dori nodded as she strained off the bacon grease, then
poured the eggs into the hot skillet and began to stir.

"I know, Granddaddy. I'm going to leave just as soon
as I feed Luther."

"I'll feed ol' Buster here, and you sit yourself down
and eat breakfast for a change. You're wasting away. I
can eat after you're gone."

She hesitated. He already did so much for her, but his
offer was tempting. She sure didn't want to work all day
in wet clothes.

"But your breakfast will get cold," she said.

He tweaked her ear.

"I know how to heat it up, now, don't I?"

She grinned and handed him Luther's bowl of cereal. She dished herself up a serving of eggs and bacon, grabbed a piece of toast as it popped up, and ate standing up.

Meeker frowned. "Honey, the least you could do is sit down."

"No time," she muttered, talking around the mouthful of food she was chewing.

Within minutes, she was in her bedroom, throwing on clothes without care if they matched or not and brushing out tangles in her long, dark brown hair. She used to take pride in her appearance. Before her parents were killed, everyone used to talk about how much she looked like her mother, with her baby-doll features and little turned-up nose, but she couldn't see how it mattered much anymore. Her pride, along with everything else, had taken a great fall when she turned up pregnant, and like Humpty Dumpty, she didn't know how to put herself back together again. She grabbed an umbrella and then stopped off in the kitchen before she left.

"I'm going now," she said and kissed her little boy good-bye. "Luther Joe, you be good for Granddaddy."

Luther grinned and blew bubbles with a mouthful of oatmeal, which made Meeker grin.

Dori rolled her eyes. "Don't laugh at him, or he'll just do it again."

"Why not?" Meeker said. "You used to do the same thing, and I laughed at you."

Dori hugged her grandfather's neck.

"I hope you know how much I love and appreciate you."

Meeker squinted and gruffly cleared his throat.

"I love you too, girl. Now hustle or you're gonna get wet. Luther and I will be just fine."

Dori blew him a kiss, then put on her raincoat and, after she stepped out onto the porch, opened her umbrella.

The sun had yet to come up, but the streetlights lit the way out of her neighborhood toward downtown Blessings. She took a deep breath of the cool morning air as she came down the porch steps. It even smelled like rain. Without hesitation, she lengthened her stride and shifted into work mode.

She'd never made it to a high school prom, and her days of going to football games and school trips were over. She'd tried homeschooling, then decided it was a waste of time and took the GED. Now she was almost through with online college courses on building websites. She could have felt sorry for herself, but all she had to do to get past it was think about her baby. She wouldn't trade him for all the parties and dances in the world. She paused briefly to check for traffic as she reached the corner, and when the first drops of rain began to fall, she started to run.

—⁓—

When twenty-year-old Johnny Pine's alarm went off, he rolled his long-legged self out of bed with a groan. Five a.m. came far too soon, but he needed the extra hour to do a load of laundry and make breakfast for his little brothers before he sent them off to school. When he was little, his mama never made him breakfast, let alone got out of bed. But he remembered what it felt like to go to school hungry and was determined that wasn't happening to his brothers.

Marshall was ten and in fifth grade, and Brooks, a.k.a. Beep, was seven and in second grade. Although they were young enough to still need a mother, that wasn't happening. Their mother had overdosed on meth two years ago and was buried in the Blessings Cemetery. Their daddy was doing time in prison with no hope of ever getting out. Johnny was all they had left, and he wasn't going to be the next one to fail them.

He headed for the bathroom on bare feet, wincing at the feel of grit on the floor. He'd meant to sweep up last night after dishes and the boys' homework, but he'd forgotten. Maybe he'd have time if he hurried through his shower.

A short while later, he was in the kitchen, stirring oatmeal and sipping his second cup of coffee. The washer was on the spin cycle—so far, so good. He eyed the oatmeal, then turned off the fire and set the pan on a back burner as he went down the hall to wake up the boys.

The Ninja Turtle night-light in their room used to be his. It was cracked, and one of the turtles was missing an arm, but it still worked, shedding a pale green glow on their faces. They both had black hair like Johnny's, and when they got older, he suspected they'd look a lot like him, as well. He did what he could to keep them in line but feared he was a poor substitute for a parent. If he hadn't already been eighteen when their mama died, the state would have taken them away from him. Now he kept everything on the up-and-up for fear they still might.

He turned on the light in the room and then leaned over the bed they shared and shook each one gently.

"Hey, Marshall. Hey, Beep. It's time to wake up. Oatmeal is done. Get up now and don't dawdle. You can't be late for school."

The boys were mute as they rolled out of bed and padded across the hall to the bathroom to pee. He got out their clean clothes and then set their shoes side by side on the floor before he left the room. He could already hear giggling inside and knocked on the bathroom door as he passed.

"Quit piddlin' around and get dressed!" he yelled.

Silence followed his footsteps as he went back to the kitchen. The washer was through spinning, so he dumped the load of wet clothes into the dryer and turned it on. The clothes would be wrinkled when he got home this evening, but at least they'd be clean and dry. They might be living life at the bottom of the barrel, but they didn't have to live it dirty.

He glanced at the clock. Already a quarter to six and he still hadn't fixed their lunches. They qualified for the free lunch program at school, but he wasn't putting that kind of stigma on the boys if he could help it. He got out a can of Spam and began making sandwiches. Marshall liked mayonnaise, Beep wanted butter, and he liked mustard. He made one for each of the boys and two for himself, added a banana apiece in their lunch boxes and a honey bun in his, and then left them on the corner of the table as the boys entered the kitchen. They were dressed, but their hair was a wreck. He'd work on that later.

"Sit," he said. "I'll dish up the oatmeal."

"Can I have raisins in mine?" Marshall asked.

"I don't want no raisins," Beep muttered defensively.

"You don't want *any* raisins," Johnny said, absently

correcting the grammar as he dished up the hot cereal and dumped a handful of raisins on top of Marshall's serving.

Beep frowned. "That's what I said."

Johnny grinned and kept dipping. Conversation ended as they began to eat. Oatmeal was not his favorite breakfast food, but it was hot, cheap, and filling, and that was that. Maybe when he won the lottery, they'd eat bacon and eggs.

He swallowed his oatmeal in eight bites, turned around, washed and rinsed his bowl, and put it in the drainer.

"Put your bowls in the hot water when you're through," he said and then pointed at Beep. "And don't be putting any oatmeal in the dishwater again. Eat it. Don't waste it."

Beep nodded without looking up and shoveled another bite into his mouth.

"If he don't want it, I'll eat it," Marshall said.

"If he doesn't want it," Johnny said, correcting his grammar too.

Marshall shrugged.

Johnny frowned. "Don't shrug that off," he said shortly. "When you don't speak properly, people think you're dumb, and we've got enough to live down without people thinking we're stupid, understand?"

Marshall blinked. "I'm sorry, Johnny."

Beep looked nervous. If Marshall was in trouble, that probably meant he would be in trouble too.

Johnny eyed the anxious expressions on their faces and sighed.

"Look, guys, you're not in trouble, okay? I just want you to be the best you can be, and that means no lazy talk, okay?"

"Is *ain't* a lazy word, Johnny?" Beep asked.

Johnny nodded.

Beep beamed. "Then I ain't gonna say that no more."

Johnny grinned and left the kitchen shaking his head. It was time to cut his losses and end the grammar lesson, or they'd all be late.

He scratched his chin as he paused in the hall. He had time to shave or sweep, and he opted for sweeping. He didn't want to walk on that gritty floor again tonight, and since he drove a bulldozer for Clawson Construction, no one there cared if he had whiskers.

By the time he was through, the boys were too. He sent them to brush their teeth and then went to look for rain gear. Marshall was outgrowing his hooded jacket. If Johnny had time this coming weekend, he'd stop by the Salvation Army resale shop and see what they had in stock.

"Guys, hurry up!" he yelled as he tossed the jackets by their backpacks and strode across the hall and into the bathroom. He eyed their hair and grabbed a comb, yanking it through their hair just enough to give it a semblance of propriety.

"Dang, Johnny! You messed up my 'hawk," Marshall said as he re-combed his hair with his fingers until he had his Mohawk hairstyle back the way he liked it.

Johnny rolled his eyes and grabbed his youngest brother.

"Stand still, Beep. I just need to get this…" Johnny stopped and frowned, then looked closer at the knot in his little brother's hair. "What the hell is that in your hair?"

"You cussed," Beep muttered.

Johnny parted the knot with the tip of the comb.

"Is that gum? Did you go to bed with gum in your mouth again?"

Beep shrugged.

"Crap on a stick, boy, you aren't gonna have a lick of hair left if you keep this up," Johnny said and pulled a pair of scissors out of the drawer in the vanity.

Marshall eyed the latest surgery absently, then pointed at the other bald spots near his little brother's right ear.

"At least it's on the same side," he offered.

Johnny rolled his eyes. The kid's head was beginning to look like he had ringworm, which would definitely set him up as a target if any of the kids noticed it.

"Don't let anybody pick on you," he said.

Marshall put his hand on Beep's shoulder. "If they do, I'll whup 'em," he offered.

"Every man has to fight his own fights," Johnny said as he tossed the hair ball into the trash. "No more gum for you at night, bud," he said gently and gave Beep a quick hug.

Marshall frowned, listening as the rain began to hammer on the roof above them.

"Oh man, it's raining. We won't get to go outside at recess," he grumbled.

"There's always recess another day. Go get your stuff," Johnny said. "I've still got to drop you off at Miss Jane's so she can take you to school later. And don't make her have to wait for you when school's over. Get your butts out to the van."

"Okay, Johnny, we promise," Marshall said.

He was old enough to realize how fragile the framework of their little family really was—Beep not so much. If Miss Jane got mad at them and quit being their babysitter, then that would mess up Johnny's job, and

Johnny couldn't lose his job, or they'd be homeless, and he didn't want to be homeless. Daddy was in prison and wasn't ever coming out, and Mama was dead and buried. He lived in fear of what they'd lose next.

Within a few minutes, Johnny had loaded them into his old SUV and was driving across town to Miss Jane's Before and After. She called herself a part-time day care, but since she refused to wipe baby butts, her only service was taking kids to school and picking them up afterward. She furnished an after-school snack and expected them to sit quietly and do homework until they were picked up before suppertime. Miss Jane also did not tolerate roughhousing, which meant the Pine brothers were on notice at least once a week.

Johnny accelerated slightly as he approached the incline where the old railroad tracks used to be. Even though the train no longer ran through Blessings, it was still the demarcation point for the wrong side of town. While Johnny had grown up there, he had himself a plan. He was going to take his family into a better way of life or die trying.

—∿∿—

Ruby Dye frowned when she heard the rain peppering against her windows. Rain was never a good sign for a beauty shop. The Curl Up and Dye had a reputation to maintain, and humidity played hell with a hairdo, especially Vera's and Vesta's creations. The Conklin twins were inordinately fond of hair spray and used it liberally, although it had a tendency to turn hair into a helmet on high-humidity days.

She glanced at the clock. It was almost seven a.m. If she left now, she'd have time to do a load of towels at the shop and mop the floor before Willa Dean Miller showed up for her weekly shampoo and style.

Willa Dean ran the local travel agency. Last year, she'd booked a trip to Italy for Patty June Clymer after Patty divorced her preacher husband for fornicating with a local whore. The divorce had caused quite a stir in Blessings, and Willa Dean's business increased dramatically after Patty June came back talking about good-looking Italian men.

But Ruby wasn't in the market for travel beyond going to the salon, so she put on her raincoat, gave her own hair a last check, and flipped a curl back in place.

Ruby liked to change her hair color on a regular basis as a walking advertisement for what she sold, which was beauty in a bottle. She'd been blond and curly for the past two months and liked the look. It brought out the green in her eyes. She grabbed her purse and umbrella as she left the house, grateful for her covered porch and carport.

She had a Garth Brooks CD playing in her car and the windshield wipers seemed to swipe rhythmically to the music as she drove toward Main. On impulse, she swung by a drive-through at a local bakery and picked up a dozen doughnuts. The twins were cranky on rainy days, and a little sweetening up might be in order.

Today was also Mabel Jean Doolittle's birthday. Her manicurist was a real sweet girl, and while Ruby hadn't bought her a gift, Mabel Jean would be just as happy with a jelly doughnut and a week of free booth rent.

—⁓—

On the other side of town, semi-newlyweds Mike and LilyAnn Dalton were still sleeping. Mike had a spa/gym down on Main Street that was temporarily closed for renovations, and LilyAnn had taken off work today for her monthly doctor checkup. She was four months pregnant and still struggling with morning sickness. Added to that, her emotions were on a perpetual-motion merry-go-round. Between the daily drama of throwing up and bawling for no reason, this was getting on her last nerve. However, Mike was over the moon that there was a baby on the way, and when she felt better, she'd be on the same page. She'd wasted far too much of her life already.

―⁓―

Unlike most of the other businesses in Blessings, Granny's Country Kitchen never suffered a loss of business on nasty days. In fact, bad weather had a tendency to draw more people to warm, cozy places, and there was nothing more comforting in the South than hot biscuits, sausage gravy, and a great cup of coffee.

The waitresses were turning in an unusual amount of orders, and Walt Warden, the morning cook at Granny's, was turning them right back out just as quickly. The customers continued to come in, but then lingered because of the rain. Before long, the place was packed, and there were a half-dozen people waiting for to-go orders as well.

Dori never looked up from her job. She scraped leftovers, rinsed, and loaded dishes into the commercial-style dishwasher without hesitation. It took ten minutes for them to run through the superhot cycles, another five of rinse and heat dry, and then a couple of minutes of cooldown before she took them out again and stacked them back into service for the cook and servers. It was a nonstop process that kept her in constant motion. By the time the breakfast rush was over, it was after ten a.m. and she was ready for a potty break.

She glanced up as the back door swung inward and the owner, Lovey Cooper, came in, shedding a raincoat and umbrella as she went. Lovey smiled at Dori and waved at Walt, who was scraping down the grill.

"Busy morning?" she asked.

"Yes, ma'am," Dori said as she took off her rubber gloves and waterproof apron before heading to the bathroom.

After she finished, she washed her hands without looking in the mirror, a subconscious act reflecting the disgust she had with her life.

She was concerned about Luther's little bottom. It was pretty raw from that diarrhea, and she felt guilty all over again for giving him the whole jar of prunes. Without a woman to ask for advice, raising her baby was a case of "live and learn." Unfortunately, Luther was the one suffering the consequences.

She dried her hands quickly and went back into the kitchen. The last dishwasher load was just about done, and she was gearing up mentally to be ready for the lunch crowd. Her daily shift was from six a.m. to two p.m., at which time the second-shift dishwasher, Larry Bemis, would come in and work until close. She glanced up at the clock again. Eight more minutes on her break—just enough time to call home—so she slipped into the back hallway for privacy. When her granddaddy answered before the second ring, Dori knew Luther was down for a nap and Granddaddy was making sure nothing woke him before it was over.

"Hello, Dori. Everything okay, honey? Did you make it to work before the rain?"

She smiled. "Hi, Granddaddy. Everything's fine. It rained on me some, but I didn't get too wet. Everything okay there?"

Meeker Webb chuckled. "You are a worrywart just like your grandma was. Everything is fine, including me and buster. There's food in the kitchen, and the roof don't leak, so we're high and dry. Can't ask for anything more."

She laughed. "Okay. I hear you. I love you. See you this afternoon."

"Deal," he said.

She dropped the phone back in her pocket and returned to the kitchen, put the apron and rubber gloves back on, and began emptying the busboy's latest tub of dirty dishes. One thing was for sure: scraping out other people's leavings was a deterrent for overeating. She was as thin as she'd ever been in her life.

———∿∿∿———

The rain at Johnny's job site made removing stumps easy, and Floy Beaudine had six of them he wanted out. But Floy had also warned Johnny not to tear up his pasture with the bulldozer if the ground got too wet.

Johnny had three stumps out before the ground got soft, and now the dozer tracks were making ruts in the pasture. It was time to stop. He was in the act of loading up the dozer when his cell phone rang. He jumped up into the truck cab, out of the rain, to take the call, and then, when he saw it was the school, his heart skipped a beat. They never called unless there was a problem.

"Hello?"

"Johnny Pine?"

The woman's voice was clipped, the disdain in her voice a faint, long-distance slap on the cheek.

"Yes, ma'am."

"This is Principal Winston. Your brother Brooks was fighting at school. He's in the office, and you need to come get him."

Johnny thought of those bald spots on the back of Beep's head and muffled a groan. He'd feared as much.

"Is he all right?" he asked.

"He has a black eye, and his nose is bleeding. It seems a bit crooked. It might be broken. We thought you would want to get him checked out."

Johnny gasped. Little kids didn't usually do much damage to each other, but a broken nose was a lot more than a scuffle.

"Broken? What the hell happened to him? Who did that?"

"The children were sent to recess in the gym because of the rain, and some of them were—"

The skin crawled on the back of Johnny's neck.

"Some? As in more than one jumped on Beep?"

She hesitated. "Well, we're still investigating the—"

"I am on my way, and you better have the responsible parties in the office when I get there."

"Now see here, Johnny! You—"

"It's Mr. Pine to you, ma'am, and we'll continue this discussion face-to-face."

He hung up and got out of the truck. Minutes later, he had the dozer loaded and was driving back to town, talking to his boss as he went.

"Mr. Clawson, this is Johnny. I got three of the stumps out of Mr. Beaudine's pasture before I had to stop because the ground got too soft. I was just loading up when I got a call from school. Beep's been hurt, so I need to run him by the ER, okay?"

Clawson liked Johnny Pine and had known him for years. Johnny was the best worker Clawson had, and he never asked for favors. It was not a problem to grant this one.

"Sure, it's okay, Johnny. We can't do any more dozer work today because of this rain, so go on home when you're done. I sure hope your brother is okay."

"Yes, sir. Thank you very much."

He hung up the phone and kept on driving. By the time he got the truck parked and headed to school in his SUV, he was so mad, he was shaking.

Chapter 2

MAVIS WEST, THE SCHOOL SECRETARY, LOOKED UP from inside the big, glassed enclosure of the principal's office and saw Johnny Pine coming in the front door. He was easily over six feet tall, with wide shoulders and long legs, and his face was downright handsome. *Strange how the bad boys always turn out good-looking*, she mused. And then she saw the frown on his face and the length of his stride and glanced at the little boy on the cot near her desk. She liked the Pine boys. They had good manners and they were smart. It wasn't their fault they came from bad blood. Then the office door opened, and Johnny Pine was coming inside.

———

Johnny's anger was on simmer as he walked into the office. Then he saw Beep's swollen face and bloody hands, the ice pack against his cheek, and his backpack lying beneath the cot, and he stifled the urge to put his fist through a wall.

"I want to speak to Mrs. Winston."

Mavis sat up a little straighter. "She's in conference with—"

"Who did this?" he asked.

"It's not my place to—"

At that point Beep woke up, saw his big brother, and started to cry all over again.

"I fighted my own battle, Johnny, but there was too

many. They said I had cooties in my hair, and I told them I didn't, and they shoved me down on the gym floor and started kicking me and calling me names."

Rage washed over him in waves as he scooped Beep up in his arms.

"They kicked you?"

"Yes."

"In the face too?"

Beep nodded, his eyes welling all over again.

"How many?"

"Four."

"All of them from your class?"

"No, they were fourth graders."

Johnny looked back at the secretary and spoke, his voice so soft she had to lean forward to hear properly. "Miss Mavis, either you open the door to Mrs. Winston's office for me, or I'll kick it open."

Mavis jumped up to block the way.

"I told you she's in conference. She's dealing with this. It's not your place to—"

"Well, yes, it by God is my place. This little boy was attacked by a gang of older boys in the school gym, which is school property, and no one has seen to his welfare beyond a fucking ice pack. Did he tell you all he'd been kicked?"

Mavis hesitated, but the truth came out. "One of the teachers on duty in the gym witnessed it."

"Why didn't you call an ambulance? Did anyone call the police?"

Mavis gasped. "We didn't see a need to call an ambulance, and the police have no place here. This is a school problem and will be dealt with here."

Johnny looked down at Beep and wanted to cry. His face was swollen, and his nose *was* crooked on his face.

"If he was kicked all over by a gang of boys, that's assault, which is illegal, and he could have internal bleeding. Either I talk to her now, or you'll all be talking to a lawyer. Do I make myself clear?"

All of a sudden the principal's door opened and Arlene Winston slipped out, quickly closing it behind her.

"Please lower your voice. I'm dealing with this in the proper manner," she said.

Johnny tightened his hold on his little brother.

"I'm sorry, Mrs. Winston, but you do not tell me how to react to this outrage, and you're not dealing with shit. Four older boys attacked a little boy, and if there are broken bones in his body or internal bleeding that you have ignored, there's going to be hell to pay. I'm taking my brother to the emergency room. I *will* have the names of the responsible parties, because their parents are paying for the medical bills incurred from this incident. Their little bastards better suffer some serious suspension time too, or shit is going to hit the fan all over town."

Mavis watched her boss's skin color go from a highly incensed pink flush to pasty white so fast she had to look twice to make sure she was seeing properly.

Principal Winston flinched. "I understand the ring-worm issue started everything and—"

Beep hid his face against his brother's chest as Johnny interrupted.

"Ringworm? Did I hear you actually say that? He doesn't have ringworm. He got gum stuck in his hair, and when I cut it out, hair came with it. That then raises the question, are you implying that if Beep had ringworm, then the boys had the right to kick the shit out of him?"

Arlene Winston paled. "You are putting words in my mouth. There's no need to make such a—"

"There is every need," Johnny said softly. "Just because you don't like this little boy's last name doesn't mean he deserves less than any other kid here. I am not making empty threats, and you know me well enough to know I mean every damn word I say."

He started toward the door, then paused and turned around.

"Considering the way this has gone down, I believe I'll just get Marshall out of school now too. I feel the need to keep my family close today, since it seems I can't trust the public school system to do it for me. If Beep is able to come back tomorrow, then they'll both be back. If he's not, they won't. And if anyone looks cross-eyed at either one of them over this, I will make you *and* them sorry."

Mavis glanced at the principal, who nodded reluctantly. Mavis used the school intercom to summon Marshall Pine to the office to be checked out of school.

Sitting up in Johnny's arms made Beep's nose bleed again. Mavis handed him a handful of tissues and then patted his leg. Johnny considered the gesture as coming a little too late and focused on Marshall coming up the hall. He knew when Marshall stumbled that it was a reaction to Beep's face.

"What happened?" Marshall asked as he entered the office.

"Please pick up your brother's backpack under the cot and we'll talk in the car," Johnny said.

Marshall scooped it up, pausing long enough to give the women in the office a look of disbelief, and then followed his brothers out of the office and into the rain.

Mavis looked at the principal.

"What do you want me to do?" she asked.

"Get the school lawyer on the phone and start calling parents," Mrs. Winston said. "Don't tell them what happened. Just tell them I need them down here now."

"Yes, ma'am," Mavis said and scurried back around to her chair as Arlene Winston went back into her office to face the four boys in question.

Johnny drove to the clinic with Beep in his lap. He knew it wasn't legal to drive like that, but he couldn't bring himself to let him go. The windshield wipers swiped rapidly through the downpour as the rain continued to fall.

Marshall was quiet all the way to the clinic, but his fingers were curled into fists and Johnny knew he was contemplating revenge. It was an unfortunate aspect of how the Pine men rolled, but this time it had to be different because they couldn't give anyone an excuse to let this slide.

"Hey, Marshall."

"What?"

"I am telling you to let me deal with this. This is more than just two kids fighting, okay?"

Marshall eyed his little brother. "Who beat you up, Beep?"

Johnny shook his head. "No. I said we're not going there. Four older boys did it, and right now that's all I know."

"They said I had ringworms. They said I had cooties," Beep mumbled.

Johnny patted Beep's arm. "We're going to get you x-rayed, buddy, and if everything is okay, when we get home, we'll have a family discussion, okay?"

Marshall patted his little brother's leg as Johnny drove into the ER parking lot, then parked as close to the front as he could get. He took off his jacket and put it over Beep's head and face to protect him from the rain before he carried him inside.

Thelma Crown, the ER receptionist, quickly recognized the family.

"We need to see a doctor," Johnny said. "My little brother was attacked at school."

Thelma hid her shock, but the others in the waiting room did not. That would be all over Blessings before sundown. She slid a clipboard across the counter.

"Fill this out for me and take a seat. As soon as—"

But Johnny didn't budge as he pulled the jacket off of Beep's little head, revealing the extent of his injuries.

"No, ma'am. We need to see a doctor now. He was kicked repeatedly about the head and body by four older boys, and I need to make sure he's not bleeding internally."

This time, Thelma didn't bother to hide her shock.

"I'm sorry. You can put him in that wheelchair while I call the nurse's station."

"No thank you. I'll carry him," Johnny said.

Thelma made the call, and moments later, a nurse and a doctor came out pushing a gurney.

When Johnny laid him down, Beep cried out.

"Johnny, don't leave me!"

"Don't worry, buddy," Johnny said softly. "You're not going anywhere without us." He held tight to his hand as they rolled him back.

—⁓—

Halfway through the noontime dinner service, the busboy at the Country Kitchen began throwing up. Lovey immediately sent him home, but it left the waitresses in a bind. They didn't have time to clear tables *and* wait on their customers, so Lovey made a few adjustments in the staff.

"Hey, Dori, I need you to grab a tub and cart and help the girls bus some tables."

"What about the dishes?" she asked as she began taking off the gloves and apron.

"Just hustle and we'll make it work," Lovey said.

Dori took down her ponytail, smoothed down all the loose ends, and put it back up again. Then she straightened the blue-and-white-striped shirt she was wearing, checked her jeans to make sure they weren't wet, and pushed a tub and cart out into the dining area straight toward an empty table full of dirty dishes.

Customers were still seated at the tables on either side. A trio of men at one of the tables smiled at her and went on about their business. But the four women at the other table were parents of kids she knew from school, and the looks they gave her weren't kind. She kept her head down as she cleared the table, then wiped it down and set it back up. As she moved past, one of them called out.

"Dori Grant! You've changed so much I almost didn't recognize you. How are you doing?"

"I'm just fine, Mrs. Parrish, thank you for asking."

But Lorena wasn't through.

"And how is that baby of yours? I guess he's getting bigger. What is he now, four months?"

"No, ma'am, he's six months old."

Mrs. Parrish smiled at Dori, but it was not a friendly smile.

"Now what was it you named him? I know I've heard it."

Dori started moving away. "His name is Luther Joe Grant, after my daddy."

Parrish's smile thinned. "Well, that's sweet, but I would have thought you'd name him after *his* own daddy and not yours."

Dori stopped, then looked the woman squarely in the eyes.

"Why would you think something like that, Mrs. Parrish? It's pretty much tradition in the South to name babies after parents and grandparents."

Lorena Parrish sniffed.

"Well, I guess that's so, especially if the identity of the parent is in question," she drawled.

Dori gasped. She tried to hide it, but her eyes quickly blurred with tears, and to make it worse, Lorena Parrish was still talking.

"However, *your* people aren't from the South, now, are they? I mean, everyone knows you're a direct blood descendant of Ulysses S. Grant, the man in charge of ravaging this country during the War of Northern Aggression."

Across the room, Lovey Cooper had been eyeing Dori ever since Lorena Parrish called her down, and she could tell by the look on Dori's face that she was being insulted. Lovey never had liked Lorena much anyway and decided it was time to call a halt to what looked like an inquisition. She strode across the floor and slipped a hand across Dori's back, patting her gently to make sure Dori understood she was not in trouble.

"Ladies, I'm going to have to interrupt this fascinating history lesson and insist that you let Dori get back to work. We're a little shorthanded right now. Honey, if you'll just get those last two tables for me, that will be enough."

"Yes, ma'am, I sure will," Dori said, thankful for the reprieve.

She could hear Lovey's sharp, high-pitched voice shift into an oversweet tone as she addressed the table of women.

"Lorena, you're looking fit as a fiddle. I guess that new marriage is agreeing with you. I have to say I wouldn't have had the guts to take on a fifth husband like you did. They're so dang hard to train and all."

Lorena Parrish was laughing with everyone else, but she was pissed and Dori knew it. Her face was a ruddy shade of red.

～～～

Johnny was sitting beside Beep's bed in the ER and Marshall was sitting silently in a chair against the wall, overwhelmed by what had happened to his little brother and intimidated by the sight of all the scary equipment.

Beep's nose had already been set and both eyes were turning black. His nostrils were plugged with little wads of cotton to stop the bleeding. The clear plastic guard they'd put over his nose spanned the upper portion of his face like a mask. He was drifting in and out of sleep, exhausted from the events of the day.

Marshall glanced at Johnny. "When can we go home?"

"We don't go anywhere until the doctor tells us it is okay," Johnny said.

A single tear ran down Marshall's face.

"Is he gonna die?"

"No, of course not," Johnny said, but he was beginning to worry. Beep was getting quieter, and all he could think about were dire consequences, like blood clots and concussions.

He glanced up at the clock. They'd been in the ER over three hours, and he was ready for some answers.

No sooner had the thought crossed his mind than the doctor came in carrying X-rays.

Dr. Quick had delivered Brooks Pine, and he was pretty angry about what had happened to the little guy. But criticism was left for others. His job was to fix him. He pulled a couple of X-rays out of an envelope, turned on the viewer light, and slid them up onto the screen as Johnny and Marshall moved up beside him.

"So, here's the verdict, guys. Mr. Brooks here has some healing to do. Besides the broken nose, he also has two cracked ribs, a large contusion on his spine, and one on his thigh. Look here," he said, pointing to the X-ray. "These fine lines on the fourth and fifth ribs are hairline fractures. Other than the broken nose and a couple of loose teeth that should reseat themselves, I don't see any other injuries to his head or neck."

Johnny felt sick. He wanted to cry, but he had to be the strong one.

"What do we do? How do you fix this?" he asked. "Are you sure that's all? He's getting sleepy. Are you sure he doesn't have a concussion?"

"Adrenaline crash," Dr. Quick said gently. "No concussion, no intracranial bleeding."

"So he wears the nose guard to protect the nose, but what about the ribs?" Johnny asked.

Dr. Quick patted Beep's leg.

"Just no roughhousing or lifting for a few weeks and they'll heal. He's young and kids' bones are very pliable."

Just to prove he wasn't as sleepy as they thought, Beep piped up with a question of his own.

"Do I still have to take a bath?" Beep asked.

It was the perfect comment to lighten the moment. Dr. Quick laughed.

"As long as you let your brother wash your face so you don't mess up the good job I did on your nose, you'll be good to go. A warm bath might even make some of the aches you're going to have feel better," Dr. Quick said.

"Shoot," Beep said.

"You have to take a bath," Marshall said. "I wouldn't want to sleep with you if you got stinky."

Beep winced as the movement of facial muscles caused him pain.

"I sleep with you even when you fart," Beep muttered.

Marshall looked embarrassed.

Dr. Quick caught Johnny's eye. "Could we speak privately for a moment?" he asked.

Johnny followed the doctor out into the hall. His heart was pounding, and he felt sick to his stomach. "What's wrong? Is something else wrong that you're not telling me?"

"No, no, I'm sorry. I didn't intend to frighten you. I wanted to tell you that I have reported this to the police and they are on their way to talk to Brooks."

Johnny was relieved that decision had been taken out of his hands. He focused on what Dr. Quick was saying.

"I'm speaking out of line, but you're pretty young to have the responsibilities you have, and I don't want to see you railroaded. I think you need to see a lawyer to protect your rights. At least make sure the responsible parties pay for the medical bills and hope the threat of a lawsuit makes the school take the appropriate action."

Johnny's shoulders slumped. "I can't afford a lawyer, Doc. I threw the word around a lot when I picked him up from school, but that's not going to happen."

"You know Peanut Butterman, right? He has the law office above the old bank."

"Yes, sir," Johnny said. Everyone knew Mr. Butterman. He was one of Blessings's true characters.

"Give him a call and tell him I referred you. Every so often, he takes a case pro bono when he thinks someone is about to get railroaded. I think this would be one of those cases."

Johnny was surprised and embarrassed. "I don't want charity."

Dr. Quick put a hand on Johnny's shoulder. "This isn't about your pride, son. It's about Brooks's and Marshall's welfare through the rest of their school days. In other words, tie a knot in their tails now, before shit gets out of hand."

Johnny got it. His pride didn't matter as much as their safety. "Yes, sir. I hear you. And thanks."

"You're welcome. I'm very sorry this happened, but the police should be here soon. They will want to interview Brooks and let him say his piece. They'll go to school and get those statements as well. You let Peanut work his magic, and you stay out of trouble in the process. Peanut will get the names of the parents, and the medical bills will go to them through him."

Johnny went back inside the room as the doctor left.

Marshall was still holding Beep's hand. "Are the cops gonna sweat Beep?" he asked.

Johnny rolled his eyes. Someone had big ears, and he didn't know where Marshall got his vocabulary. That sounded like something out of an old gangster movie from the 1940s. "No, Beep is not in trouble, and the police are only going to want to hear his side of the story."

Marshall frowned. "You can't trust 'em."

Johnny stared at his brother in disbelief. "Marshall! Where is all this coming from? Since when have you become an expert on bad police procedure?"

"I watch TV. I know how it goes down," Marshall said.

"I think your TV choices could be better, and we'll be talking about that as well in our family meeting. In the meantime, you will be quiet, and you will be respectful when the police get here. Do you understand me?"

Marshall ducked his head. "Yes, sir."

Beep reached for Johnny's hand. "Don't leave me alone with the cops," he said.

"What the hell?" Johnny muttered. "Have you been watching those shows with Marshall?"

"Yes."

"Where?"

"At Miss Jane's after we get through with homework. She watches old cops-and-robbers movies."

"Good Lord," Johnny muttered. He was going to have to have a talk with the sitter too. Could this day get any worse?

There was a knock on the door, and then a uniformed officer from the Blessings Police Department walked in carrying a tripod and a camera case.

Johnny breathed a sigh of relief. He knew and respected Lon Pittman. He would be fair. "Hey, Lon," Johnny said.

"Hello, Johnny. Dr. Quick has reported an assault on Brooks Pine, who I am assuming is your little brother, Beep. Can't say as I ever knew his real name before today. I am going to video his statement, okay?"

Johnny nodded. "Dr. Quick told us he called you. Beep will answer your questions. Won't you, buddy?"

Beep blinked and tightened his hold on Johnny's hand.

Lon was shocked at the condition of the little guy's face and hated that his presence was adding to his discomfort. He quickly set up the camera and once it was in place, he moved just out of camera range. "It's gonna be okay, Beep. You remember me from Career Day at school, right? I came in and talked to your class about obeying traffic laws and how you look both ways before you cross streets. I just want you to tell me what happened."

About the Author

Sharon Sala, who has also written under the name Dinah McCall, has more than eighty-five books in print, published in five different genres—romance, fiction, young adult, Western, and women's fiction—and her young adult books have been optioned for film. She has been named a RITA finalist eight times by Romance Writers of America, and in 2011, they named her the recipient of the Nora Roberts Lifetime Achievement Award. Her books are *New York Times* and *USA Today* bestsellers and published in many different languages. She lives in Oklahoma, the state where she was born.